Nathanael Chambers

# ClusterFuck

Ridero

2025

ISBN 978-83-8440-079-1
Created with Ridero smart publishing system

# Contents

# Pre Book Witter

Smello there, congratulations, you are fortunate or possibly unfortunate depending on how we get along to have a copy of this collection of random words. Never in my life did I intend to write a book, I can barely read or write but I really wanted to make a written record of an event that occurred in March 2025.

Now that you have the book and on my part totally without obligation I assume that you will read it. Well obviously you need to read it as it's a fucking book not a bar of chocolate or a biscuit but feel free to try and eat it if you like. I used to eat tissues and paper napkins as a child so it probably won't do you any harm, I'm still a reasonably functioning member of society after consuming countless Brittany Ferry dark blue napkins in the early 1980's, I don't know why but they were my favorite.

Rather than eating it please read it if you can be arsed and have nothing better to do or very important in your diary at this moment in time, that is obviously if you can read, it's only page one but you have got this far so you can probably read or you have a helper, if you are going to struggle with long words get a dictionary or have someone to read it as a bedtime story, your carer possibly? Obviously if you have this collection of 79000 random words in digital format on your phone or tablet then for health and safety reasons I strongly suggest that you under no circumstances try to eat it.

Now you have this book in your hands or on your whatever device let's venture into the world of Clusterfuck, I really do hope you enjoy reading it as much as I enjoyed living it, recalling it and attempting to write it. As underpaid twats serving in restaurants annoyingly say “ENJOY” (j'espère).

# 1 What is?

Noun. clus·ter·fuck ˈklə-stər-ˌfək. plural clusterfucks. vulgar slang.: a complex and utterly disordered and mismanaged situation: a muddled mess.

This I think is the best place to start by explaining the title to the uniformed, uneducated or those who just don't have an inventive use of obscenities in general conversation or are too shy to use simple words like fuck, cunt, twat etc. So for those not in the know of how to use and understand obscene and or vulgar words and hence how to use the term ClusterFuck to its full advantage I will provide an explanation followed by a breakdown, I'm only at the start of this venture and could possibly have a breakdown myself before I get into the flow of it, I've thus far spent four days writing this first section, deleting, rewriting, and repeat. Time dependent I could possibly die without getting anywhere, feel free to have a breakdown yourself at your leisure in the comfort of your own home, I hear it is good to relieve stress, anxiety etc but I'm no expert on the matter of mental health as you will soon come to understand.

Apparently the term ClusterFuck comes under the classification of vulgar slang which is a new term to me and one that I very much like. Anyhoo what in this day and age is vulgar I ask? In an age when you can find any level of porn, violence, murder, explotation etc just by tapping your sweaty piss fingers on your phone, tablet or if you prefer your vulgarity in large screen format your personal computer or lap top, not ignoring another great recent invention, screen casting so you can watch whatever your piss fingers find on your phone directly on to your far too big for the room telly, I say screen casting is recent I've no idea how old it is as I only discovered it in 2024 so I'm down with the kids in my world. Screen casting I have discovered is a great way of boring the shit out of people showing them endless holiday photos casting them directly to our moderately sized TV but it is much better than hearing sighs of boredom from people huddled around a small mobile phone screen, that said some mobile phones are now bigger than my television.

I remember back in the day as a child in the 70's when my parents invited the neighbors round to share our boring holiday photos it was billed as an event, negatives were mounted in their little card pouches, lovingly arranged in the top of a projector in a thing that looked like the air filter off a Lada Niva, the living room was arranged like a theatre, father would be wearing his holiday bermuda esque shorts and would be passing round sweet wine, probably Hock, warm beer and whiskey to keep the invites interest, pineapple and cheese on sticks, smoked cocktail sausages lovingly prepared out of a tin etc, all to soak up said refreshments. I don't think garlic bread had been invented or had been introduced to the outskirts of Burnley back then otherwise I'm sure it would have been a winner to soak up the drinks! It really was an event, I remember stepping over puke left by the exiting guests on the drive way the next morning en route to catch the bus to school. Anyway I digress, lets get back in the room.

ClusterFuck containing the rude word FUCK really isn't vulgar, if you are already offended by the use of the word fuck then you had best stop reading and pop the kettle on or put your sweaty piss fingers to work on your semen smeared screen and carry on where you left off, (this applies only to males unless you share wank time with your beloved ... I dare not think) Breaking down the meaning of ClusterFuck we have the following.

Cluster, noun, a group of similar things or people positioned or occurring closely together, "clusters of creamy-white flowers". That was quite simple wasn't it, now for the rude word.

Fuck a much used, loved and well known term.

Fuck (/fʌk/) is profanity in the English language that often refers to the act of sexual intercourse, but is also commonly used as an intensifier or to convey disdain. While its origin is obscure, it is usually considered to be first attested to around 1475. In modern use, the term fuck and its derivatives (such as fucker and fucking) are used as a noun, a verb, an adjective, an infix, an interjection or an adverb. There are many common phrases that employ the word as well as compounds that incorporate it, such as motherfucker and fuck off.

Vulgar, obscene, insulting and smutty slang are high in my vocabulary of spoken words but I rarely write them, rarely I write anything, usually on account of not being able to find a pen or a scrap of paper and even if I do find one the writing is at best as illegible as a doctors prescription but alas nowhere near as interesting or worth taking the time to decipher.

Enough of dictionary corner shizzle, onwards with this collection of random words that I don't at this stage know what to refer to as, is this a memoir, novel, diary, car repair manual, holiday guide, marriage manual, who cares lets get going and see what transpires.

Before moving on while we're still in the dictionary corner there is another word I've just used that you might not be aquanted with that will be used frequently in the following ramblings so for your further education in new words and please feel free to use it in non offensive conversation with your homies while getting down with the kids, the word is Shizzle...

Noun informal US, noun: shizzle, used as a euphemism for 'shit' in various senses and phrases.

“This shizzle is givin' me a straight-up headache.”

“This is good shizzle”....

Just before we proceed to the next stage of wittering, I’ll be carrying on but you have a choice. Firstly you have the option to put this Shizzle aside or in the bin and go to bed, do yoga or do something useful, yoga doesn’t come under the heading of useful and your life will probably be more fulfilled even if you just read one word and repeat it while inhaling and exhaling slowly, I think that’s how yoghurt works but again I’m no expert, you will see if you keep up there are many things

I'm not an expert on. On the subject of not being, I am in no way an author but I feel that i'm now in the zone for gogogo on the word marathon, I've decided after a short nap it's going to be a book, nothing special just a block of A5 ish size pieces of paper glued together possibly with a sweaty piss finger picture on the cover. As you don't yet know the content or where the words might lead you we will decide later on. So, now I know I'm making a book, I prefer to say making as I make things, I don't do writing as explained before as you will hopefully remember. If you do remember then you are keeping up with me. Writing apparently requires some level of understanding of language and literature neither of which I posess or understand. I looked up some information online and as I understand it, to write a book it is only necessary to write some drivvle and have it printed. Great news I've got drivvle coming out of my ears, whether anyone cares to read it is another matter, attracting the reader and retaining their interest is also a task one must apparently take into account.

If I possessed a certain type of talent that I am yet to master or even concieve I could create a Mr Man or comic style book requiring more drawing than words but according to internet sources that won't cut mustard unless it's written in an ALGBTY+PG Tips genre none of which I understand apart from PG Tips that i am informed is crap tea compared to Yorkshire tea. In a nutshell I need to waffle at least 200 pages, 60000 words, 10 chapters and I need a story to tell. Not sure about reaching the numbers but I have a story to tell and thus far I've already depending on your reading prowess wasted possibly an hour of your ever dwindling life waffling on without even giving any clue thus far about what the story is that I have to tell. When we get going remember that this is a true story, yes a true story I'll have you know so that might make it more interesting, hmm possibly not as there will be no aliens, spaceships, monsters etc to spice it up so it could be more boring than waiting for bread to toast.

I sense you are intrigued to know where we are going? Maybe I over estimated your interest, anyhoo possibly I will see you in chapter two if you have nothing better to do my dear new unknown friend.

# 2 What Spawned Clusterfuck

I'm sitting in my place on the human sofa one afternoon during September 2024, I was arsing about on the internet as one does when there's only Cash in the Attic to tempt me to watch telly as I've just missed Bargain Hunt and watching Escape to the Country is just irritating, I left the country years ago and I am not interested in it. When I say country I mean the United Kingdom of misery not the countryside. I should point out at this stage that I'm not some drop out who sits around watching daytime time television waiting for the next meal time to arrive but living in the arse end of nowhere in France our work pattern is somewhat fluid, sometimes we have a week of Sunday's, other times a week of Wednesday's but we need to move on and leave this nonsense behind as this isn't about escape to the country this is about the journey into ClusterFuck.

Let's move on again as I'm itching to get to the actual events that form the nineteen chapters of this yarn, yes nineteen chapters I've set up and for each one of them I need to find 3157 plus words, I think I've possibly overstretched my little ability to write as thus far I've only achieved 1378 words in the first chapter so I need to either think more proactively to spin out a tale or start typing with a stammer or maybe even throw in a touch of Tourette syndrome to increase the word count, maybe I could insert a joke at the end of each chapter just to put the word count up, we'll see how it goes. If we are still together when we arrive at the page with THE END printed on it in big letters then I'll have done good and you will be more educated about what a Cluster-Fuck is and you will have hopefully had a laugh or cry on the way.

If I was reading this I'd probably at this point go to the page with THE END written on it read the last paragraph then count the pages back from what I've already read to see how much longer I have to endure the book for.

Someday back in September last year or thereabouts, if I don't finish writing this for a few years it was September 2024, my partner Terri (Terri is female by the way, it's a constant misconception of names with us two, Terri woman, Nat man, me Nat as a caveman would have said) was doing the WhatsApp phone thing with her mother, or should I say her mother was wittering into thin air as Terri is nowhere near the phone, she's sipping Top Buget beer and not really listening. Terri's saying yes occasionally just to keep up the pretense up that she is engaging in conversation, I'm on standby feeding Terri more Top Buget beer when required. Same old boring conversation of complete shizzle, unreliable hospital appointments in Wales, lack of doctors appointments, court case against the Taffy who took her money and fitted or didn't fit a new kitchen, the health care is better in Gibraltar, church accounts and arseholes at the synod in Gibraltar etc. This is Terri's mothers weekly witterings, they are a routine weekly recurrence which can switch in the level of tedium depending on whether Audrey (now you know my partners mothers name as well as ours) is resident in Welsh Wales or the hell hole that is Gibraltar, that's only my take on Gibraltar that it is a shit hole as I have only visited once a few years ago which incidentally was to move a van full of shizzle for Audrey from Gibraltar to somewhere in south Wales. I have nothing against Gibraltar in itself, it's clearly a popular place on account of the massive number of people inhabiting it and people visiting by the cruise ship load to visit what is just a rock. Anyhoo, Audrey flits between the two places depending on health associated appointments which are a constant cause for complaint. Older people I find love to complain about pretty much anything, note I said older not old. Anyway during said conversation Audrey made us an offer that we reacted to without delay before she forgot what she had said or changed her mind, the reason for us getting on this offer like a car bonnet was that sometimes lemonade flows and or medication kicks in and Audrey can often forget what she's said, I'll briefly explain that Audrey is the woman who has four steam cleaners still boxed to mention just a few other items that appear by magic in her home both in Wales and Gibraltar that are anonymously delivered from Amazonian apparently for no fathomable reason. To expand on this topic, when she brings Christmas gifts it is very much a lucky dip as she has no idea what she had bought and wrapped up and who each gift is for!

Said offer went like this. "What would you both like for Christmas"?

"Not sure", we don't need anything. Over the last 14 years together we have pretty much accumulated everything we could ever need and more, we have everything we need other than a couple of thousand spare Euros.

"What about a proper holiday I know you like camping around France but it's not very exciting is it, how about a trekking trip in Sri Lanka or maybe a city break in Hong-Kong? There are trips available for about 2000€."

Well thats all well and good in principle but we don't have the means to find the spending money for such a trip. When we go camping locally we don't spend much more money than staying at home, just a few euros on fuel and camp sites.

The seed was known though and not wanting to miss out on a couple of grand's worth of holiday I instigated an online search. I didn't even need to instigate a search because as if by magic a page popped up on Facebelm.

"Feraille Raid" I had to investigate what it was as the video looked very alluring.

Let me explain what Feraille Raid is, it's a rally in Morocco 3000km+ (not including getting there and back) for scrap vehicles. You travel from Tangier Med ferry port to Marrakesh over 6 days, going east through Morocco in to the desert then south and then turning back west to Marrakesh. When they say scrap vehicles it's a vehicle over 15 years old for a car or van and 20 years old for a 4×4, not really that old by modern standards. There are 50 vehicles allowed to register on the Raid. Each vehicle needs a co-pilot to navigate and if you have room passengers are also allowed so there will be at least 100 people on this trip plus the support crew, medics and mechanics.

The question I asked Terri without going into any detail was, "Are you interested in a desert road trip in Morocco?" I then backed this up with a brief description of what the trip entailed but to save words just showed her the videos on the website.

Without any hesitation or need for constipation or contraception the reply was, "Yes please ta muchly thanking you kindly."

On the face of it, it looks like the adventure of a lifetime, driving through the desert, vast open plains of gravel and dust, sand dunes to nose dive your vehicle into and get stuck in and then heroically rescue yourself, overnight stops at desert camps, meeting the locals and donating educational or medical items to their local charities, using road books for directions, full back up team for vehicle repairs or recovery, medical care at the camps should you need it, translators, people to help with paperwork etc, all of this was important to me as I have old vehicle anxiety issues about traveling anywhere other than the local supermarket in our old cars and even that can sometimes be touch and go, so with a guestimated 8000km+ trip I knew there would be anxiety issues ahead if we went for it.

After not much deliberation in fact none whatsoever we didn't hesitate to register on the Feraille raid with our scrap car of choice.

Our scrap vehicle of choice was my 1979 Lada Niva called Svetlana, if you don't know the Lada Niva they are basically a Russian tractor with seating for 4, we'll not bother with the details of said vehicle at this stage as if you don't know the Russian Niva tractor you will come to know and love Svetty in time, in a nutshell they are noisy, rattle a lot, consume lots of petrol and nearly as much oil, and even with seats shoe horned in from a 1980 Alfa Romeo GTV the seating is still uncomfortable and the noise is totally intolerable on the auto routes when traveling at 90kmh on account of no noise insulation, just a metal floor and a rubber mat between you and the engine or road depending on where you are looking. This does however at times have its benefits as due to the noise I can't hear or can pretend not to hear anything Terri is saying which can be a blessing. In a nutshell Svetlana is slow, noisy and smelly but will get you almost anywhere (almost).

So it looks like we're going on an adventure to Morocco in a 1979 Lada called Svetlana, I hope you are keeping up with names, if not we'll recap in future chapters and introduce more names for you to remember, I think putting a name to a description makes it real, maybe it does maybe I doesn't, I'm just guessing and trying to sound intelligent, anything to help you make sense of this collection of words that as I re-read them I am pretty much just creating nonsense.

Before moving on to the next chapter there is a fairly important, no wait a moment, pause, stop! There is a very important element of what caused the birth of ClusterFuck that I need to explain in brief detail.

Audrey posed the question, that as we will be stopping at her place in Gibraltar for a couple of days on our route to Morocco, why don't we get married at City Hall? We had been planning on getting married for many years but had not got round to it in France on account of the French bureaucracy. To get married in France was far too much faff so we just kept putting it off for years.

Marriage in France is a must do as there isn't the will system that exists like there is in that place called the United Kingdom of Shitdom as I now refer to it, where you can leave everything to your loved one, animal rescue centre, pub, favorite street worker etc just by creating a will online.

To explain it in a nutshell, If we are not married and I cark it Terri gets nothing, the house goes to my sibling's although Terri would have the right to stay in the house. My brother wouldn't be bothered about the house, he has a family and life in Tenerife with a nice house of his own on the Plaza in Guaza, he has a good job and a happy life. My sister however (in reality referred to as the person my parents spawned who I can't remember the name of) but for narrative purposes I will describe her as a complete fucking knob who cares about nothing more than getting stoned, letting the family down, and posting angry items on social media. I feel it is good and safe to vent these feelings in this book as she probably won't read it anyway.

We went along with Audrey's wedding idea and via a few emails, finding our life in paperwork to be scanned and 500 notes later transferred to Gibraltar we had a wedding ceremony booked for the 6th March 2025, this would be followed by the start of the Raid on the 8th. I also remembered to get a new passport as apparently they don't let you in to Gibraltar or Morocco with a French Carte de Sejour and a BricoMarche loyalty card, fussy fuckers they are but they are both independent countries so I guess they can make their own rules.

If you are still with me let's go to chapter 3 which I think might be a bit boring depending on your gender or 'A' status as it will be mainly procuring wedding outfits and carrying out car maintenance on Svetlana before her 8000 ish kilometer trip. Not wanting to waste your time I will split the next chapter into two parts, the first part is the acquisition of wedding attire, if that is of interest then read on, the second part is car maintenance on a Russian tractor, ahh no on second thoughts we'll do car preparation first, wedding second otherwise you will be thinking what the fuck are these two idiots on. If you can't be arsed with wedding and car maintenance shizzle descriptions please feel free to go directly to chapter 4 when the journey into ClusterFuck will begin.

I'm delaying chapter three because as mentioned above I need to get the chapter word count up using various means so I'm going to give this a try using the three aforementioned methods, as a footnote to this chapter, I think footnote is the literary word for it but I'm probably wrong, I also need feed back before moving on, for feedback I have a proof reader, not in a grammatical or spelling sense just someone who reads a chapter well obviously he's only read one thus far and gives me his honest comments.

Chapter one he thought was and I paraphrase in my favour a little “edgy but comic genius”, nice comment i thought, he is however an eighty odd year old idiot called Robin or more commonly referred to as idiot neighbour, I’m sure he will be thrilled to be mentioned in my ramblings. You will meet the idiot neighbor in a later chapter, number eighteen I think but that’s a long way off so he could appear anywhere in between. Anyway here we go in a first attempt to up the word count, veering wildly from the script, not that there is a script and I’m trying to keep the edgy comedy level up but not too high thus keeping the book accessible to all ages, genders and species, I hope.

Here we go with one of my favorite jokes written in the form of someone with a stammer and tourette's, this could be a total fucking disaster.

Fuck cunt tits, DD-David ww-wanker -HH-Hasselhoff ww-anked nn-no ff-fuck my bb-bastard ss-stammer, ww-walked into aa-bra, nn-no fuck cunt bastard I – I m-meant tto ss-say bb-bar and oo-ordered aa dd-drink.

“It's a pleasure to serve you, Mr. Hasselhoff”

ss-said the fucking bastard bb-bartender twat cunt arsehole.

“Just call me Hoff”

He rr-replied bollocks cunt face twat hole.

“no hassle”

Ss-said the bastard cunt bb-bartender.

You would not believe how difficult it is to imagine and try to type as if you have Tourette's and a stammer. I mean no offense or disrespect to anyone with these issues, at least you have a condition, I however am just a dick and unfortunately being a dick is not recognized as a medical condition and therefore no professional medical help or medication is available, so unfortunately, I'm stuck with it until the day I expire. Wittering on, should the Hairy Hoff Meister ever read this drivvle, big up respect oh curly haired, leather jacket wearing, sometime rock star, particularly popular in Germany for some reason. Hang on folks I've just had a thought, the only Germans I know are “three speed walking sticks” as my father used to call ladies who prefer to munch a rug rather than suck a bockwurst. So with Hoff as the biggest pin up poster cutie in Germany in the nineteen eighties I think I would also have become a rug muncher, hang on a minute I already am, I like women, to a point, that is unless it's a Wednesday which for many years this special day of the week has always been declared as “Gay Wednesday”. This is a day that is dedicated to and still is a homage to the male form, where men are encouraged to embrace other men's form, be it mentally or physically or both depending on if you really love cock worship. This is what gay Wednesday is all about. Bugger me, bollocks, I've gone wittering wildly off piste again.

So there we go, a bit of a result, we have registered a few more hundred word's on the counter, you've read a few paragraphs written in a weird and strange way, I've shared with you one of my favorite jokes that probably made no sense at all however many times you read it and re read it, more importantly no one thus far despite mental, physical, gender or discrimination issues has been ridiculed or offended so all is good. There is still much time yet for me to offend everyone.

A dyslexic walks into a bra!

# 3 It's All in the Preparation

Here we go with only 5 months to go before said trip, my anxiety levels are already very high at the thought of what could, might and will inevitably go wrong.

Before we go ahead I want to reiterate my limits as a word / book / novel / car manual etc creator. When words arrive in my head I need to get the words down as soon as they arrive otherwise, ping and they are gone into the ether, so obviously I need to type them before they leave the premises of my brain, the narrative ahead can therefore be a tad haphazard, the result of this increasing haphazardness is becoming more and more obvious, after a whole two chapters thus far in which sometimes what I put down I re-read and it is complete and utter fucking nonsense, I say put down as it sounds intellectually romantic in a writing/authoring sort of way doesn’t it, really saying put down is just prodding the screen of my tablet with a dobber which is already wearing out as the rubber dobbing element is already getting a bit sloppy.

I'm told by my idiot neighbor, the pre reader of this shizzle, that the narrative is written as if I'm telling this tale in person to some bored, disheveled, stinky, probably homeless person who's at least six pints in sat in a Bra (see what I did there), which is probably the same imaginary Bra that I'm sat in writing this shizzle. I'm not sure how the Idiot neighbor can concieve the notion that a homeless person can afford six pints but we must get on with the tale that I want to share with you as I'm wandering off again. Let's get back in the room and get going with the preparation.

As you will recall we are booked and Audrey has paid for us to take part in the Feraille Raid in Morocco. There are many things we need to accomplish and require before we depart on what will be an epic journey. Firstly after registration you need to choose a bib number for your scrap car, any number between 0 and 9999, I wanted 007 or 8008 as 8008 upside down on a calculator as a child as most of you will know spelled out BOOB. Terri however had other ideas. Back in the UK she had a tarts car, hairdresser's car whatever you want to call it, it was an AUDI TT turbo with a red leather interior, we are not interested in this story about the tarts car, however what is important to mention is that the registration plate was T666COW, which roughly translates to Terri the devil bull. So there we go Terri decided and I didn't get to be James Bond or BOOB and we opted for bib number 666. The number of the beast.

The email checklists from Asier started to arrive thick and fast. Asier is the coordinator and main organizer of the rally, we will meet him again later so keep his name in your memory bank. Bulletin number one is all about equipment, I'll not recount the list exhaustively but these are the main items as I'm still wanting to get to the story, without you getting too bored.

Essentially we need a vehicle obviously, two spare wheels, 20 liters of spare fuel, 2 fire extinguishers, first aid kit, tablet for navigation, two mobile phones, small tent preferably of the pop up type, sleeping mats or camp bed and sleeping bags, map of Morocco, compass, head torches, diahorrea tablets, paracetamol, oil and coolant for said vehicle, basic tool box etc.

Next we have the vehicle pilot and co pilot details to register. This should be easy enough, we need to send a copy of the Carte Grise and car insurance, I thought to myself at this point, is my insurance valid in Morocco, probably, hopefully, I suppose I had better check. Driving license, hmm yet again, my driving license had been out of date for at least five years but I'm reliably informed that it is only the photo that is out of date, I don't know why because I don't look a day older than when I passed my test way back in 1989. I would have had a new license by now, however the French government have thus far turned down my application for a French license three times, their system is great, you fill everything in online, copy all of your paperwork except for your death certificate wait six months then receive a text saying, please reapply. At the time of writing this I have at last received a new license so I can now drive legitimately.

Next we need to address the controle technique or MOT as you understand it as it needs to have been passed less than six months ago otherwise there might be issues at the Moroccan border, Svetlana's CT runs out just after we plan to get back from Morocco so I need to book her in for a test. I went off to SecruiTest in La Souterainne, the test went OK apart from one issue that the headlights are falling to bits and need replacing, no great shakes, I'll order some new headlight's, pop them in and boom, control technique done. If only it was that simple, since "Poo Tin" started being an arse with Ukraine the acquisition of car parts for Russian vehicles have become very scarce locally, when I say locally, France, Holland and Germany, none of the suppliers have even basic parts so we need to get them from LadaPower in Estonia, LadaPower were very clever and quickly hot footed it and moved their warehouse from Ukraine to just over the border. Estonia is a fair distance away so it takes a while for parts to be donkeyed to France. We're on our four week countdown and we have no headlights.

Proper job, two weeks later the headlights have arrived. Anxiety levels are rising as there were only a few days after the lights arrived before we were due to depart. I went back to SecuriTest and had to sweet talk the bloke at the control technique to fit my contre visit in the next day and I promised that if he would I would send them a postcard from Marrakesh when we get there. Anyhoo, Svetlana had her contra visit and succeeded at the control technique and passed with flying colors, my levelling and directing of the headlights using chalk lines drawn on the gayrage doors obviously worked a treat, either that or he felt sorry for me and passed Svetty anyway, as at least I had gone to the trouble of replacing the headlights. The only other issues to attend to were the minor oil leaks from the engine, gearbox, transfer case, front differential and back differential, big jobs that I don't have the time or will to carry out but I took comfort in a comment from one of the other teams on the Raid via the "get to know the other teams" Group on WhatsApp "If oil is leaking out you know there is some in there, when it stops leaking fill it up." Wise words indeed.

I'm going to dwell no more on Svetlana for now as it's a bit boring and I don't want to loose your interest and we are only about 500 words from actually starting the adventure, I will probably go off piste between now and then to try and get to the required minimum of 9000 words for three chapters.

We'll leave it there for now apropo Svetty, she goes, sort of stops and thanks to the new headlights we can now see where we are going in the dark. She's still dripping oil so we know there's still some in there! We know what we need to take with us for the Raid and I think we have everything ready so that will do for me for now. Let's move on to the other side of the preparation, wedding shizzle.

I think at this stage you should congratulate me on not using any foul language thus far in this chapter apart from 8008, I did prefer 80087355 at school and still do as an utterly immature 52 year old adult it's still up there in the childish humor stakes. While we're on numbers let's go back to T666COW and our raid bib number 666. There is a prize on the raid for the best fancy dress. The fancy dress must be worn for two of the six stages. This was only one prize available in addition to the best decorated vehicle, oldest vehicle, most breakdowns but still smiling, who gets lost the most, who helps the other teams the most and last and least important who wins the raid.

We had a plan, Svetty was born in 1979 so looking at the other teams online I think we are in with a shout at the prize for the oldest vehicle, that is of course depending on if we finish the raid as you don't get a prize if you just turn up for the raid. Second chance for a prize is fancy dress, obviously we are stopping off to get married in Gibraltar en route so if we dress up for the wedding then boom we have some form of fancy dress with no effort involved other than finding suitable wedding outfits. With the number 666 in mind Terri started her outfit search online, when I say online it was pretty much exclusively on the Temu app, her online shopping weapon of choice.

Before this venture I was unaware of such a place where you can buy anything under the sun from Mr Wong for pennies instead of pounds or should I say cents instead of euros. The fact that Mr Wong probably uses child labor in sweat shops somewhere in China or that part of the world to provide goods for next to nothing is of no issue to me. I sense some of you human rights people might be angry by that statement, but the way I see it in my simple brain is that if you can buy something online that can be sent to Europe from the other side of the world for a fiver that a child was paid 5 pence to make and then have it delivered for free, then boom, cheap average quality goods for us, the child has a job, the suppliers of the materials have a job, the postal service have a job then also the crew of the container ship transporting hundreds of containers of Mr Wong's shizzle that I guestimate eighty percent of the merchandise people bought didn't even know they needed, wanted or had never even contemplated buying until they saw how cheap it was and quickly filled the basket before the bonus discount timer ran out (at this point I refer you back to Audrey and her steam cleaners).

I'm a bit last minute, always have been always will be, so the woman commenced her shopping list first, that way I could follow suit with her theme for what might be wedding attire or could be fancy dress or a combination of the two. The genre appeared to be emerging as devil, steampunk, stupidity, wedding, fancy dress.

After many hours of muttering at her tablet and repeating why can't I find that again I assumed Terri was slowly filling her online shopping basket, emptying it, refilling it, emptying it, editing it and finally placing an order.

Two weeks later a parcel arrived from Mr Wong, the contents were interesting, I'll review the contents of the package for your information in the order that they will be worn from top to bottom or bottom to top I can't decide yet which way works best. Traditionally being the groom I wouldn't see the wenches outfit until the big day as they call it, big day? Having been there before I can inform you from experience it's not really a big day, It's a fecking long day, designed to appease everyone, mainly the mother in law or mother in laws to be, at great expense to me as I'm paying for the whole chabang just pretty much to sign a piece of paper to give half of what I own to someone else. This time it will be different.

Right then, let's describe Terri's wedding / fancy dress outfit. I was party to the viewing of it as Terri did it as a fashion show in front of what I affectionately call "her ladies", the collection of ladies is actually called "stich and bitch" or "Wooly Mammoths". I happen to be included as their monthly gathering is hosted in our house, generally I escape to the workshop to busy my self doing anything apart than listening to women bitching while stitching. Just to give you a brief insight into this monthly chore, women arrive with food of different sorts depending on the season, they eat food and drink tea. Why they don't replace tea with wine and beer is totally beyond me. They then eat some more savory stuff, drink more tea, eat cake, then eventually get some wool or other craft material out to stitch or such like while bitching. It's then my job to clear the table and floor of their food as it is clear that when their gobs are bitching at full speed they don't have the dexterity to get food into their mouths at the same time as bitching which is strange to me as apparently women can multi task but when it comes to sausage rolls and wool I very much beg to differ. The bonus of this monthly invasion is that I get the leftovers. Normally there's not much left but in winter when soup is on the bitching menu my favorite leftover is Terri's friend Cathy's home made chicken soup which is absolutely delicious but is however clearly extracted out of a tin probably procured from the English Shop in Gueret or illegally imported from the United Kingdom of Shitdom, anyway, tinned soup is absolutely delicious so I'm not complaining, it reminds me of school. I intend in no way wish to offend Cathy in her ability and dexterity as a chef to open a tin of soup, pop it in a pan warm it up and pass it off as her own creation. I do hope she will be thrilled to be mentioned in this book, the reason being, apropo the book title, Cathy unwittingly and unintentionally comes into contact with and in some way has to deal with nearly every wanker in the Ceruse region of France where we live, hence the relevance to Clusterfuck, Cathy is lovingly referred to as a "Shit Magnet" essentially the same venture as ClusterFuck but involving wankers rather than life events and you never know who might read this book and take a hint! Sorry we've veered off again, back to Terri's wedding outfit.

We will work from the top down, Black pork pie hat with what I will describe as a funeral veil over it with red skull motifs. The hat quality from Mr Wong is a tad questionable, it's not the black plastic shite you get with a "Kiss Me Quick" pork pie hat that you can buy on the promenade in Blackpool should you be unfortunate enough to visit the godforsaken place. Working down we will pass straight by the face paint as that really is something else and not part of the clothing outfit, we will discuss it in some detail at the end of this chapter, followed by red +1.5 steampunk sunglasses so she can see and have a vague idea where she's going while looking cool providing that is that she takes them off indoors otherwise she will enter the I'm in the dick zone of wearing sunglasses indoors, that said wearing sunglasses indoors will become an essential fashion accessory later so dear reader bear that in mind for the relevance of it in I think chapter eighteen or possibly 19 I don't know yet, regardless of sunglasses or not she is still a dick. So we are down to the neck, a black band choker thing with a plastic tacky purple rose on it, I like the idea of a choker on a future wife as you never know when you might need to use it in anger, I'll have to investigate if there is a loop to attach a dog lead or possibly a chain to it depending on Terri's behavior. Next we have the black net curtain cardigan thing, I can't describe it any better than that. The idea of this is to respect the coverage of women's arms and shoulders as an element of body coverage that will be needed when we wear our fancy dress outfits on the Raid in Morocco. You are probably aware that women should be covered up in Muslim countries, I agree and think women should be covered up wherever they are, especially with the size of women you see in our neck of the woods and looking online while carrying out my research about Morocco I am led to believe the larger lady is favored by the local Moroccan men.

Just to clarify, I've not been looking at fatty lass Moroccan porn, just scanning information about what Morocco is like, honest, cross my heart and hope to die.

Terri's head and shoulders are now covered, not in dandruff but a combination of pork pie hat, funeral veil and black net curtain cardigan. Just as well because over the net cardigan is a red and black satin basque with a tie up back, this I'm sure will excite the grubby Moroccan men with their sweaty piss fingers. Moving downwards a long red skirt of the type where women can't move their legs properly without shuffling along like a homeless person taking their begging cup to the off-licence, over this a full sized black net curtain that I think is called a petticoat which forgive me if I'm not mistaken is normally worn under the skirt to provide volume to the skirt, but Terri being Terri and a bit of a knob she's put it over the skirt not under it, anyway each to their own, and to be honest it did look pretty good. That just leaves the flower patterned Doc Martin esque boots, no glittery high heels here but it would have been hilarious if she had gone for heels and watching Terri fall off them. Finally a full length Gandalf cape with pointy hood should the weather be inclement, weather inclement I ask, for fucks sake, we're going to Gibraltar then Morocco which during my research into fatty women has advised me that Morocco is in Africa so it should be sunny and warm or even hot should it not?

Now onto the face paint, think of Morticia from the Adams Family, pale foundation, black mascara, generally black round the eyes, black lipstick, combine this lot with the red and black satin and lace outfit, when she pouts the whole ensemble makes her look like some sort of Japanese fuck doll! Hopefully using the above information and your own imagination you can conjure up your own image of Terri's wedding outfit.

The now wife had previously read this description of her outfit and corrected me on a few items, I decided not to alter my words and leave it just as it is as a reminder to how as a male how little notice or interest I take about anything!

Next on to my attire, this is much more simple, I wanted to wear shorts and T shirt, felt fedora saved from my first wedding and maybe invest in some of those pointy shoes that twats in suits wear where a third of the shoe is wasted because there is no foot in it and you look like a penguin with pigeon toes. This idea of my proposed wedding attire was spectacularly shot down in flames. The future bitch wife however must be obeyed so, tablet in hand I'm going on a mini adventure and entering the Temu zone, going down the rabbit hole to see what lurks in the depths of Mr Wong's sweat shops and see what a man in his fifties might procure as a wedding outfit.

Three days later I re-emerged, grinning and triumphant from the rabbit hole with a shopping basket filled to the virtual brim with in the region of fifty items in it. Next task was to whittle the basket down to a hat, suit, shirt and accessories, yes I opted for a suit and thought maybe I should splash out on some of the pointy twat toe shoes. After another three days of deliberation my basket was finally sorted.

I had decided on, black suit and shirt with red flames rising up from the bottom, red braces, an Austin powers style bejeweled cravat neck thing, felt bowler hat with red feathers and blue +1.75 sunglasses to match Terri's sunglasses but in blue, the sunglasses would in no way match the outfit but they go with the color of Svetlana. I already have matching undies in slinky black with red lips on them saying "KISS" that I bought in La Rochelle on our last adventure away from home, this was out of necessity as I forgot to take clean pants with me for ten days away camping. They were a bargain at only one euro a piece in a clearance box in a Carrefour supermarket so I thought bugger it, I'm on holiday and at that price I'm going to splash out and buy two pairs, the other pair has "BIKE" printed all over them which to me was confusing to see that emblazoned on men's pants.

Back in Burnley on Sea it was the women at the infamous dive known as Zanzibar night club that would wear such a label on themselves as a sign of their Friday night prowess. Often it was permanently tattooed somewhere obvious or hidden somewhere to be found bleary eyed under a flab roll at three in the morning in the bedroom of some dank dark council house on Stoops council estate. It wasn't always a council house, sometimes the Burnley slags had reasonably nice residencies but they were generally fat slags. You have to remember this was before the days of Internet porn, nowadays you can have a daily wank by watching whatever genre of porn you choose to look at. Back then you would have a weeks worth of pent up spunk ready to discharge on a Friday night or early Saturday morning and you didn't really care who you spunked it on. Often you would be too pissed or disinterested to discharge or the image of Margaret Thatcher would come into your head while banging a Burnley fat slag from behind and everything would go limp. When fucking a fatty going from behind was always best as backs aren't generally fat and you also don't need to look at their face so you could imagine you were banging anyone. My top tip from back in the day is that when you have had enough and need to get a taxi home and sleep until Sunday and you have no chance of discharging your pent up spunk, the best thing to do is get plenty of phlegm in your mouth or a gob full of whatever drink that might be within reach, pretend you are going to spunk, pull out and spit the phlegm on her back or fat ass, fat slag then feels like she has achieved something by making you spunk and you can get a taxi home for a well deserved rest and pleasurable wank.

Back to the wedding attire again. When my items arrived from Mr Wong the quality of the shirt and suit were of the highest quality thin flimsy polyester, my immediate thought was, don't have a smoke while wearing this lot or I could end up being a living towering inferno not just a polyester printed pattern of flames, the bowler hat was actually really good quality and had a note in it from Mr Wong's niece who had made it asking me to rate it five stars as she makes felt hats to pay for her university tuition fees, I did what the note said and gave her a five star rating even taking the trouble to comment on how good the packaging was.

All in all the ensemble looked pretty good and at sixty European pounds for the whole lot who cares if I burst into flames. Apropo the footwear situation, I opted out of buying any pointy twat toe shoes, I'm more than happy and do actually enjoy doing fancy dress but having pointy footwear worn as a fashion accessory by some twat toed person who sits in an office all day and doesn't see anyone that they need to impress or look stupid too other than the other twat toed personnel in matching shoes and polyester suits probably purchased from Temu, also I bet they have a floppy hairdo teamed with a cheap plastic briefcase containing nothing more than a sandwich that mummy made for them just to finish the business man but I really work in a call center look, therefore that is where I had to draw the line on the shoe decision. I bought some boots instead! Boot, boots you understand not wellies.

Nearly organized and ready for departure. Svetlana's been trial packed to check we can fit everything in, boom, bonus we can just fit everything in. Wedding outfits have been sorted as you have just read, main dates have been put in the diary, we are almost there.

Terri however decided on one more modification to Svetlana, she wanted to put carpet on the floor! What the? What the fuck would you want to do that for? Was my response. Terri's argument was that it was to provide a touch of sound insulation and to help keep the engine fumes out of the cabin. Most of you will have forgotten or be too young to have lived with the lovely smell of petrol and air passing through the cars carburettor. It's a stupid idea to put carpet in but I let her get on with it. Off she troddled up to the barn and came back with two rolls of carpet, why we have rolls of carpet stashed in the barn I have no idea.

Let me explain why applying carpet to a Niva is a stupid idea. Niva's like Land Rover Defenders and the like leak like fuck, in my experience they leak even when it's not raining, water drips from the window seals, drips into the boot, sprays up through where the steering column and pedals go through the bulkhead. Driving in wellies is recommended in inclement weather. For this reason they have no carpet on the floor just rubber mats and holes in the floor for drainage, some of the holes are formed in the factory, the rest are formed by rust to drain the ingress of water back on to the road. But we're going to the desert and it will be dry so the carpet will stop the sand coming inside was Terri's final say on the matter. We now have a beige and blue piece meal carpeted floor, fortunately covered with the rubber mats as it looks totally shit.

One of Terri's other projects was to cover Svetlana in stickers, not sponsorship stickers like the other raid participants but basically covering all the anti rust painted areas of which there are many with stick on spiders, bullet holes, skulls etc, again as with the carpet it keeps her happy and quiet so I left her to it.

Our departure date was set for the 2nd of March 2025, the wedding would be on the 6th, the raid registration is on the

7th, the raid starts on the 8th and finishes on the 12th and we then aimed to be back home on the 21st. We have destinations booked and places to visit in between, hotels have been booked for the first part of the journey, we will book the return accommodations on the way back just in case anything untoward happens and we need to change plans. We will get to each chosen destination in the following chapters.

One final preparation to take care of is to organise baby sitters for the children. This is fairly easy as we have a reciprocal agreement with Audrey, when we go away on trips she comes to France and stays at our house which suit's her as it's part way between Welsh Wales and the hell hole of Gibraltar. This works well as essentially Audrey gets a free holiday home and we get to go on holiday without the hassle of taking three children with us. Believe me she treats our house like a holiday home, the mess, oh the mess, when we return, it can be epic. I'm not complaining, two days getting the house back to normal is a small price to pay for a hassle free holiday. Audrey brings her toyboy Steve with her or should I say Steve brings Audrey, fortunately for Audrey Steve loves driving so he happily drives from Wales to Gibraltar three times a year, suffice to say he doesn't drive a Niva. Despite being Welsh, Steve is a lovely man who even has an Audrey Amazonian storage area in his house to accommodate the online purchase overflow as Audrey cannot move around in her house without falling over an Amazonian box that she has no idea what is in it. More about Steve later as he becomes one of the heroes of this rambling story.

Our children, Pippa, Billy and Desmond are home schooled so in our absence Audrey makes sure they are given breakfast and dinner, she continues to provide them with some form of basic education, they are all retarded dicks hence the need for home schooling as they are not fit for public interaction yet and probably will never be but we are slowly working on it, an uphill losing battle springs to mind and as they say two mong's don't make a right, and three mong's just make the situation even worse. Most people would pop retarded children in the cellar or euthanasize them using the black bag, brick and lake interface, but they are our dicks and we feel obliged to do the best we can whether they are retarded dicks or not. Steve lovingly provides the children with their educational physical activities which they enjoy very much, the problem is the children don't take in or engage in mental stimulation very much other than watching the television. In my recent experience teaching them to count for example is a total fucking waste of time and their speech skills are somewhat limited. Anyhoo we have the baby sitters sorted, and they have arrived and are in d'house, wick down with the kids word moment.

Tomorrow or chapter four if you prefer we will be ready to set off on our adventure, Svetlana's packed and ready but we have an issue, tonight it is forecast for snow and I want to put Svetlana in the gayrage so Terri's shit carpets don't become frozen or water logged before we even leave Le Bost, the problem is, with big fat tall tires and raised suspension (I'm talking about Svetlana not Terri) she is too tall and won't go in through the gayrage door with anything on the roof rack. Executive decision, we'll fuck it for now and we'll do the roof packing in the morning, I've had enough for today, I've still got dinner to cook and departure anxiety levels are at the roof level, normally I'd go down the pub but there isn't one so we just stayed in and got pissed, well I did.

Just as a note, you will have read the word gayrage a few times thus far, it's not a typo, a gayrage is the same as a domestic garage, somewhere that you probably put your modern hybrid or electric shite vehicle or just use your garage to store shite that you might one day need or can't be bothered to take to the tip. The difference is firstly the size, a gayrage is more of a workshop where you fix your shit old cars rather than storing shit new ones. In the gayrage when you fuck something up which often happens, break something, spend a day putting something back together only then to find that the first bastard part to be reassembled is still on the floor, then you mutter to yourself, fuck, cunt, bastard, twat, cunt and you shed a little man tear. These mutterings are then followed by throwing something heavy, and having a hissy fit in the fashion of a gay in a rage. Hence the term gayrage.

Congratulations for reading this far and you have now learned a new word, you can rename your garage if you like and use the word Gayrage on a daily basis, I hold no copyright on my made up word. I would however offer a bit of a warning here, if you are going to use the term Gayrage please do use it with caution. Lets say for example that you are on a night out on cAnal sTreet in Manchester, there could be a slim possibility that your use of the word gayrage might backfire on you. Should you be involved in a random conversation where you slip the word in, you might be misconstrued and aggressively bum raped by a not so "gentle man" in a YMCA bikers outfit with ass out chaps or get knocked out by some tattooed dyke with a mohican who is probably wearing a rugby shirt, both of which you could have inadvertently sent into a gay rage.

I'm stereotyping here but I have witnessed both in the real world. I knocked the dyke out using the gay bikers truncheon and then shoved it up his ass. This is just a warning, I wouldn't be able to live with myself if you were injured by someone in a gay rage whilst using my made up word, that is unless you have renamed your garage to gayrage and injured yourself doing something discusting in there in which case it's your own stupid fault.

On the plus side we are at 8940 words, 60 short of what is apparently required for the first three chapters. I'm proud of myself and I'm on writing fire and I think that I am now actually authoring, I'm dobbering so many words it will soon be necessary to replace the dobber as it's wearing out again! Happy days. No celebration planned yet though apropo the possible achievement of actually writing a novel. Some of the following chapters will be short and my all over it like a rash word count I'm sure will soon drop. I don't want to interrupt the main story event by veering off on a tangent from the story anymore, so from now on we'll drop the crappy anecdotes and jokes.

I've done a little research online and based on expected final word count what we might be creating here could be a novella rather than a novel but you know what? Novella sounds much more romantic than Novel and let's face it, with a wedding ahead romance should be at the forefront of our minds. My ass, romance, have you ever met my future bitch wife! Let's get going, no more shite, no more wittering, let's go on an adventure.

# 4 Stage Minus 1 – Le Bost to Gibraltar

Departure day has arrived and I'm wide awake at five, I didn't sleep much thank you very kindly to the intrusive imaginary friend on my shoulder who I lovingly call anxiety, the main worry being, will we actually get to our first destination or fail on day one which would be a totally fucking embarrassing disaster especially after all the bravado of how bullet proof Svetlana is. Bless Svetty she's done eighteen thousand kilometers on her new engine so I should be feeling more optimistic but I'm not. There's no going back now though so we have to take my anxiety with us on a road trip.

As I was up at five, I'm on it like a car bonnet, well not really. Why is it that when you wake up and have fuck all to do all day you get up at dawns crack, when you have somewhere to go or something to do all you really want to do is pull the duvet back over your head, turn up the thunderstorm white noise on your phone and just pretend you are going to die. So I got out of bed to stop the washing machine of my mind going round and round before it got to the spin cycle, if it does get to spin cycle I might have to go to urgence in Gueret and spend a week in intensive care followed by three weeks in prison camp at St Vaury, it's happened before, obviously it has otherwise I wouldn't have said it but I think that episode in my life is another book in itself.

Comme d'habitue I popped outside for a morning rillo and, fuck me, it's fucking freezing, I'm glad we put Svetlana in the gayrage last night. While I wait for anyone else to bother getting up out of their pits, I'll busy myself putting the last few bits in Svetlana, a couple of cases of Intermarche top budget lager, red and white wine in 3 liter bags in a box, hopefully this will keep us going before we get to Morribobs in Gibraltar to do a pre Morocco shop. I've noticed that we don't appear to have packed any food but I'm sure we'll find something to eat en route, I'm not really a pack up picnic person, pass me a tinny at mid day and I'll soldier on to the days destination.

What's left to do? Chuck some toiletries in and pop the shizzle on the roof. When I say pop some shizzle on the roof, try lifting 2 massive spare tires mounted on rims above your head trying not to just throw them on to the roof rack to avoid the high possibility of breaking something. It was fucking cold but after my tyre throwing olympics I'm sweating like a nigger on a rape charge, or not to be racist a nun in a whore house. My fingers however are so cold that I can't even feel them so I took a pause to regain blood circulation. Next are the easy items to apply to the roof, I'm doing this in between making cups of tea for the baby sitters and future wife now they have bothered to get out of bed as it helps in defrosting my fingers. Next on the roof is an agricultural cric jack, essential to lift Svetlana high enough to change a wheel and has many other uses, sand ramps, camping chairs, umbrella and I bet you can't guess what's on top of this lot?

No you didn't guess it and I think you would never have guessed it, we are transporting a wheelchair from Le Bost to somewhere in Morocco, the reason for this is, one of the rules of the raid is that we have to take stuff for the Moroccan desert communities. Audrey decided to donate and bring from Welsh Wales to Le Bost a brand new wheelchair for us to transport to Gibraltar and then to be donated to someone somewhere In Morocco.

I've seen wheelchairs for sale or rent in our local pharmacy and the cheapest is 800 notes. Audrey wouldn't say how much she paid for it but I suppose it's money better spent to fund a developing or devolving country rather than buying yet another steam cleaner!

We, or should I say I have packed the roof of Svetlana including the fecking wheelchair, my fingers are still freezing despite making many more cups of tea, it's still a mystery to me why when you are clearly stressed and trying to achieve items on your to do list that you are alone in your endeavors.

No one bothers to stand up and say, hey do you need a hand strapping that fucking wheelchair to the roof? (The future wife says this is untrue and she did help but I beg to differ)!

The baby sitters and Terri are safely attached to their electronic devices in our gracious living room feeling nice and toasty in front of the roaring stove I lit two hours ago.

We are ready finally, I'm getting more and more anxious now so without further ado we say toodle pip and set off in the direction of Spain.

First stop is Intermarche at Bessines, easy stop off point as its just off the A20 heading south. We need to fill Svetlana with petrol for the first part of the journey, obviously we do and many times we will need to give her a drink as she doesn't run on thin air. Svetlana isn't a modern sip sip fuel vehicle, the old bird swigs at best 11 liters of fuel for every 100 kilometers of travel. The total journey will be in the region on 6500 kilometers so we will need to fill Svetty up about 22 times.

Proper job, we're full of fuel and heading to our first stop over in Spain, it is about 650 kilometers to the hotel Tudanca Miranda in the town of Miranda De Ebro. Before this venture the furthest we've been on a journey in one hit in the Svetty mobile was 212 kilometers from Brantome in the Perigord region of France to La Rochelle on the coast, so 650 kilometers in one go is going to be a mind numbing, ear ringing, rattly ride. On the plus side its all motorway so hopefully I can sort of switch off.

Svetlana's running like a dream, the sort of dream where all is good but something might go wrong and you will soon wake up in a cold sweat with the pillow looking like you've got up to go to the toilet, forgotten where it is in the dark and pissed all over it. It's ok though, I'm awake, obviously as I'm driving so we are plodding on at 90 kilometers an hour watching the wagons overtake us. We got our Svetty sat nicely behind a Spanish wagon letting him pull us along in his slip stream, no need for directions from Sally sat nav as he was probably going the same direction as we are.

Terri in her superb infinite wisdom had ordered Svetty a “Bip & Go” device as there are quite a few sections of toll roads en route especially around the French and Spanish border. This gizmo that you attach to your rear view mirror let’s you pass through the tolls without having to stop and get a ticket and then pay at the next toll station. Genius idea, you just get an online bill every month if you use the gizmo. The time saved will cut literally seconds off our 10 hour first leg.

We approached the first toll section somewhere between Brive and Toulouse, obviously you need to slow down for the gizmo to bip and then you can go without actually stopping. I’ve not changed gear or used the brake in two and a half hours and fuck me my left foot has gone to sleep, it’s totally dead! I mean totally dead, there really is no feeling at all, I took my right foot off the go pedal and fuck me that felt the same as in no feeling, I had to look at my feet to check they were in the correct place in the footwell and on the pedals! Prolonged vibration and holding aging joints in one position is clearly going to be an issue as we are about 2 hours or 100 kilometers in and have about 6400 kilometers yet to cover.

Anyway we plodded on, me doing ankle and foot stretching exercises as we went, this does involve using the wrong foot on the go pedal from time to time but it helped to keep me amused. Talking of amusement, Terri kept asking for the hundredth or so time like a child saying are we there yet? Are we there yet? Annoying fucking bitch. Anyhoo she is however doing a sterling job of rolling cigarillos for the pilot every half hour. We played I Spy for a while but if you pass the time playing I spy on a motorway it gets really boring after half an hour.

Before we know it, maybe I nodded off and the Spanish wagon in front had just dragged us along for a few hours in its slip stream we are now in Spain. Going from France to Spain is great, the only way you know you have passed from one country to the other is the change in language on the radio, I learned that several years ago driving a vehicle with a radio and also the language on the road signs and the people change.

French people are in general rudely polite, slow and honest. Spanish people and this is based on my limited interaction to date thus far are rude, fast and have a look in their eye's that says they will rob you blind at the first opportunity when you turn your back on them.

A few hours later we arrived at hotel Tudanca Miranda. This hotel was booked as a stopover on the basis that there was secure private parking, this was a requirement so I can sleep easy as there was a couple of grand's worth of shizzle strapped to the roof. We circled the hotel a few times and found some parking out the front but that's about it. Some BMW driver, obviously a cunt as he'd earned some money and thought the best way to spend it was on a BMW, anyway he left the car park so we managed to get a space for Svetty near the reception. At the reception I asked where the secure parking area was? It's out the front where you have parked was the reply from the gay receptionist, he informed us that there is a security camera so we can see from the reception if someone is stealing something from your vehicle. Well thanks for that dickhead, I feel I can rest easy and I can count on your high tech security measures to prevent theft not from but off my vehicle. Thanks Spanish gay boy that's not really fucking comforting ta muchly.

I'm usually artificially polite to underpaid reception staff but right now I'm tired, irritable and I'm about to have an episode.

I don't know if it was the rising stress of the journey, lack of afternoon alcohol, lack of food or 10 hours of being rattled in Svetty but in the hotel reception I was about to have a moment, not induced I will add by the gay reception man and the parking situation but that probably added to my anxiety levels.

We were standing in the hotel reception and I was immediately drenched in thick sweat from head to toe, shivering and shaking like a shitting dog doing a walking shit and felt like I was about to pass out, fortunately there was a comfy sofa in the reception so I sat down to have my moment while Terri finished checking us in. We were given the room key, the eighth floor was where we were heading. Walking to the lift was weird, it felt like my feet weren't connected to my legs and my legs to my body. We found the room, not sure why we had to find it as we hadn't lost it in the first place, but that's how my brain was working. I must have been bad as I refused a rillo on the balcony and lay down sweating on the bed thinking I was going to die. After half an hour or so I came too a bit, feeling chipper enough I went down to the non secure car park to procure some evening refreshments out of Svetlana.

A couple of Top Buget beer's later, I can't remember the details exactly, I was feeling more human than before and we both had the need to consume food.

It's about six in the evening, I'm starving, not literally starving you understand, to see real starving you need to travel to Africa or Gaza or watch the news from twenty years ago and view coverage of the Ethiopian famine to see what starving is actually like so lets settle with me saying "I was a bit hungry."

There was someone different at the reception when I went to ask where the restaurant is. It's next door, the building with "Canteen" in big letters illuminated above the entrance. Into the canteen we went for dinner and ordered a beer, sorry food service doesn't start until eight. Eight! Balls, I forgot we were in Spain where they eat at a ridiculous time of night. We had an hour and a half to kill before we can eat, I would have gone for a mooch around town but it was raining, actually to be more precise it was a combination of sleet and hail so we worked our way through the different beers that were on offer while waiting for the chef to arrive and cook our dinner.

When we got food I recall it was basic, meat, potatoes and veg but lots of it, I can't tell you exactly what was on the plate due to previously working our way through every brand of beer on offer at the bar while waiting to be fed. Anyways it was very good so I ate it like a good boy and went to bed.

I Can't sleep again, eating late in the evening is bad for sleep, it was at least half past ten before we finished eating. I've consumed a belly full of food, more beer and wine than I care to remember and just finished all this no more than twenty minutes earlier. Fortunately to soothe my brain the rain was still hoofing down outside, listening to the pitter patter of the rain dripping on the balcony, I eventually drifted off for a few hours of disturbed sleep.

It's seven, still dark, and still pissing it down. We are ready to set off to our next stopover at Camping Caseres. It's going to be a shorter journey today, only about 450 kilometers but in a Niva that is still a long way.

As ever we need to refuel before departing. I like refilling Svetlana in Spain as it's ten cents a litre cheaper than the petrol in France. Also some additional great news, the hotels limp secure parking appears to have worked as I can see the fecking wheelchair is still in place from the view from our balcony on the 8th floor and without removing the wheel chair you can't steal anything vaguely useful off the roof unless you are disabled and only need a spaz chair.

We're off and it's not just the way we smell. I'll sanitize myself when, or if, we get to Gibraltar.

No need to waffle on about the journey today, it was just a boring motorway for the whole 450 kilometers. We did have a minor altercation when we needed to stop for a piss with no services coming up so pulled off the motorway to relieve ourselves and Sally Satnav tried to take us back to France, not really a drama but Sally Satnav might have been trying to tell us something. Sally's intuition and all that.

The only other mentionable moment en route was going past junction 666 on the N630 motorway where we felt it necessary to give the junction sign a little Svetty toot, toot, toot.

We arrived at Camping Caceres early afternoon, we had booked what was billed online as a hostel room. For 40 euros a night I was expecting something like a Youth Hostel in the United Kingdom of Shitdom. Oh contraire dear reader, I think the camping site which incidentally didn't appear to have anywhere for tents apart from the camper van places might have at one time been army barracks or the like. It was ace, we had a big room with a comfy bed, a bathroom bigger than most hotel rooms, outside there were patio chairs and a table sat under a massive covered area. The door to each hostel room was painted in a graffiti style but with more brush work rather than spray cans. I forget the name of the artist but should you visit you can see it signed on all the doors, the paintings were really smart.

We asked where can we park? As previously discussed we have the fecking wheelchair and other shizzle on the roof that I don't want to be robbed of especially as we are now in deepest darkest Spain.

What a comforting reply we received from the young lass at the reception, you can park just round the corner from your hostel room and the main gates are closed between 10 PM and 7.30 AM, your car registration is read by a camera to let you in through the barrier during the day. I'll hopefully rest and sleep easy tonight.

Time to find somewhere for lunch. I spotted a place on google maps about a kilometer or so from the hostel. The kind young lass at the camp reception said the restaurant is open pretty much all day.

Off we troddled for lunch, it was only about a kilometer away and usually we would have walked but it was still pissing down so we went in Svetlana.

I made a deal with Terri, I'll drive there and Terri can drive back. That's a fair rule that I like to implement a lot. Said eatery was tucked behind a petrol station, you wouldn't even know it was there if you didn't know and obviously lots of locals, workers, truck drivers, camper van drivers and the likes were obviously in the know. It was heaving but the waitress managed to shoe horn us in to a table. Neither of us speak, read or understand Spanish, what we did fathom was that it was a set menu with a choice of 3 starters, 3 mains and 3 puddings, the puddings we thought were an optional cost extra but we really had no idea.

Even in French when we read a menu we don't understand what is written as we don't eat out much so with a Spanish menu in hand, there was a "what the fuck" are we reading moment, we couldn't understand a word of it except for, chorizo, soup and pollo, Terri went for soup with chorizo apparently with other things in it, I went for the other soup that I think could possibly contain some form of fish. I always like to try something different to Terri just incase what Terri chose was shit so we could share or vice versa. For the main course we only understood pollo so we both went for that.

Soup arrived, Terri's was as thought chorizo with some form of meat, it smelled delicious and apparently Terri slopping it everywhere it also tasted pretty good. It appeared that I had gone for gazpacho, the contents of which are still unknown, suffice to say it was fishy, meaty and veggie, it was really good whatever it was and the luminous orangey pinky color brightened my day. Next arrived the pollo, and fuck me I've never seen a plate full of food like it. It was essentially a whole deboned roast chicken shared between two people, the chicken meat had been compressed then all the skin and fat put on top and re-roasted, this could be a heart attack on a plate, on the side or should I say the other half of the plate there was a heap of potatoe dauphinoise or whatever the Spanish equivalent is. We both tucked in and and soon gave up, delicious as it was, my belly can only take so much food in one hit, there was so much food for the twenty euros it cost, I now understand why the Spanish don't eat until at the earliest eight at night, with this quantity of food at lunch you can't fit anything else in until you have had at least two good shits. I'll probably opt for just a salad tomorrow, but as we'll hopefully, fingers crossed be arriving in Gibraltar a carryout out curry night might be on the cards?

Lunch over and it's sill raining, (rain becomes a theme) we are back at the hostel, we don't appear to have any neighbors so we are making use of the covered patio, terrace whatever you want to call it area, we found a music channel on the telly, opened the window and set up a makeshift bar on the provided patio table. It was Fairly basic, we had a box of stubbies, red and white bibs, nibbles and the road trip box of happiness containing a camping stove, kettle, long life milk, Yorkshire tea for Terri and menthe et reglise tea infusion for me.

There's nothing much to do as it's still raining so a chilled late afternoon and evening was ahead. With everything that's planned for the next few days I think we'll need an early night and early start tomorrow. We popped round to the reception to ask if we can leave before the gates are open at 7.30 as we want to be away early. There's now a different lady on reception and she had the air, no, not the air of but the attitude of a complete fucking bitch, said bitch abruptly muttered, no the gates open at 7.30, if you want to leave earlier you need to park outside. Just here outside the front of the reception I asked? No that area clearly says no parking, you will need to park over there on the street. Thanks for the non secure parking offer you miserable Spanish bitch woman.

Executive decision we'll leave at 7.30 and keep Svetlana nice and cozy in the secure barracks compound. Terri had a human rights rant at this point, they can't stop you leaving at anytime you want, this isn't fucking Auschwitz, what if you need to leave urgently should you for example have a family emergency to deal with or your arm falls off and you need to go to urgence? Anyhoo it was getting late, I put the camping kettle on and had a pre bed brew of menthe et reglise outside on the terrace listening to the rain.

Sleep was quick to arrive tonight listening again as ever to the rain. Tomorrow we are going to Gibraltar.

We are up and on it at six, camp bar was packed up and the morning brews were made. I could hear the movement of campervans, we went to look and the campervans were escaping the Auschwitz gates under the cover of darkness. Without further ado we joined them, escaped and now we are heading Gibraltar bound.

Oh the joy of going to Gibraltar again, I can barely contain myself with the sense of dread being surrounded by English twats and cunts for a few days. Hopefully we will arrive there early afternoon or I thought to myself it would be better to crash and die en route to save the hassle and the misery of visiting Gibraltar. It's going to be a boring few hours so we'll reconvene as soon as I see the Cock of Gibraltar. We did amuse ourselves while tootling down the very boring motorway by shouting Rupert every time a Renault 4 passed in the opposite direction. There were loads of Rupert's going the opposite direction all raid prepared and covered in sponsorship stickers. We assumed they had all enjoyed a raid in Morocco and were heading home. The wife has a 1982 Renault 4 or a Quatrelle as the French affectionately call them, he is called Rupert, hence the shouting of Rupert every time we see one.

Some time later and now I think I can just see it through the rain, the miserable Cock of Gibraltar, I find it as disappointing in the distance as seeing the White Cliffs of Dover from a ferry unless you are leaving the white cliffs then boom, happy days.

Terri is currently driving, I'm peeping through my fingers, even though we are on a motorway, Terri's driving is somewhat erotic, yes I did say erotic not erratic but we'll leave that observation there for now.

Terri didn't want to negotiate the approach into Gibraltar, nor negotiate the passport and custom's control's, Morribobs car park and then getting to Audrey's place in Gibraltar as you need biceps the size of Bournemouth to steer Svetlana in your desired direction in confined spaces.

We stopped just off the motorway, swapped seats and had a piss. It was raining so hard that when we got back in Svetlana it looked like we had pissed in our pants, maybe we had? Onwards we went to Shitbraltar.

I don't know dear reader if you have ever driven into Gibraltar? There are about eight million roundabouts on the couple of kilometer approach road to the border crossing, everyone is in a rush for no reason as when you arrive you will be stuck in a queue at the border, who the fuck would rush to get in the border crossing queue into Gibraltar anyway? Well obviously dicks overtaking us in expensive electric SUV's, us being in a French registered Russian Svetlana I used all the roundabouts as a chicane cutting them up and making them shit their pants. If Svetlana should happen to nudge into one of them it would be thousands of notes worth of repairs to their vehicle and zero to Svetlana. On the down side I might have to wipe blood off the home made bullbars.

Eventually after playing roundabout roulette we arrived at the Gibraltar border crossing, to get to this enclave you have to negotiate proper chicanes with dicks managing to use all three lanes instead of following one single lane, eventually we arrived at the border.

Anything to declare or nothing to declare? Nothing other than my eccentricity, stupidity and being a dick which I will happily declare.

We approached passport control where there was a busy body in a high vis vest waving me towards him, I had put Svetlana in low box so we could just crawl along to him. When we arrived at Mr High vis and stopped we were greeted by the sentence. "Do you speak English"? Yes Mr High Vis I am unfortunately British and can understand you I replied, I do however live in France and as you can see I have a French registered vehicle, British passport and French residency card, is there a problem? (dickhead under my breath) I asked?

This is a border crossing was the reply and you must stop when told. I did dickhead, I stopped when you told me to, maybe your mate in the cabin checking passports might have asked me to stop before I got to you by putting his hand out of his booth as in my experience people in their high and mighty booths do so and I would respect their notion for me to stop, but he didn't, why didn't he? Possibly he'd snuck out for a poo or a smoke or maybe his arm wasn't working well enough to put it out of the booth window to stop me? Maybe he was so bored checking passports in the confines of his totally black tinted windowed cabin he decided to caress his winky in private? Scanning passports must be a fucking boring job so winky stroking might be acceptable or even encouraged as a pass time. Anyway he asked if we would be more conscientious when at the border crossing in the future. I nodded in some sort of recognition or agreement and as soon as possible I disinfected my passport of sweaty piss fingers and the possibility of border man's spunk residue on my official documents. This attitude that I just have experienced is why I fucking hate anything associated with the United Kingdom of Shitdom.

Anyway after all that shizzle we are now in Gibraltar! Great news? First Etape Minus 1 of the Raid done without incident, we have thus far managed 1800 kilometers without a hitch other than the obligatory top up of engine oil.

Our first stop in Gibraltar is to pop into Morribobs to procure refreshments, it was going to be a quick pop in and out as we didn't have a pound coin for a trolley so we had to carry everything. Pound coins look similar to a euro coin but they are not similar enough to borrow a trolley for twenty minutes. So we used a shop and stroller basket. Essential shopping item's on our list are, John Smiths, Punk IPA, IPA Mixed pack & crisps, a very healthy shop indeed.

Final leg for Svetlana for now as she really deserves a rest. We departed Morribobs on the treacherous journey up to Audrey's apartment. Said residence is located at something or other Terrace, near Rosia bay, locations are not important as Gibraltar is tiny.

During the very short commute from Morribobs to somewhere else, we had to have our wits about us, defending ourselves as best as we could from the myriad of mopeds hurling themselves at us from every direction and the cunts in Range

Rovers trying to drive at speed to their yachts moored at the marina. We arrived at something or other Terrace and put Svetlana in the underground garage so she could have a nap for a couple of days before she would take us to Morocco.

We ordered a carry out curry, went to collect it on foot in the rain, yes it's still raining. We ate much mediocre curry, obviously we ate it as even in my caveman brain that is what you do with food regardless of how disappointing it is. The food wasn't up to the standard of five years ago and the naan breads were especially dry and shit. Anyway we ate everything, watched telly for a bit and went to bed.

There is much administrative shizzle to achieve tomorrow. Sweet dreams dear reader see you in the morning.

# 5 Doom Day Approacheth

Morning dear reader, did you sleep well? Are you still with us? Apparently this morning we need to take much paperwork to the Births, Deaths and marriages office in down town Gibraltar. We have been advised by Alix who has arranged the ceremony to get there as early as possible as the office can often have people queuing out of the door, probably only for births and marriages, if you are dead you probably don't have much need to be queuing. Would you believe it but it's still raining and like a retard I've discovered after unpacking everything that I haven't bothered to pack a rain coat. Yes, I agree I am a dick but I was expecting clement weather on this trip going to the north African desert and all that.

We were first in line at birth, deaths and marriages, soaking wet and when the doors opened, there's a tiny little room with three booths and only one person manning them, or in this case womaning them. We explained we were arranged to be married at City Hall tomorrow and we need to present all of our known documents except for our death certificates. The Spanish lass behind the screen didn't really seem to understand fuck all of why we were told to be there and what she needed to make copies of so gave us both a random form to fill in.

Why I ask when in a Gibraltarian government building and therefore a British government building you need to converse with someone Spanish who either doesn't understand English or is pretending not to or just can't be fucking arsed to be helpful in anyway. Anyhoo, half an hour later help arrived in the form of the person responsible for organizing the ceremony. Apparently Alix had emailed Terri saying he would meet us at said three booth no staff government office at 9.30. Terri being Terri and somewhat slap dash in communication obviously didn't have a look at her emails otherwise we could have had an extra half hour in bed to arrive at 9.30 and not rush to be first in line in the pissing rain.

We were united with Alix, he walked in, pissed wet through into the 3 booth 1 staff increasingly busy and wet room. I was disappointed, Alix was and probably still is a man! I was expecting some fit young wedding planner chick, but nope, he was a middle aged slightly rotund Hispanic man.

My first wife had a friend called Alix who was female and fit as fuck as they say! They used to go to tap dance sessions on a Monday night and the first wife would usually not return back home until nearly midnight, there's only so many hours of dance practice you can do in one evening is there not? I always thought there was little or no tap dancing going on but just a bout of rug munching but I never asked and I just let the fantasy roll on hopefully thinking that one day I might be invited to join in.

Anyway, Alix was apparently expected by the one staff member to arrive in the office and he promptly started to sort the paperwork out, he exchanged words in "Gibberish" with the one Spanish lass working there. Gibberish is the English / Spanish crossover language that is popular in Gibraltar. The paperwork was given to Alix and off we went wandering in the never ending rain to a rather posh looking Hotel to fill out some more forms. When we arrived it looked to me like the palatial hotel lobby is a free for all meeting place for anyone to use and engage in form filling, conversation, drug deals, weapons transactions etc without actually being a resident of the hotel.

We were both given our partially completed forms apropos tomorrow's wedding. All we needed to do was just fill in a few details which should be simple enough you would think. The easy bit is where I have to write my name and sign, I wrote Nathanael Andrew Peter Chambers, obviously as it's my full name and was instantly berated for writing across the part where Alix puts his name and signs it. The form should be bigger or wider dickhead! Anyway not wanting to dwell on the form filling fiasco, we'll leave it that Alix couldn't read or make any sense of anything I had written but he hoped the one staff person at the three booth office would take an average of the three completed forms and make some sense of them. We were told in no uncertain terms to check the official register tomorrow at City Hall before signing it after the wedding ceremony to make sure all the details we're correct before being on paper married to someone with a totally random name who doesn't exist.

Proper job, that's all the paperwork shizzle sorted. We parted company with Alix in the rain, he said he wouldn't be coming to the ceremony tomorrow but he said we just need to turn up at City Hall and everything will be taken care of, no problem we've already got too many guests invited without having a non fit non female Alix attending.

My next task is to go and buy a rain coat before the rain washes my skin away. I don't know if you have ever been to Gibraltar and enjoyed a walk along Main Street? It's a bit like Deansgate in Manchester, all the shops you need if you are a fashionado, hypochondriac, jewelry thief, or need a new cover for your phone, all the shops are here on this one miserable rainy street. Gibraltar is so small it only has room for one Main Street and it is about as impressive as going to Burnley market when all the stall holders are there on a Saturday, at least if you want to buy tripe you can get it in Burnley or if you prefer to go further afield to Bury market where you can apparently buy the best tripe and black pudding in the world. Alas we are on Main street in Gibraltar not in Burnley or Bury.

We were walking along popping in and out of stores trying to avoid the rain, why does no one sell reasonably priced rain coats in this god forsaken shit hole? Rain coats are obviously not high on Gibraltarian inhabitants shopping lists. Then boom we went in to the Superdry shop, I'm not really into brand names but I had heard of Superdry from my skiing days and all I really needed at this moment was something to keep me dry but if they are quoting SuperDry I'll have some of that. Fuck me 100 English pounds for a rain coat, smart looking as it might be with the biggest inside pocket I've ever seen, I could secrete a bottle of anything in there without anyone being any the wiser or pop down to Morribobs and do some pilfering. It was however not as pricey as I thought though, I had missed the massive and multiple signs saying 50 percent of everything, so I thought fuck it we are on holiday then moving onto honeymoon so I'll take it. No need for a bag thanks very much, please just cut the labels off and I'll wear it to keep myself SuperDry, if I'm not kept SuperDry I'll be back very soon for a refund.

We are now in the hen and stag partying territory, the only problem is that there's only the two of us so we decided to stop on the way back to our temporary digs at chez Audrey and stopped for lunch at a little Italian restaurant. We ordered a jug of sangria and ordered some food, I can't remember what it was that we ordered and ate on account of the large amount of sangria consumed. I do however remember the very friendly waitress who was chatting to us as the rain appears to have stopped the locals and holiday people eating out and she was clearly bored. You really would have to be very bored to willingly talk to us two knob ends! Anyway, we had some conversation about our planned trip and she kindly said that if we call in tomorrow after the ceremony in our wedding outfits we would get free drinks. So that's about it for hen and stag doo shenanigans. I did consider pushing the boat out and also having a curry for dinner but it was, as you can probably guess, still raining and I couldn't be arsed with the walk to the curry house even in my SuperDry coat which appears to be doing exactly what it says on the label. Instead I rummaged in Audrey's freezer and found a thing to eat for supper, I have no blooming idea of what it was even though it had a scribbled label on it, I think it was mushroom based but feck knows it could have been anything. On the plus side I didn't die or puke my guts up or shit everywhere and lived to see another unfortunate day so it must have been ok. Instead of going out clubbing we watched some crap on telly and went to bed, rock and roll then for our hen and stag outings.

# 6 The Day Into ClusterFuck

Here we are, it's the wedding day. Wedding number two for me and number three for Terri. All the paperwork is done, all we need to do is to just turn up on time at City Hall and sign a few papers.

The nearly but not yet current wife has yet to dye her hair red to compliment her outfit and the general Morticia look, that I think is to try and look like the living dead. This is an easy task for Terri as she looks like the living dead almost every morning unless she's having a good day then she looks more like someone in a self-induced coma.

First attempt at hair coloring looked like a disaster, well, didn't just look like it, it was a disaster on the color front. It looked like a Les Dawson purple rinse but only with a slightly pink tint, clearly not red. Another go and we now have a touch of red color but nothing spectacular. It doesn't really matter as Terri will be wearing her kiss me quick, pork pie style hat and funeral veil so no-one will notice her crap hair coloring failure.

Time to break with routine, it's not Sunday so I don't need to clean myself but I'm all over this wedding shizzle like a rash, in the spirit of enduring the inconvenience of getting married again I will treat myself to a shower, not just a normal shower like I have at home, I'll turn the water on and rub soap into my nether regions and orifices, you know, as it's wedding day and all that, then I thought fuck it, If I can find some nail clippers in the many drawers and cupboards in Audrey's bathroom I'll treat myself to a manicure and pedicure, possibly an ear and nose hair trim but the latter might be pushing it a bit, I'm not a machine you know and I don't have a personal stylist to pamper me and the nearest I have to such a person is still failing miserably in the bathroom at hair coloring.

So dear reader, we are both clean 'ish' that is to say Terri and I are clean, to reiterate you will note that I state Terri and I are clean 'ish', you however are probably sat in your week old piss stained undies, smearing the pages of this book that I have lovingly created with your sweaty piss fingers and god knows what else you might have on your grubby digits. Anyway let's move on from your dear readers lack of personal hygiene and carry on with our wedding day.

Terri's finally managed to achieve a weird pinkish hair color and we are more or less dressed in our fancy dress / wedding outfits. It's now time for the traditional wedding breakfast.

Previously the wedding breakfast would have consisted of sharing a bottle of Stolly with the best man and chief usher followed by a few lines of snort. Today we had vodka thanks to Audrey, well I did and there was a very pretty looking bottle of Prosecco that might or might or might not have been left in the apartment for us but we would consume it anyway. I was later advised by the now wife that Janette Jenison had left it there on a previous visit because her body could not consume any more alcohol. I'm sure if we wanted to in Gibraltar we could procure class A narcotics, but I'm past that these days and a class B smoke doesn't really cut the mustard anymore as they say.

We are dressed and ready to walk down to City Hall to be weddinigified. One or two items of my wedding attire were missing, firstly I need to affix my pocket watch to my suit jacket that shit magnet Cathy kindly gave me, next unfortunately or fortunately I had like packing a rain coat forgotten to pack the studded dog collar and lead that Cathy had also given me, shame. I had also borrowed a cane, I couldn't have a suit and bowler hat without a cane. I had borrowed it from idiot boy next door and a rather spiffing cane it was too. Idiot boy suggested it might be at least one hundred years old so I must not loose it. Anyway I had forgotten it and it was somewhere in the back of Svetlana, presumably it was packed next to the golf putters and sand wedge clubs we had packed.

Now dear reader you are probably thinking to yourself, why the fuck is this moron going on a rally in the Moroccan desert and taking golf sticks with him? I can happily inform you that neither Terri nor I play golf as it is a totally fucking boring and pointless pastime. We have children to walk which is a much more enjoyable way of walking a few kilometers rather than hitting a small ball around 9 or 18 manicured fields depending on how much money or time and patience you have. We do however when we get bored on camping trips like to set up our own crazy golf course to pass the time or if there is one available within walking beer distance we will always make use of it. Crazy golf in our household is a very competitive sport. Obviously for crazy golf you need a putter and a ball or preferably a ball each to reduce arguments.

Up there for thinking down there for dancing, I'm planning ahead. We are planning on playing home made crazy golf in the desert. Obviously we will also need to take a sand wedge with us as it will be like playing crazy golf in one massive sand bunker.

Off we go hot footing it towards down town Gibraltar. I now have idiot boys cane in hand having retrieved it out of Svetlana, for comedy value I should have taken the putter as a cane but I really can't be arsed to rummage in Svetlana's bum again as we have to repack everything ready to head in the direction of Morocco tomorrow.

We are heading to an upmarket looking wine bar next to City Hall to meet all of our privileged invited guests, it's going to be heaving and I'm glad I didn't offer to pick up the bar tab.

Walking through Gibraltar in our wedding attire / fancy dress was proper ace. I doffed my bowler hat with the aid of my cane to greet everyone we passed with a cheerful 'good morning to you' and 'morning sir' or 'morning madam'. You get the general idea of a knob head in a polyester flame suit, generally being an arrogant dick strolling along acting like he's the lord of the manor of Gibraltar. In my mind I was just trying to brighten up other peoples day, some of the people on the other hand just thought I was an annoying cunt. One item I missed from the soon to be wife's attire was her supposedly sexy garters. Either the size didn't fit her thighs or Mr Wong's elastic wasn't up to the job and they kept falling to her ankles and tripping her over. After a few trips they were removed and secreted in the glamorous bag for life we were carrying.

There was a distinctly different reaction from the locals who were on their way to work or to drop their children off at nursery which I assume based on the look on their faces took to mean, fuck off dickhead, wanker, fuckwit etc. On the other hand, the American, Chinese & Japanese tourists asked politely if they could have their photograph taken with us. We were even asked if we were employed by the city to walk round in fancy dress, alas we are not paid to be idiots but there could be a business opportunity there in the future.

We arrived after many photos with tourists en route at the posh wine bar place, the guests are already here, they being Rachel & Val. That's it, we or should I say Terri only invited two people who would serve as witnesses for the ceremony. Rachel had made sort of an effort and was dressed up as an elf, Val had dressed up as Val! Rachel and Val are friends of Terri's from many moons ago when Terri lived in Gibraltar. Bless them both for accepting Terri's invite or should that be plea as they were both taking time out of their busy lives to join us on our paperwork marriage day. Without them we would have had to pay an extra fifty English pounds for rent a friend, or to be exact rent 2 friends as witnesses. I will reimburse them both later by buying them a lavish wedding day lunch.

We all downed a few drinks in readiness for the marriage, it's the unwritten law of wedding days, it really is amazing how rowdy four people can be and it's not even twelve o'-clock, I suppose considering the wedding breakfast that we had consumed it was inevitable. Time now to drink up and go next door to City Hall to do the wedding thing.

City Hall wasn't as grand as I was expecting it was a bit like walking into Burnley town hall on dole and child benefit day but without the dolie's, is dolie's a word? Perhaps doley's would be better, anyway lets for now call them the unemployable. Gibraltar has many unemployable people but they have money and probably lots of it to afford to live there and therefore don't need to work nor do they have any intention of doing. There was another wedding party waiting in the entrance hall, clearly with more friends than we have as there we're about ten of them. They were obviously dead keen to tie the knot as they weren't on stage until after us. Our huge wedding entourage was ushered into the big white ceremony room. Then a gate crasher joined us, one of Terri's mother's friends from the church who came along as a spectator, boom, we might as well make use of her so we now have a free no cost to us wedding photographer, proper job!

We're loitering around for the registrar, ceremony person, I'm not sure what they are referred to in Gibraltar, we are the first ceremony of the day so maybe they had overslept or were waiting for it to stop raining before venturing out, anyway a man arrives tucking his shirt in to his pants and putting on a tie. I need to point out at this point he wore pointy twat toe shoes but his suit was clearly of better quality polyester than mine and might have been bought on Gibraltar Main Street and not from Mr Wong via TEMU.

Let me introduce you to Mr Adrian Traverso, we were told by Alix the previous morning that this gentleman would be carrying out the ceremony. Mr Traverso by all accounts is the chap who carries out the wedding ceremony's on a French reality television show called 'Married on First Date', if you haven't heard of it don't worry, neither have I, my life might be boring as fuck but I draw the line at any form of reality program, apparently the show is very popular and there are many different countries offering the same or similar crap on television.

The idea of 'Married on First Date' is that two people, that's how in my understanding marriage normally works to know each other on line and the first time they actually meet in person is their wedding day, the ceremony of which is carried out by Mr Traverso. If you want to look him up on Instagram he goes under the name of Mr Happy Traverso, he's always on the lookout for new followers and maybe if you say you heard about him in this rambling collection of words he might buy a copy or 'patronise' the immaturity of this book.

Despite his pointy twat shoes he was very polite and engaging and who would have thought it that a French television celebrity would be carrying out our paperwork ceremony. As a side note, when I saw the quality of the lining in Mr Traverso's suit it was clearly rather more expensive than I had at first thought it looked. For the first time in this book something strange happened. I didn't want to offend Mr Traverso so I didn't ask if his suit was from TEMU or TK MAX? I hadn't driven all this way to be kicked in the balls by a celebrity with his pointy twat toe shoes and shown the door. Also possibly we could end up on television a bit like my 'friend' handyman Paul who features on Chateau DIY, being on television however has turned him from a grumpy old twat into an even grumpier miserable old twat.

We were advised that the ceremony is only brief, good job as you are already running late Mr Traverso and after my wedding breakfast I'm ready for a spot of lunch. Mr Traverso asked if we had the rings, of course we have, you might laugh at our outfits but we are not total retards? Bring on Elf Rachel with her Morribobs bag for life. Contained therein is an embroidered ring cushion lovingly made by our friend Lynn Bonnet. Not the sort of ring cushion you need when the piles pop out of your arse to allow for comfortable sitting. This is an embroidered cushion with ribbons on it to hold each ring in place. The rings are where the laughter started again following the laughter about our outfits.

Let me explain, Terri had an idea that she wanted a nut for a ring, yep that works for me as we spend more time fixing shit in the gayrage than we do doing anything vaguely romantic. The most romantic thing I've done recently was to buy Terri 4 rolls of spooled MIG welding wire as they were in stock at LIDL, who says romance is dead.

Back to Terri's wedding ring. She opted for a 10mm nut. To be exact it was a 10mm internal diameter nut that nearly fit over her wedding finger, the outer diameter of the nut will fit a 19mm spanner so it might be a tad too big to wear. Taking some rudimentary measurements the nut looked as if it would fit ok between the other fingers without chaffing. This is as far as we can guess without said ring being bodged and put on her finger.

When I say the 10mm nut nearly fit, some modification was required without putting Terri's ring finger on a diet or grinding a bit off it, so it was off to the gayrage for Terri to modify the nut for a first fitting.

I quote now directly from Terri, 'I'm going to the gayrage to ream out my ring'. What the fuck? 'Ream out my ring'! Whatever the fuck floats your boat darling future wife, just don't expect me to clean up the mess. After a few attempts at reaming out her ring she reappeared from the gayrage triumphant with a reamed out ring that fitted her wedding finger snugly.

Next onto my ring, you really don't want to go there, its dirty and clinkered, so I just got a 19mm ring spanner off the tool board cut the handle off it, filed a bit off it and boom it fitted. So Terri's reamed out ring sits nicely in my butchered spanner.

Back to the ceremony, rings are on the cushion. Mr Traverso started the ceremony with the usual boring shit, we are here today to witness the joining of, bla, bla, bla.

Skipping ahead,

'Do you Nathanael Andrew Peter Chambers take Teresa Rainbow to be your lawful wedded wife'?

'I take Teresa bitch whore slag bag to be my wedded strife'.

'Do you Teresa Rainbow take Nathanael Andrew Peter Chambers to be your lawful wedded husband'?

'I take Nathanael Andrew Peter knob cheese cunt face Chambers to be my awful wedded husband'.

'By the power invested in me I now pronounce you man and wife, you can now kiss the bride'

'Do I have to? We're past all that shizzle and it might smudge the Japanese fuck doll black lipstick'

So that's all that done and dusted, we're officially married.

Does it feel different you might ask? Nope not really, I just need to amend my phrasing henceforth to 'bitch wife'.

I could have elaborated more on the ceremony but you have all been to one and they are all the same so there's no need to waste your time continuing waffling on about wedding formalities. I will however in the next chapter describe Terri's, sorry my wife's wedding bouquet as it plays a part in the future of our adventure.

To unofficially finish the ceremony Mr Traverso joined us for a fag outside, well a fag that was illegally smoked in the entrance hall as it's a no smoking area and guess what it was still pissing it down but Mr Traverso being a celebrity no one complained. I don't know how his suit would have faired in the rain, the color might have run out of it but while still being polite I made no mention of it and just wondered what might have happened. We all did hugs and handshakes and went on our separate merry ways. Mr Traverso was a bit despondent that we were the first ceremony of the day as he guessed all the rest would be boring as fuck.

I have a gut feeling that everything is going to go in the downhill direction from here.

Time now for the wedding reception. Wife's mother's gate crashing friend did one early and fucked off, she probably had to go and pray, down the alter wine or do some other ecclesiastical lunch time chore. I have just made the first married mistake here, I should have said mother in laws friend.

Off to the wedding reception it is then, we hot footed it or should I say we wet footed it to the Clipper for lunch, I'll try and remember everyone to give them a mention, we have the wife, Elf, Val and me. Quite the party is planned I'm sure you will agree. The Clipper was heaving not with our guests, just tourists and locals talking Gibberish. The reason we chose this venue is the pies that they make, hopefully they will be as good as I remember from five years ago, not a tad limp and untasty like the takeaway curry house was.

What could be better for a reception lunch than pie, mash, peas and gravy or chips in place of mash if you prefer but I'll have you know chips with a proper good pie is a great big fat wobbly no, no, in my book, not this book but in my mental book you understand? Pies all round it is then, I don't care to remember what the wife, Elf and Val ordered. I however knew immediately what I was going to order. As the wife has a habit of vomiting mushrooms back up looking the same way as they went down as she doesn't digest them, for this reason I don't get to eat mushrooms very often and I like them a lot. I decided without hesitation or fear of constipation to seize the opportunity and ordered the chicken and mushroom pie, obviously with mash, just because I can and it's the law. When it arrived I was a little disappointed, there were vegetables on the plate, however delicious looking the fresh vegetables looked on the plate I have to ask myself why the fuck are there vegetables on my plate? You Gibraltarian idiots, where the hell are my mushy peas you fuck wits? I made this comment to the waiter who appeared to take my comment on the board and he came back with a small bowl of garden peas, I would mush them up on my plate with my fork or in my mouth and spit them back out nice and mushy onto the plate ready for eating. These people need some training in Northern English cuisine.

At a very big table behind us in the Clipper many people arrived, well about ten of them, not a huge crowd but more than the four of us, It was by chance the wedding party that were on after us for their ceremony with Mr Traverso at City Hall. We compared random notes with them, not sure why we bothered but it seemed polite and passed the time. The men wore trainers with their suits so I was more than happy to converse with them about absolute fucking bollocks that I have no idea what it was about as is the norm for a wedding reception. We didn't go the whole hog of wedding reception delights and felt no need to get into any fisty cuffs with anyone or any inanimate object, I didn't even enter into a heated argument or debate and thus far no one has puked or pissed anywhere inappropriately.

Elf and Val made their excuses to leave which was not necessary as we have already taken up too much of their time and we parted company, they had more important things to do with their lives than waste a full day of their time with us two dicks in fancy dress. I was told off by the pair of them for paying for drinks and lunch, this wedding reception cost 80 quid, the last one was about three grand so I'm not complaining.

We wandered back in the direction of something or other Terrace calling in at every hostillery en route, several pints later we arrived back at chez mother in law, it was only about four in the afternoon so time for wedding rude time. Ha ha, nothing rude going on here, we are past all that mess and the cleaning up, repairing furniture, I really cannot be bothered with that shizzle anymore. One thing is puzzling me on the discussion of rudes which is, we are using mother in laws bedroom and bed, obviously not with her in it as she is at chez nous looking after the children, my query is why when we arrived to stay there were handcuffs attached to the bed that the wife had already neatly tucked out of sight under the mattress!

In true wedding fashion we had a nap, normally you would have to get up after a short nap and meet and greet, dance with, be polite to a hundred or so people of which 50 percent you don't really like but felt obliged to invite. You feel obliged to invite family who are generally wankers, friends on the other hand you invite because you like them and they like you, hence they are friends not someone you are unfortunate enough to be related to that you really fucking hate.

The benefit of getting married in Gibraltar and not inviting anyone else is there is no need for an evening reception to bother about so we can have an afternoon nap for as long as we like. The evening reception mainly consisted of watching telly, drinking wine and cups of tea, an early night is in order as we have many things to accomplish tomorrow before the honeymoon starts, hang on a minute we're not at home so the honeymoon is technically already in progress. We left the mother in laws handcuffs tucked safely under the mattress and went to sleep.

# 7 Decoration

Honeymoon day one, the first job was to take little pea as we call her to the church to pick up donated items for the poor and needy of Morocco in addition to the fecking wheelchair strapped to Svetlana's roof, little pea is the mother in laws little Kia Picanto, Gibraltar registered runabout that she left at chez nous in France a few years ago when she couldn't be arsed to drive it back so we used it for a couple of years before Pea being eventually returned to Gibraltar.

Off we popped to the church, I don't know what it is about churches but they always smell foisty regardless of how often they are used or aired. I have a theory that the foisty smell comes from the dead skin falling off the aging congregation floating around in the same way that you can smell a fart by inhaling miniscule elements of poo particles. That's only my theory and is probably complete and utter shite.

We were given bags and bags of stuff, I have no idea how we will get all this shizzle in Svetlana, we've already had to put the god forsaken wheelchair on the roof. Oops I just said god forsaken in a church, do I say hail Mary or something? One lovely item that had been donated was a full team's football kit, I hate football but I think the underprivileged Moroccan bin lids would be very appreciative of it when they receive it.

Next item on the to do list was repacking Svetlana, which will now be a struggle to get everything in and more importantly all the essential items visible for the pre raid technical check this afternoon. The wife was going to decorate Svetty my old Russian bird so I left the two of them in the comfort of the underground garage to get on with it. Meanwhile Asier had emailed another bulletin apropo the ferry crossing and requirements we had to adhere to in order to be allowed to enter Morocco at Tangiers port tomorrow, a mere twenty pages to translate and save on the tablet, I would have along with the other hundred or so previous pages translated them and printed them out for reference, however the mother in laws printer was I think manufactured in the same century as the humble typewriter, and was as much use as an ash tray on a motorbike.

The wife's repacked and decorated Svetlana, we are full up to the roof inside and on the roof rack we're nearly to the ceiling of the underground garage, hopefully we will get out of the underground garage without loosing the fucking wheelchair at the exit door. There's just room enough for the wife and I to get in the front seats.

Lets proceed to the decoration, the wife had wrapped red and black tinsel around the roof rack and front bull bars, just married paper bunting was hanging on the back window, and then on the back bumper where you would normally as is or was tradition to tie tins to the back of the vehicle to clatter off down the street, for environmental, noise and litter pollution reasons the wife had attached paper cups to the back bumper with guess what color of ribbon? If you didn't guess black and red then you really are a thicko and must have someone read this drivvle to you while dribbling from the mouth while sat in your bedsit with piss oozing out of your jogging pants that alas you have never jogged in, Jizzed in maybe but I'm fairly certain never jogged in. Apologies, I promised that I wouldn't but I have digressed yet again.

I mentioned earlier that I would explain the wife's wedding bouquet in more detail. I will forewarn you now that this tale will go off on a tangent so please bear with me, there is a link between the Bouquet and a childhood trauma leaving me with a hatred for football. I feel the tenuous link is worth talking about here as I will probably never write another book and this off shoot story should be written down for prosperity. Please still remember that in and amongst my ramblings all of this is a true story and not fiction although there are a few embellishments added here and there en route. Are you still with me?

The bouquet then. The wife person had bought from, guess where? Yep TEMU, red and black plastic roses and other small flowers with berries on them to make a bouquet. She had assembled them in some sort of order with a bit of vehicle emergency wire to hold them all together. They looked ok I suppose but don't tell the wife that what she had done was make a totally shit job of it.

Enter stage left, Bernadette Atkinson or Bernie as she prefers to be known, she is an acquaintance of ours who is a friend of the shit magnet Cathy who you may or may not remember from earlier. Don't get me wrong Bernie isn't one of the shits that Cathy's magnet attracts, she is a down to earth say what I like, like what I say northern lass who happens to now live in Bourganeuf, not anymore in the north west of the United Kingdom of Shitdom where she lived as a child. Anyhoo, Bernie, before moving to France used to have a flower shop somewhere up in Scotland and very kindly modified Terri's attempt at making a bouquet into something very beautiful and sturdy. It was for Bernie simply a case of using a good eye to rearrange the relevant items in a more aesthetic manner. The finished bouquet looked proper smart, Bernie had also fashioned a handle on to it that resembled a big black cock dildo. Enough of that though, the handle worked a treat to attach the bouquet to the front of Svetlana's bull bars. Svetlana looked epic in the style of what shall we call it? 'The wifes covered Svetlana in glue and ram raided an arts / crafts / Christmas and flower shop'.

The reason I want to elaborate here is due to a conversation that I had with Bernie at a lunch we went to. She described herself to me as a witch, not just any old witch but a Pendle witch. 'A Pendle witch' I asked. 'Where are you from'? I asked, 'Sabden' was the reply.

Here is where I found out the world is a small place or perhaps just a place of pure chance. To cut a long story short as this is still a deviation from where we should heading I will briefly explain.

Bernie was dragged up in a village just a stones throw from the village where I was dragged up, although we are 10 years different in age we had possibly crossed paths as Bernie used to frequent the village I lived in. Bernie asked if I knew Mr Derek Lambert from Higham, that's the village where I was dragged up. Yes I knew Lambo as my dear departed father used to call him, Lambo was a pillar of the community, he worked as a justice of the peace in Burnley on Sea, and he used to arrange in his grand barn many soirees of all types. Thinking back to the late 1970's early 1980's they could well have been swingers nights, I'm only surmising this as most properties in Higham had Pampas grass growing in their gardens, a sure sign of swingers houses back in the day or is that just an urban myth? Anyway Lambo as we'll refer to him was Bernie's uncle, not a real uncle, many of you like me will have had an aunty or uncle back in the day as a pretend relative, they were in no way related, just close friends of our parents who looked after us when our parents were going out for a child free adult romantic meal or popping their car keys in a bowl at a house with Pampas grass growing in the garden before getting pissed on Blue Nun or Hock and doing fuck knows what.

The introduction of Lambo brings us on to talk about the Niff Naffs. Lambo and my father used to take the spastics from the spastic home in the near by town of Padiham to the Turf Moor football ground to watch the Burnley team attempt to play football. This was part of the community care that the Burnley and Pendle Round Table did.

As I recall from what my father told me about the Round Table their activities mainly consisted of meeting for a meal once a week, getting pissed and watching porn in the back room of wherever they were eating. I don't know about you but I've never found that group watching of porn which would inevitably lead to masturbation would be an appealing thing to participate in. I prefer to oil up and crack one off alone using the screencast thing. Back to the Niff Naffs, this was my father's pet name for the spastics (remember we are still in the 1970's and spastics still existed).

We were standing on the terraces at Turf Moor and as I remembered it was fucking freezing, at the time I would probably just have said I was cold, being an eight year old I hadn't yet learned the word fuck but when I learned the word I would and still continue to use it at every opportunity in later life.

Let me picture the scene for you I'm standing fucking freezing on the terraces at Turf Moor watching football minding my own business. The Niff Naffs are watching the crowd which consisted of Burnley's finest looking thugs waiting for the match to finish so they can run out of the ground and kick the shit out of the opposing teams supporters or vice versa. There were eight of the Niff Naffs stood in front of us in a row, dribbling and drooling as spastics do or did before they weren't called spastics.

One of them said 'Mrrster Tlumbers ii kneed u goo tu ta toilet'. My father replied, 'sorry I can't understand you', Niff Naff repeated 'Mrrster Tlumbers ii kneed u goo tu ta toilet'. 'Sorry I still can't understand you' 'Mrrster Tlumbers ii kneed u goo tu ta toilet, ohh too late'.

So one of the eight spastics is still watching the crowd and started pissing himself, possibly on account of how fucking cold it was or more likely because he was a spastic with no bodily self control. Why did they dress spastics in gray trousers? It is possibly the worst color other than beige to highlight the fact that one has pissed one self. Then as is the sheep or lemming mentality of a gaggle of spastics (I don't know what the collective noun is for a group of spastics so I'm sticking with gaggle) the others decided to follow suit and piss themselves.

Meanwhile on the pitch there was a player called Kinder. Lambo was quite into the game and was shouting, cheering and booing at totally inappropriate moments much to the annoyance of the meat heads waiting for a fight, obviously they couldn't beat up Lambo as he was on their side of the terraces. Lambo then pipes up in a very justice of the peace posh accent

'Kinder just kick the fucking ball you absolute fucking wanker', at this moment the meat heads moved in, I can't recall what happened next apart from putting bin bags on my fathers car seats to protect them from Niff Naff piss when we took the spastics back to the spaz home.

I have hated football ever since for obvious reasons. That my friend is the link to the creator of my wife's bouquet that is now strapped to the front of Svetlana with cable ties! Onwards, we have spent far too long talking about Svetlana's decoration. We are nearly ready to leave Gibraltar and set off to Algesiers for the pre rally registration and technical inspection at a random car park. Asier has given us coordinates of where the car park is, presumably to see if we can use coordinates rather than an address as there are few if any streets in the Moroccan desert.

# 8 Algesiers Registration

You can see Algesiers from Gibraltar, I guess it's no more than five kilometers away but someone stupidly put the sea in the way so without a boat its about an hour's drive. Before leaving Gibraltar there are a few necessities to procure, back it is then to Morribobs, we're not sure what the raid registration will entail or how long it might take, this is a raid organized for the French so you can guarantee there will be much conversation and pontificating without fuck all being achieved.

We bought provisions, sausage rolls, sandwiches, pork pies, crisps, John Smiths, Punk IPA and a couple of boxes of wine. I was really pissed off as there were no Scotch eggs to be found in Morribobs, I asked myself what sort of a deteriorating world we live in when you can't buy a Scotch egg at Morribobs? Picnic and refreshments sorted we exited Gibraltar, one of the best directions to go. Coordinates are in the sat nav and we are heading off to a car park in Algesiers.

We arrived at said car park and it looked like all the other teams had already arrived. The reception we got was lovely, everyone wishing us felicitations on our wedding, I have just had to recorrect the auto correct as it brought up fellatio instead of felicitations, I've no idea where that came from on my tablet, the chance would be a fine thing but as we're married now we are past all that and the thought of being fellated by about 100 middle aged French people I feel would not really add anything to the story, also it would be fictitious so we won't pursue that line of thought as we are trying to keep these ramblings as true as possible.

Mr Super Mario man even gave Terri a chocolate red rose that she rather disrespectfully chucked behind the passenger seat and it might even to this day still be there. I call him Super Mario man as that was what was drawn on the bonnet of his rather tired looking Renault 5, he did introduce himself but I'm no good with name's especially when being introduced to more than a hundread people in any language so for the purposes of the other teams we will refer to them by vehicle or looks but not names apart from Asier who's name we remembered from all the email bulletins and WhatsApp messages we had already received.

The range of vehicles parked up was very varied, everything from the very small including a 35 year old Fiat Panda, a few Renault Twingo's, then on to mid size vehicles with a few Peugeot 205's, Renault Express Vans, Renault Kangos and a collection of Citroën's including a knackered old C5 family saloon. Then we were up to the big 4x4 boys, LandRover Disco's, Toyota Land Cruisers, Nissan Patrols and somewhere in between all of this my Svetlana.

I was expecting to see a random collection of vehicles in a car park but this was more like the start of the 24 hour Le Mans, there were small marquees set up, one for registration, the next for inspection of vehicle and equipment, the next for road book and navigation and finally GPS and emergency SOS tracker installation.

We were all directed to park in two opposing lines at 45 degrees to the exit from the carpark, hence the reference to Le Mans where you see all the cars lined up ready for a run to your car start, there were 25 cars on one side and only 24 on the other. One of the teams had already pulled out and had not even got as far as Spain, from what I understood they didn't even set off from wherever they were setting off from due to the lack of an engine! Sad as this was for them I felt good that we weren't going to be last as we had managed the 1800 kilometers from Le Bost to the registration in Algesiers.

First off, we need to do the registration, this is where you get your cars bib number, it's a simple procedure, hand over your carte grise for inspection so they know it's your car, next a copy of the car insurance to show your vehicle will be insured in Morocco, health insurance in case you get the shits and crap yourself inside out and have to be repatriated to France inside out in a bin bag and boom! You get two big stickers with your bib number on them to stick on the drivers and passenger side doors. Ours as you already know is 666.

First job, clean some of the shit off the door and apply said sticker, Svetlana and the other 48 cars now look like they are going on a Raid. We also have a Feraille Raid window sun band thing that is lush as Svetlana's sun visors are totally shite. For some reason that I could not translate or understand we aren't supposed or allowed to apply the banner to the windscreen until we are on the ferry to Morocco tomorrow.

Next was the vehicle inspection, a nice man with a clip board in hand and a pen attached to it with a bit of string holding the pen to save him bending down to pick it up should he drop it came along to check on Svetlana to see if she had everything required. If I remember correctly I went through a list of what we needed in chapter three so there's no point wasting time repeating ourselves now so let's just say Svetlana and team 666 got a clipboard full of big fat ticks in all the boxes. Onto the next marquee.

Onwards onto the road book and navigation area, we have used road books before and they are fairly simple to use and follow. For those of you who don't know about a road book the easiest way to explain one is that if you have ever watched rallying on the telly where the co pilot has a book in his hands and he shouts, 'one hundred meters hard left', 'over the ridge hard right', 'caution at the water crossing' then 'straight for eight hundred meters' then 'right at the pylon' etc etc, that is a roadbook. Hopefully you get the idea?

Many of the teams did not understand this simple idea, its essentially just a very detailed sat nav that doesn't talk to you so your copilot has to give you the directions as its difficult to read and drive at the same time. At this point in the proceedings I'm going to change from using the word teams to équipe as we're now in ten percent English speaking land and 90 percent French language. Many of the équipes appeared to have no fucking idea how a road book works even though full details and instructions had been previously sent out by Asier to all équipes so everyone can familiarize themselves with how the navigation works.

We are now tediously waiting in line for the uninformed or just plain lazy who have not read the instruction bulletin to understand how the navigation works and be educated by the very patient members of the Raid support team. What makes the lazy fraternity appear to be more clueless is that the road book is not only in paper book form it's also installed on your required 'essential equipment' tablet which will basically be used as a SATNAV using it's built in GPS. Some of the thicko's however seemed to have forgotten or bothered to install the application, maps and route tracks. I think we might be waiting here for some time and I'm getting increasingly bored.

Unanimous decision with the wife, fuck this for a game of soldiers, we're gong to wander off for a pork pie and a luke warm IPA then we'll go back when everyone else has been seen to. Being a good participant on the Raid I have already installed and test run the digital version of the road book to see how it works so when it was eventually our turn, last but not least, it was a quick resume to make sure we understood everything which for once in our lives we did.

In my simple mind if you are going on a 3000 kilometer Raid through the Moroccan desert would it not be a sensible thing to understand how the navigation system works before arriving at the start of the Raid? For no other reason than it providing you with a vague idea of where you are going?

The Moroccan desert according to my paper map is a rather vast area with not much going on other than sand. This French tardiness got my brain into thinking, is there a French word for spastic or retard that I could use in conversation? Just for your information, I've looked it up and to save you the bother of doing so the words spastic and retard are very similar in French as they are in English, the French have just added a few more letters that serve no purpose and are not pronounced so on the spastic and retard reference front we will continue using the English language.

Finally we are at the last marquee, this is where we receive the GPS emergency thingy. Super quick it's just a box stuck on your dashboard, when it's activated hey presto anyone who wants to go online via the Raid website they can sit, watch and track our route and position on the Raid, that is only if you have fuck all better to do. There is a big button on the tracker which vaguely translates to HELP we're fucked, or should I say Svetlana's fucked and we need rescuing! Pretty please come and rescue us soon ta muchly.

Right then all administrative shizzle is done, big ticks all round and the 49 vehicles were all lined up ready to go to our own choice of digs for the night, as the Raid doesn't actually start until we cross on the ferry to Morocco tomorrow morning and we all meet up before we leave the ferry port in Tangier, tonight we had to find our own accommodation.

Oh no, now it's getting really French, everyone's enthusiastically wittering about fuck all again! It's getting dark and I'm becoming more and more increasingly bored. There's six days of chewing the cud ahead so save some conversation for the coming days so we don't end up sitting around in silence in the coming evenings. Everything's sorted for today, we all have big ticks in all the boxes and we are all good to go. Let's all go to our hotels and have an anxiety disturbed sleep.

The reason for me wanting to fuck off is that we need to be at Algesiers ferry port departures car park at 5 in the morning for the ferry in the direction of Tangier Med, it's now 7 in the evening and I'm fucking knackered and in need of food, I've survived the day on pork pies and warm IPA, do these people not remember that I got married yesterday?

We all gathered for a photo opportunity and a speech by Asier, the speech was obviously entertaining as there was much laughter and cheering but to be honest I didn't understand much of it apart from Asier reiterating we need to arrive for the ferry at 5 tomorrow morning.

At last we are leaving the registration car park. For video purposes we have to leave the car park starting from the end of the two lines of equipes, there are drones flying above filming the event and a cameraman next to the vehicles so there's a lot smiling and waving for the cameras going on. Tooting your horn when departing is apparently obligatory, some of the équipes had the American police and fire engine siren horns fitted and some of them had what you might remember from the 1970's horns that went 'didididldododoodo', we had none of these so made do with Svetlana's 46 year old limp toot toot toot.

At last we are on our way to the hotel for a well needed kip. We were going the same direction as one of the old Fiat Pandas for a short while so being childish we went side by side on a dual carriageway tooting our hearts out. I liked their car as there was a sticker on the back saying 'In Rust We Trust'. Again I don't remember their names but the female copilot always appeared to have a beverage of the non soft drink or tea and coffee variety in her hand. She was my type of lass. After a few kilometers they turned off to wherever they were staying and we continued on to our digs.

Oh fuck, not now, not today Svetty please! The battery light has just come on, that means either the fan belt has snapped so Svetty will soon overheat and the battery will drain itself very soon and we will come to a grinding halt. The other alternative is the alternator might be fucked so it isn't charging the battery, we won't overheat but will still soon come to a grinding halt when the battery is drained of all it's power, the second option at this point in time is preferable but acquiring an alternator for a 46 year old Russian tractor in Spain would be like trying to score class A narcotics in a nunnery, the hotel is only 5 minutes away according to Sally Sat Nav so we carried on to the hotel.

Mr Anxiety had vanished for a few days, probably because we weren't traveling anywhere other than on foot which is apart from avoiding being run over by a moped in Gibraltar is fairly anxiety free. Then just one red light on the dashboard illuminates and BOOM, here is the miserable fucking cunt right back on my shoulder, why can't he fuck off and annoy someone else for a few days, surely I've not been that bad other than ridiculing in a humorous non offensive way, spastics, homosexuals, thalidomide's and the like. I'm on honeymoon for fucks sake, give me a rest! He's literally filling the car with the air of doom, gloom and disaster. Even as I smoke my roll up the wife has made for me, as the smoke exits Svetty's ancient front quarter light windows it's spelling out the word 'anxiety'.

Please take a moment to remember Audrey the shit magnet is now my favorite mother in law so we are technically related, this is unfortunately going to be the beginning of the end.

We arrived at the hotel, I don't care to remember the name of it, suffice to say it was one of the minimalist swanky looking places that for some reason or other the developers who build them like to plant them at the arse end of an industrial estate. Good sign for Svetlana's security as there were only two parking spaces outside and we witnessed a vehicle coming out of the gated underground garage. Proper job, secure parking tonight not just a surveillance camera. We went to the reception, well the main door, it was locked, we knocked a few times, nothing, we peered through the windows, there was nobody about even though there was a huge bar and restaurant area all illuminated. We knocked again and waited a while, surely in a hotel of this size there must be someone, somewhere?

I gave up and used some of my mobile data allowance to look up the hotels telephone number. I rang the number and a very polite lady advised me that in the evenings the hotel has a virtual reception, she said we sent you the reception door code, your room number, room code and underground garage access codes earlier today via WhatsApp. Thanks for that dickhead! I didn't say that obviously, I've been either traveling or having to endure French wittering all afternoon so haven't seen any WhatsApp messages. Could you text me the various codes please? No problem was the very helpful and friendly reply.

We eventually accessed the hotel and more importantly the underground carpark. Time for an IPA to briefly remove Mr A from my shoulder and a quick John Smiths for good measure, no time to rest and get comfy though lush as the room might be. We need to find out why Svetty's battery light is on as we have a ferry to catch in the morning and need to set off to Algesiers port at stupid o'clock.

We went to put Svetty in the underground carpark so we could have a recky at the fan belt, battery and or alternator, to hopefully fathom out what it was that wasn't working or had broken. Just to add to the trauma the fucking wheelchair on the roof reared it's ugly head again and was intent on causing more issues. The underground carpark had a 2.1 meter height restriction so we couldn't get Svetty in to the garage without taking the fucking god forsaken wheel chair off the roof or without risking ripping the wheelchair off, which I think would be a good thing, or possibly not such a good thing with the risk of pulling the whole roof rack off the car at the same time as the wheelchair was strapped on proper good. The possibility and actuality of ripping the roof rack off we will review in a future chapter but more importantly at this moment in time god forbid we risk damaging the hotel ramming a wheelchair into it's perfectly rendered walls. Even though there are no staff at the hotel I think they might notice a wheelchair to rendered wall interface collision moment at some point and it will probably be retained on the CCTV cameras for future prosecution purposes.

After much faffing and swearing the bastard wheelchair was removed from the roof and Svetty rumbled into the underground garage. We found a parking place with plenty of room and lights directly above to work on Svetty if we needed to, the wife drove the wheelchair in and parked it nearby, comically she parked it in a disabled bay.

As Svetty's battery charging issue and depending on what's not working or had broken could possibly also lead to engine cooling issues we were in a very urgent situation so that we can hopefully resolve the issues before 4AM tomorrow morning, with this in mind and with much haste I slowly sauntered my way up to the room for a tinny and a glug of wine or two to prepare myself mentally for what might be a very short Clusterfuck of a raid, or not even a raid at all. If there's something serious going on we would miss the ferry. My initial thoughts were that it's probably best to have car issues in Spain rather than in Morocco, at least we are still in Europe and can be repatriated to Le Bost without crossing any water.

I tentatively lifted the bonnet and using my trusty 2 foot length of roofing batten propped the bonnet open. Once upon a time there was a proper bonnet stay but I took it off two years ago and put it somewhere safe and never found it again, my bonnet stick as I like to call it works equally as well as the original Russian designed item. Proper good news the fan belt is intact, just as well as I forgot to pack the spare one, I was supposed to put it next to the golf balls and being a dick I obviously thought desert pitch and put and crazy golf was more essential than a basic car part, sometimes I can be a complete fucking retard. The next job was to check that the alternator was charging the battery, I did remember to pack a voltmeter but unfortunately it's in the "hopefully not to be needed" tool box underneath all the camping gear and all the technical inspection stuff, so lets unpack the car yet again. Fortunately while unpacking we had to uncover more cases of IPA so after a quick tinny break, there it is, behold the volt meter. I set the meter to 12 volts put the contacts onto the battery and the battery is fully charged. Strange, I started Svetty and she started ok and the volt meter is reading 14.5 volts, perfect voltage for battery charging. No shit Sherlock it's obviously just an iffy connection on the dashboard. Much panic, stress and ado

about fuck all. We repacked Svetty and went to die for 5 hours.

The best part about today is after leaving Le Bost on the 3rd and today is the 7th this is the first day when it's not pissed it down, if it had been raining at the registration and inspection it would have been an intolerable nightmare. The worst thing is, I just remembered that the USB charging things we put in Svetty, USB ports hadn't been invented in 1979, anyway the charger has a little digital display on it that tells you the charging voltage of the battery, I really am a stupid fucking cunt sometimes, I could have saved much stress, six tins of IPA, an hour unloading and reloading Svetty and could be tucked up in bed wide awake stressing about starting the raid tomorrow just by looking at the LCD display.

Before ging back up to the room we rammed the wheelchair on top of all the stuff in the boot, we will deal with it tomorrow, I don't fancy strapping it back on the roof at 4 in the morning when we exit the underground garage and it will probably after todays respite be pissing it down again. You know what I really need at times like this? A Scotch egg but alas I had to settle for a rather dry sausage roll. Goodnight dear reader, I'm going to stare at the ceiling for five hours.

# Intermission moment

Tomorrow as you are now aware we are planning to board the ferry to Morocco which as you probably or might not know is an independent country in north Africa, independent as in the same as Gibraltar. The reason I point this out is that Gibraltar is currently number one on my most hated shitholes on planet earth so my expectations are not high for what Morocco might be like. Despite my extensive non porn based research into the country and it's fat women, it looks like it might be worse than Gibraltar. That said we are going on a raid not being tourists.

So far in this novel / novella, I hope, no I'm sure I have succeeded in not insulting any one thus far by either using their real name in vain. This is a true story and no one's identity has been changed as no one is innocent, also any references to gender preference, disability, stupidity, being a dick, being a spastic or the like is all true.

I need to stop here and review the term spastic, I am aware that it is not a term acceptable to use today, however when I was a child we as a family would weekly on a Saturday morning visit the market in Burnley where there was a thing outside, I say a thing as I can't think of another name for it. Essentially it was a box 2 foot by 2 foot, possibly bigger but I was smaller then and everything looked big, said box was adorned with a plastic or more likely fiberglass child stood on it. Said child wore orthopedic shoes teamed with leg calipers and a Joey Deacon face with a sign on the front saying please donate to the "Spastics Society". For the younger readers Joey Deacon was a spastic who featured on children's News Round and Blue Peter back in the 1980's, I'm not going to elaborate on Joey Deacon but you have the means and should you have the desire you can Google who Joey Deacon was.

Back in the day spastics were used to raise money not raise awareness or improve treatment for spaz issues. If you felt sorry for the plastic calipered boy sat on a box full of pennies you would put a penny or two in his head, I thought that it was great that you could put pennies in a spastics head. The money went to help the spastics society, that is unless, Burnley's equivalent of Cider Ronnie who was a life long resident on the bench outside the library in nearby Colne, I don't know the name of Burnley's equivalent, but whatever his name he would have already nicked the pennies and popped to the local SPAR shop for a tinny or if it was the weekend when more donations would be deposited in to the spazzers head, possibly two tins of special brew. While on this subject of spastics and disability who remembers 'flid' fighting at school, this is something my friend Handy Man Paul who is mildly famous for his appearances on Chateau DIY reminded me of recently, I say he is my friend, we basically have similar interests in shit old vehicles, tolerate each others stupidity and generally dislike people or come to think of it hate everyone and everything apart from a kebab.

For those of you who are too young to remember, I'll give you a brief recap on flid fighting. Basically you put your hand up to your shoulder, tuck your hand into the sleeve of your t shirt so you just have the stump of your elbow visible. You then have a scrap using just your elbows as it looks like you have thalidomide arms. There we go, another disability hopefully not offended.

# 9 Getting to Stage 1

4AM and we are up, well I say we are up I didn't really sleep so technically speaking I don't need to get up just change from a laying down resting position to a standing vertical position. This hotel is either near a transport interchange or is used as there are no staff around to turn a blind eye to it by women or let's not be sexist here it could be men of disrepute as there were comings and goings in the corridor outside the room all night, or the part of the night that I was laid in a horizontal position.

Anyway, whichever way you see it we are up and on it like a Svetty's bonnet! Talking of which I didn't check the oil last night, I'll pop down to the car park and do that while the wife does her teeth cleaning and other bathroom ablutions, while checking and topping up the oil I had a quick mouth wash with IPA, it's not medically proven but in the circumstances it's better than mouthwash. Cleaning my teeth first thing in the morning makes me wretch my guts up so I opt for nothing or just a mouth rinse of something, today my choice was IPA.

The wife's ready, we put the bags and travel cave / bar in the boot on top of the as it will henceforth be known the 'godforsaken fucking wheelchair', don't worry we will manage to dispose of it soon, much as I would like to I don't intend on fly tipping it in a parking place or lay by as the favorite mother in law had paid good money for it. We are aware that the godforsaken fucking wheelchair is destined for a needy person in the wilds of the Moroccan desert, hopefully it is not destined for one of the fat non porn based Moroccan women that I researched on line who are either too fat or lazy to walk. If it is one of the former mentioned fat lady's who receive the godforsaken fucking wheelchair they will be disappointed when they see that it doesn't have wide sand tires fitted to it so it will probably just sink into the desert sand leaving their fatness marooned.

We are off to the port to meet up with our other 48 equipes, at a very specific location that we have the coordinates for. Guess what, after yesterdays brief interlude of sunshine it's pissing it down again, obviously there's no sunshine just now as it's between 4 and 5AM. That was a stupid comment as obviously it is dark at 4AM unless you are in the arctic circle. Google sat nav is set with the coordinates of where we are heading, this is the last use of the phone sat nav before we switch to the raid's app on the tablet in sunny Morocco later this morning.

Todays first issue, we went towards the super secure car park gate and it didn't open. There must be a button somewhere but we couldn't find the exit button anywhere I don't think it was stupidity on our part just a lack of sleep and high anxiety levels. Dickhead moment, there is a big sign on one of the columns that were holding the hotel up directing you to where the exit button is, like the rest of the hotel it wasn't obvious, the button was hidden behind a different column, what's wrong with a big red arrow saying 'Press Here To Exit' or whatever the Spanish equivalent is. We escaped the car park and headed towards the port, until we got to the first roundabout where we went in completely the wrong direction, again not human error, well sort of, the phone was upside down and the screen hadn't turned itself the right way up. Modern technology, you can't live with it and you can't live without it. Slight change in direction and we appear to be heading to Algesiers port.

I don't know if you have ever been to the port in Algesiers? It's fucking huge, I was expecting something like the port of Dover with a bit of freight and mainly Ferries, this place appears to be where anything from Africa and beyond arrives for distribution throughout Europe. To give you an idea of the size of the port, we drove through the port entrance check point, there was no one there to check anything probably on account of the hour of day, the rain and the Spanish being even more slapdash than the French when it comes to country border control and bureaucracy. Anyway after passing the port entrance there was according to the sat nav on the phone still another 4 kilometers to go. The sight of the cargo cranes and gantries everywhere all floodlit was quite a sight to behold, just brilliant engineering if like me you like that kind of stuff, the scale of it was amazing. One thing that the Spanish haven't yet quite accomplished in the port is a proper road system, lots of it appeared to be under construction or using the Spanish term, we'll do it 'mañana'. We could see where we were supposed to be but the sat nav was struggling to get us there. In desperation we swapped to NATnav and followed someone else. After going round a few makeshift roundabouts several times we eventually arrived at the specified coordinates. Hopefully in the desert we will be able to take the most direct route between coordinates as there aren't many roads or roundabouts.

Half the équipes had already arrived. It was similar to the ferry waiting area at Dover or Calais, vehicles parked up in lines, bleak, miserable and guess what, very wet. Time to deploy the Superdry coat and have a wander about, I would have stayed in Svetty smoking myself to death but there were people standing in the rain chewing the cud and wondering why we were all here at 5AM when the ferry doesn't leave until 7 so I decided to be as sociable as I can manage. It's not as if there's anyone else waiting for the ferry other than the équipes that had arrived, the off-road support wagon, three 4x4 support vehicles and a support 4x4 ambulance which hopefully I will not need to make use of.

I sauntered around being polite saying bonjour, shaking hands again and making small talk, at 5 in the morning my talk in French is very small indeed. I need to go for a piss to remove the mouthwash from my bladder, where is the ferry terminal building? I could do with a brew as well. I spotted the terminal building, it's was a stinky old porta cabin with a toilet that I wouldn't dare to sit on so I had a stand up piss and returned to Svetty without touching anything other than my cock. Meanwhile the wife had busied herself sat sheltering in Svetty, in addition to the previous vehicle decoration, she had applied to the interior perimeter of the windscreen what I can only describe as a red neon strip light. It looked when illuminated and I have to be honest at this time of the morning totally fucking tacky and shit but as before it keeps her happy. The wife did leave the vehicle briefly to apply 'Harry Maskers' around the bib numbers on the doors to stop them falling off due to Svetty's rather rough Gladiator paint being more like wall render for a car instead of a nice smooth surface that you can apply an adhesive sticker too without it falling off.

There was a tap on the window, its Mr Peugeot 206 man who started to befriend us at the registration yesterday. He is quite old, I don't know how old he was and it's impolite ask but his copilot is his nephew and he looked much older than us or maybe he just had a very heavy paper round when he was a child. Mr 206 was therefore we are guessing in his 70's or maybe 80's, he had very bad teeth, that observation is totally unimportant but I thought I would share it with you anyway. Mr 206 liked practicing his English and was very tolerant of our French so we got on ok in small talk conversation but there comes a point when small talk in the pissing rain starts to peter out and you are looking for the polite way to say fuck off I need to get back into the dry of Svetty and continue smoking myself to death. I don't know about the smoking killing me but the wife put the tacky windscreen lights on strobe setting and I nearly became an epileptic! Perhaps I will need the use of the support ambulance after all.

Back to the godforsaken fucking wheelchair, it can't live in the back of Svetty, It's going to need taking out and reinserting every time we want to get something useful out or in. I set too strapping it back on the roof, I was still SuperDry thanks to my new coat, well my body parts under the coat were dry anyway. The wife woman then has a light bulb moment, that is a light bulb moment that is a good idea, not epilepsy inducing windscreen decoration. Why don't we ask for it to be put in the support wagon? What a fucking good idea wife woman! The support wagon aside from providing a mobile repair workshop also transports for the equipes with very small vehicles like ‘in rust we trust’ Fiat Pandas luggage, camping gear etc. Very kindly a nice Germanic man of the support team took the godforsaken fucking wheelchair off our hands and popped it in the back of the wagon. Someone else must have had the same idea as there was already a wheelchair in there. This got me thinking, maybe the favorite mother in law had like her steam cleaners had ordered from Amazonian several godforsaken fucking wheelchair’s, contacted the raid organizers and had them sent to different equipes!

Hurrah! We are rid of the godforsaken fucking wheelchair. The rest of the équipes have arrived, French tardiness at it’s best, when advised to be at the port at 5AM that to the French means 6AM, it’s just starting to come daylight, it’s still raining and there’s still another hour before the ferry is supposed to depart. I should of sided with the 6AM arrivals as nothing has occurred yet that is other than getting wet apart from the SuperDry covered areas. Some random bloke in a high vis jacket was wandering around with a very soggy baguette demanding something or other, I assumed money so I passed him off as a beggar masquerading as someone important.

Someone at the front of the lines appeared out of nowhere and started waving frantically for everyone to move forwards, it’s amazing, the soggy baguette beggar wore high vis but the port officials didn’t, they just shouted and pointed in their black rain coats. Everyone’s excited now as we are off to Morocco, tooting our horns and flashing our lights, the raids camera man is soaking wet filming each of the vehicles as they pass by. I can’t see shit, Svetty’s windows are thick with condensation, I’ll clear my side of the windscreen with the outside of my SuperDry covered arm. That was a disaster, the velcro on my cuff interfaced with the epilepsy inducing windscreen lighting and removed said lighting from its resting place balanced on the sun visors.

Quick untangle of flashing red rope light and we were off for 300 meters then came the joy of passport control, good job there only appeared to be the raid vehicles going on to the ferry as there was only one booth open and it's nearly departure time.

As part of the registration day we were given our ferry ticket. It looked like an IOU that I had written while wankered. Anyhoo we eventually passed over our passports and the IOU to some miserable Spanish bitch sat hunched over in the booth, like most people that work in booths of one sort or another you can tell by their attitude that they really don't want to be there. She sighed, huffed and puffed a bit then gave us our return IOU ticket and passports back, some other person then sauntered over to us in the rain, possibly the husband of the miserable booth bitch with a piece of paper with Tangier Med written on it to put somewhere on our already cluttered windscreen.

Unlike say on a Dover to Calais crossing you don't actually book a departure or return time. You get an open ticket and just turn up and hope there is room for you on the ferry that you want to board otherwise you sit around for four hours waiting for the next one. When you check in to depart the return IOU ticket you receive is valid for two months. I was soon to discover that a two month open return is very generous and totally unnecessary indeed.

We are parked up in lines again, there's a big green ferry in front of us and another on to the right of where we're parked that is blue. I think from looking at the signs that we were going on the big green one. I don't know if this waiting area had at some point been bombed or there is a really bad mole problem but we appear to be parked in one of the many craters. Obviously it's still pissing it down, Svetty and the surrounding vehicles are creating their own islands of safety in the ever deepening puddles. Nothing else for it but to continue my pursuit of an early lung cancer induced grave. Everyone was getting bored, the tooting of solidarity had died down and apart from the people with the foresight to pack wellies, well who wouldn't pack wellies when you are en route to Morocco, everyone else was sat in their vehicles getting nice and moist with condensation.

Another line started to form three rows to the right. Remember that we are in scrap cars and we have between the 49 équipes some form of solidarity and camaraderie on our upcoming mission. The new line consisted of Chelsea Tractors, all of these were United Kingdom of Shitdom registered Range Rovers, Land Cruisers, new Defenders, Mercedes G wagons, basically all tosser vans highly polished but surely destined for an ill fated raid in Morocco!

Without anyone really starting it or gesturing to do so almost all of our équipes started tooting and making a fucking racket, I assume this was as a sign of disgust of twats with money, or it was possibly just a French hatred of the English or it might more likely have been been the sheer frustration that we were still not on the big green boat, My other thought was that it might have started with just one équipe tooting in morse code 'UK Posh Wankers fuckoff' then the rest of us ruined it for them.

Come on ferry people, it's 7.30 and we are still sat here bored as fuck, further inducing our risk of lung cancer and still looking at the 7.00AM ferry. Being British by birth, not my choice I hasten to add but it was however the place on planet earth that I was formed, I actually think that I would have been more appropriate to have been born in Germany that is apart from my distaste of the obligatory German leather shorts. However being British and not proud, we are trained from an early age to queue and there is some skill to do it properly but today is not the day.

After the ferry the first stage is 476 kilometers to Azrou. I don't have any hope that we will be going anywhere soon. I assume that we are waiting for either Spanish or Moroccan workers to do their thing, I've not witnessed Moroccan workers yet but they can't be any better than the Spanish who by all accounts make the French look like workaholics.

I don't know what the issue is that's going on with the big green boat but finally a handful of vehicles come off, then straight away as if the ferry people are in a rush, BOOM we are being waved on. Green boat is massive and there's about 75 vehicles in total to get on. The vehicle area is on 3 levels and is bigger that Le Bost, but twats being twats the wankers directing us where to park still wanted to put the 75 vehicles nose to tail against a steel wall while shouting aggressively at us all the time until they achieve their seemingly pointless goal of getting you exactly where they had decided that they wanted you to park.

What's the issue Mr or Mrs Spanish or Moroccan wanker? Are you planning on sneaking on to the boat a Boeing 747 or a Sherman tank or two to park in the rest of the area? Is it the one that your Moroccan rag head brethren might have hijacked? The plane that is, although I suppose you could hijack a tank, at least there would be less passengers to dispose of. To be honest the same can apply if they were Spanish hijackers but to be fair the Spanish would have just stolen the plane and run away from the tank, the Spanish don't have the time in their working day and or even the intelligence to hijack anything, I say working day as I assume Spanish terrorists or freedom fighters or whatever the fuck they call themselves still have a daily routine like all Spanish people do, that is, have a lazy morning, eat some tapas at lunch, take a siesta, get up later if they can be arsed, think about doing something constructive like stealing a tank or hijacking a plane and then say to themselves, you know what, fuck it, I've done enough for today, then spend most of the evening eating while presumably leaving the Moroccans to do the pilfering of airplanes, tanks, small nuclear facilities and the likes and secretly pop them on a nearly empty green boat. Anyhoo we parked where we were told after doing an 8 point turn, Svetty's not designed for maneuvering on a big green boat.

I remember back in the P&O and DFDS Dover to Calais etc ferry route era that there were doors at front and back on the boat or should I say fore and aft, the idea was that you could drive on at one end and off at the other. This thing only had one massive door at the back, presumably if there was once one at the front it had been welded up for health and safety reasons following the Zebrugge ferry disaster that occurred in the 1980's or the boat was possibly designed by a total fuckwit who thought it was a good idea to get everyone to do an eight point turn while being shouted at by a wanker in greasy once high vis overalls. I would not like to negotiate a 40 tonne arctic on this big green boat.

We left Svetty, took a photograph and went upstairs while they put whatever it was they were sneaking across to Morocco into the big green boat and went to get a brew.

Big mistake, the information bulletin we received informed us that it is necessary to fill in a form and have it stamped along with a stamp in your passport by an official while on board the big green boat to allow you to enter Morocco. It's sort of a visa, I suppose it is a visa but I don't travel much so I'm a bit thick in these areas. Anyhoo, As I understood it, albeit as we were soon to discover totally incorrectly was that in the lounge on the big green boat someone in authority would work their way round while you sat and sipped your coffee and carry out the required administrative shizzle when they got around to you. I had totally fucked that translation up, dickhead. What you actually have to do is join a line in the other lounge at the front of the big green boat where you take your pre filled in form and wait for your turn to have your form examined, frowned at and likewise your passport before being given the two stamps to allow free access to Morocco. Remembering my birth country I'm born and bred to queue, I think that I'll probably enjoy it.

There was a flaw in the Moroccan administrative procedure on the big green boat. There was one official person sat in the lounge if you could call it that with many passengers to process. As a rough calculation, there are 49 équipes with a minimum of 2 people per équipe, let's say 12 support crew, a couple of campervans were also on the boat so lets say 2 people per van, the posh wanker UK 4x4's, let's say there were 4 wank mobiles with 2 cunts in each so there are by my rough calculation in the region of 122 people to be processed by this one man with his laptop and portable passport scanner.

This is where the plan of having one Moroccan official on the big green boat doesn't work. It's just a matter of simple math's to see why they are so fucking dumb, the journey takes about an hour and a half therefore 90 ish minutes. Each person on board was taking 1 to 2 minutes to process by the lone very irritable looking official, I keep calling him an official but I should say he was actually police and had a gun so you do what you are told, anyway, as Steve Wright used to say on radio 2, 'you do the math' 122 people x (lets say) 1.5 minutes per person = just over 3 hours. The big green boat has docked in Tangier which is a blessing as staying in line with the boat swaying here there and everywhere was a bit of a chore when you were not in the que near a piece of furniture to hang on to. There are still about 30 of us in line or 45 minutes worth of bureaucracy to complete if you prefer. This is where being in équipes of at least 2 people pays off, one of you can slope off out on to the deck to work on your lung cancer while the other stays in line. It didn't really matter where in the line you were as no one was allowed off the big green boat until everyone had been processed so you could have had a brew and a nap and just sauntered up at the end of the queue feeling refreshed and relaxed. If everyone however took this approach the big green boat might never go anywhere.

I left the line and went out on deck for a smoke. Fuck me, it's so windy I can hardly stand up, we are not even out at sea, we are docked in Morocco. Welcome to Morocco we hope you have left your shorts and T shirt's at home and brought your windcheater. I brought a Superdry that appears to be doing the trick. After fumbling for a while to light my fag I took a moment to look around, Tangier docks didn't look much different to Algesiers or Dover or Dieppe to name a few I have had the irritation of passing through, I suppose docks and their surroundings are fairly generic the world over, masses of concrete waiting areas, ramps and floodlights.

Smoke finished, my face was red raw from the wind, on the plus side it's not raining, I went back inside and resumed my place back in the queue. Mr Official had obviously twigged that we had docked and had upped his game and was processing passengers in under a minute. Our passports are quickly stamped and temporary visa's ticked off. Policeman plod packed his things away looking really unhappy in his mornings work and buggered off. I don't blame him for being a miserable cunt, I suppose I would be if I had to come over from Morocco on the big green boat, then wait around for hours before doing boring administrative work whilst on his way back to Morocco. He had probably been up all night and now it's daylight and in the middle of Ramadan he can't even have a drink of water or pop out on deck for a smoke, I think in his shoes I would look pretty miserable as well.

Finally the access to the car deck is opened, back we go down too many flights of stairs and we are back in Svetty. I have a theory that the obtaining of visa delay on the big green boat is a deliberate cover to allow the thieving terrorists running the boat to unload their contraband before anyone else is allowed down on to the vehicle decks so no one sees what the thieving cunts have been up to? It just a thought, or perhaps I've just created a totally meaningless conspiracy theory.

Svetty started which was a blessing and we were revving up, needlessly revving but it's what you do when 49 équipes are excited to get going on the raid, we're tooting again along with the all the other équipes as we leave the big green boat and head off into Morocco.

That's it we have made it to Morocco so now we are off on etape 1 to Azrou.

Lets GO GO GO! We are all headed in a tooting convoy in the direction of the exit, well obviously we did, we were not going to turnaround and use our return ticket and get back on the big green boat just yet.

# 10 Stage 1 Tangier Med – Azrou

We are on it, the tablet is turned on and the first stage of the road book is loaded and active, the paper copy is in the wife copilots hands on standby should we need it, in the unfortunate instance for example that the tablet falls out of it's holder on the windscreen and drowns on Svetty's rather damp water logged under carpeted floor, I still don't know what the wife wench was thinking when she essentially installed a sponge under the rubber mats but we are here now and will have to live with it. For the first time on this trip I'm actually quite excited rather than anxious about this venture now that we've managed to get this far. Let's face it, if it all goes tit's up then it all goes tit's up, we are a long way from home and if things should go tit's up there's not a lot we can do about it, so I'm going to put Mr Anxiety to one side and try and enjoy myself.

Not so fucking fast sunshine or sunshine's if I include all of the équipes! Before you can leave the ferry port your car, van, truck or whatever you are driving has to be x-rayed. I'm going to explain this contraption as it might interest you as I've never seen one before and as tedious and time wasting as it was I found it to be quite an interesting piece of kit. The process involves driving said vehicle up onto a concrete ramp about 30 meters long, the official police type people with guns, obviously, as everyone above toilet attendant status in my so far brief time in Morocco appears to be packing a piece, for all I know they might just be water pistols but it's probably best to not try and find out. Anyway they get as many vehicles onto the ramp as possible and I mean as many in one go as they can, you are literally 2 centimeters off the vehicle in front, this takes fucking ages but, they're the boss. Next to the ramp is an articulated wagon, a big 40 tonner, attached to the side of it is what resembles a car wash but without the whizzing round brushes, soap and water. After being instructed to leave your vehicle you are directed to wait in a big bus shelter. Said wagon then moves very slowly, I mean really fucking slowly cleaning the vehicles with x-rays instead of big brushes, soap and water. It's like an MRI scanner for vehicles. I assume in the back of the silent slow moving electric wagon, I say it was electric powered as it was silent, not your normal juddering diesel lorry, there were lots of people like the ones sat at airport scanners boringly looking at screens to see if anyone is transporting anything that might be a threat to the integrity of the Moroccan empire. You have to ask yourself the question, why do this after you get off the big green boat and not before boarding?

If I was a terrorist which I will point out that I definitely am not, I might be many bad things but a terrorist certainty not. I don't think that I really have the stomach for terrorism or the will to die for something I was brainwashed in to believing and don't really understand.

Back to my question, if you were a terrorist would it not be fun to blow up the big green boat and not have to risk taking your bombs and ammunition into a country that is eighty percent sand and not much else? I suppose the terrorists are the ones that policeman plod was delaying everyone else for while doing his administrative shizzle so they had time to remove their stolen tanks and the likes off the big green boat without any of the passengers being any the wiser. My current argument that I clearly haven't really thought through falls down here, why would a terrorist blow up the big green boat that their bounty was on?

Continuing with the x-ray machine, the batch we were on were waved off and the next batch waved on, hurrah, it appeared none of us were carrying munitions of any type as no one was arrested. This could take time. I'm imagining if the big green boat had been full, it would take hours and hours to x-ray all the vehicles, if you had chosen to go to Morocco for the weekend you would be really pissed off because as soon as you actually got anywhere near to leaving the port you would with the experience of what we have thus far endured you would need to immediately start the return journey before leaving the port and we are soon to find out we are not even close to leaving the port just yet.

There was no point in getting too excited yet as there were three quarters of the équipes still waiting to be x-rayed. After being waved forward again we arrived at administrative bollocks pointless fucking waste of time number 3. We were waved into a parking space, it was possibly customs, but we had no fucking idea what it was. Fortunately the support crew were loitering around to help us. This area is where you get what is essentially a visa for your vehicle for it to enter Morocco! Fuck me, I am very much aware that the French love their paper work but this is on another fucking level of creating jobs for the boys and girls or those who identify as something else with the sole purpose of fucking everyone off and making them miserable.

It's now 11am, we set off at 4am and the total distance traveled is in the region of 60 kilometers including the big green boat taking us through the Straights of Gibraltar and most of those kilometers were driving around Algesiers and now Tangier concrete jungle big boat ports. You will note my increasing use of the word fuck, this is mainly due to my increasing frustration that we've been on the go for seven hours, haven't traveled very far and we are still not on the raid, we have not even left the fucking big boat port and there's still more administrative shite to accomplish before we can begin the 476 kilometer long leg of etape 1.

What acquiring a vehicle visa or whatever it is actually called involves you handing over your, passport, card grise and insurance document to the policeman in a very long coat. What then happens is he saunters around the vehicle several times, looks inside, why he needs to look inside is beyond me as we've just been x-rayed for fucks sake. The next step is he fucks off to a cabin with our papers, then someone else comes over, walks round a few times, has a look inside, gives us a 'whatever' sort of look and wanders off. I would have got out for a smoke to further my chances of dying from lung cancer (if that happened right now it would be a fucking blessing) but I didn't.

I know you are eagerly waiting for this as I haven't updated you on the meteorological situation for a while. It is wait for it as this is quite special considering we are now in Morocco, its fucking sleeting, yes sleeting I tell thee, I reiterate its fucking sleeting for fucks sake! With the gale force wind still in force that I referred to on the big green boat it's fucking horrendous, even under the mundane concrete covered bit we are currently marooned under waiting for the wanker to return with our papers and a visa for Svetty it was biblically fucking soaking. Poor old Svetty was getting battered.

The water from the top of the copilots door is dripping on the wife, even though we're not moving there's water dripping on my feet from the clutch and accelerator apertures in Svetty's front bulkhead. the sleet turned to rain and eventually the water ingress got worse. Good job we have a sponge installed on the floor thanks to the wife so Svetty is holding water like a fucking bucket instead of it draining out. I should have packed my wellies

Eventually, some time later, I really don't know how long later it was, I've given up on keeping time as it's a pointless time consuming exercise, a different man appears back at Svetty, he's soaking wet through in his long police coat, he flashes his gun while removing our documents from his inside pocket and passes our papers through the quarter light window that's also leaking like fuck. The soaking wet support crew members who obviously had a job to do otherwise they would be sat in their truck were directing the équipes in the general direction of where we needed to go.

We were directed to a parking area where we will all line up for a photo opportunity before we hopefully and I pray to God, who incidentally I don't believe in but just now I'll try anything to get me out of this fucking port. That said when I say I'll try anything, Buddhism is a complete no no, the constant clanking of the small cymbals you have to chime on your fingers while mumbling some foreign shite would drive me mad.

We appear to be past all the administration shizzle and are now free to leave the port and enjoy the beauty of Morocco and all it has to offer. One last chore to do while the other équipes have to sit around waiting for Mr cant be arsed to sort their paperwork out. We need to obtain some Dirhams.

Unlike any other country I've visited on my limited travels where you can exchange your local currency to the currency of where you are heading for a small fee and an exorbitant exchange rate at a post office or such like, but at least you can do all this before you leave home. When in Morocco you can only exchange your currency or buy Dirhams on Moroccan soil or sand, I've not seen any of the sand yet but hopefully we will see some desert sand before it gets dark.

You will remember that I said the rain and wind was horrendous in the previous paragraph, I hope you do remember that as it was mentioned only recently and if you don't recall it you are a thick fucking cunt! Sorry for the deteriorating language but I'm becoming more and more frustrated and really doing my best to enjoy the experience, fucking tedious as it is at the moment.

This cheered me up though. Whichever daft Moroccan cunt designed the massive concrete roofed covered area about the size of a football pitch in the now you are free to go on your adventure in Morocco but don't forget to get your Dirhams and very importantly a Moroccan phone card if you didn't arse to think of doing this before you left home. Anyway some daft Moroccan cunt decided to put the toilets, prayer room and ferry booking booths so you can book a big boat ticket back to Algesiers and also to a number of other destinations that I did not understand as they were written in squiggly foreign writing. This was all situated under the massive concrete canopy. These useful amenities were fused and linked randomly with avenues of grass, blocks of concrete to sit on and flower beds.

The cash machines, phone card kiosk and bureau du change however are not under cover, they were at the opposite side of the parking area where all the équipes were starting to line up, as you already know the rain is coming down at a good 45 degree angle with the sole intention of getting you totally soaked unless you are under the football pitch sized concrete canopy which is great should you wish to go for a piss, poo, pray or get a big boat back home. Having endured a career in architecture for 25 years, it doesn't even to the thickest of cunts seem sensible to put flowers and grass outside and public amenities such as bank machines undercover.

Anyway, the wife went off to procure some Dihrams from one of the weather exposed cash machines, it's now not only pissing it down but there's a bit of hail mixed in. She went to the first machine, card not accepted, second one, card not accepted, third one, you know the score so she went to the bureau du change, bit of a twat as they wanted euros in folding money and would not do a bank card transaction so we gave up the 500 ish notes we had and bought 5000 Dihrams. Now to the cheery bit. The wife wench was so soaking wet that when she came back with the spondulies and got back in Svetty, she reached into the back for her clothing bag and got completely undressed in the car and then obviously redressed in dry clothes.

We now have our official papers and some spondulies in hand so now can we please, please set off on the raid soon?

Everyone's sort of assembling ready for the photo and video opportunity, however, everyone's also hiding in their vehicles. Even the support crew were sat in their moisture steamed up trucks. One of the équipe's who we did actually know the name of was Olivier. We had made acquaintance with him before we had even set off from Le Bost via the WhatsApp group as he lives in the same department of France as we do so we had a bit of a bond and I think he wanted to travel down in convoy with us but alas our wedding plans didn't coincide with his itinerary.

Olivier decided he was going to set off. After a quick conflab with the wife we followed him. 100 meters later Olivier pulled up further along the car park. Ten or so of the other 49 équipes followed and pulled up beside us, well to be fair everyone who had briefly set off just abandoned their vehicles waiting for some form of official start and not just setting off with sheep mentality. Sheep mentality eventually won over and an équipe driving an old Toyota Land Cruiser decided they were going for it as no one could be arsed getting out of their vehicles to have a conflab and as we all knew via the road book app and paper road book vaguely where we were going everyone else followed.

Now we are on it, we're finally in Morocco and on the Raid, fair enough the first stage will be a tad boring. As I've said previously the first stage or etape 1 if you prefer is 476 kilometers, to start we have 239.82 kilometers on the road, mainly on motorway traveling south along the coast. We then have to turn left at Kanitra and head south east on the off road section to take us from the 239.83 kilometer marker to the 304.33 kilometer marker where we will be back on the road, a fair distance to travel considering we set off at 4AM this morning. We are looking forward to arriving at the first overnight camp which has fortunately been replaced with a hotel on account of the shite meteorological situation.

This is how etape 1 panned out. First off I became a tad confused, we left the port which is obviously at sea level and then we appeared to be going downhill for about ten kilometers before being back at sea level. I say sea level, there was sandy tidal mud at each side of the road. I'm happy we're now starting to see sand albeit wet and muddy beyond the overworked windscreen wipers. Then boom, there was a camel standing in the wet sandy mud at the side of the road. We must be in an exotic country or passing by a very small zoo.

The raid vehicle we were following took the next slip road, this sent the wife copilot into a frenzy, are we going the right way, we can't get lost in the first few minutes of the Raid otherwise we would look like a total pair of dicks. According to the electronic road book we are following this road for about 90 kilometers so I wasn't bothered. We carried on and all was good, the vehicle we had been following had probably just popped off the route for fuel or lunch or to turn round and go back home.

There's a section of peage motorway coming up ahead. I don't know if I wasn't really looking or if the lane signs directing you to the lanes for tickets or straight through telepeage were not idiot proof but we stopped at a barrier with a ticket machine, I pressed the button, no ticket, pressed again still no ticket, then some cleaning type person came over and shouted you need to be in the next lane for a ticket you are in the telepeage lane. The bip and go we have doesn't work in Morocco, hence why we had aimed for a ticket machine. I assume the man was of the cleaning person status as he wore a high vis jacket but I couldn't see a gun. The problem right now is that, right up Svetty's arse is a 40 tonne arctic and there are more vehicles behind him and we need to reverse out of this lane. I got out and gestured that the 40 tonner needs to move but I just got a shrug from the driver in return, well mother fuckers, none of you are going anywhere until I reverse out so I'll sit here and leave it up to you as to whether you choose to move or not. Normally driving in the Svetty monster I would drive towards or reverse towards someone until they moved as nine times out of ten they would come off worse. Today was the one in ten time I didn't think this theory was a great idea and I didn't want to argue with a 40 tonner so I slowly reversed towards him until he jack knifed his cab a bit to leave me just enough room to reverse out and get in the next lane.

Button pressed and success we have acquired a ticket, the barrier opens and we are on our way again. The first thing

I would like to share as we have some time while we are tootling down the motorway is how dirty Morocco is at first sight. There appears to be a mentality that, if there is a banking, tip a wagon full of rubbish down it, it's even more prominent if it's a river bank, every river we passed or crossed the banks of were covered in rubbish. Possibly the idea is to tip the rubbish in to a river and it will eventually with this lush Moroccan rain eventually be washed into the river and then out to sea, the rubbish is then someone else's problem.

Thus far as I was anticipating I'm not feeling the love for this country. My next observation was that as every possible area where grass or vegetation could grow was covered in rubbish the sheep and goats were reared on the embankment's of the motorway which were reasonably clean looking. This was obviously the fat Moroccan woman's work as every flock was reared by a fat woman. Let's face it, any woman hidden under all of that you can't see me garb would at a glance look like a fat fucker even though she might be a young fitty underneath but I doubt it and like people with potential water pistols and no high vis I have no intention of finding out.

Back on the route, the other équipes are passing us by on the auto route, cruising by in their fairly modern vehicles compared to Svetty who plods along but I don't mind as we will seek our revenge when we start the off road section. It's still lush though as everyone's flashing their lights and tooting their horns as they pass us, obviously we did the same in return. The raid isn't a race but an endurance event where the aim is to have fun. There are a number of timed sections which are logged on your tablet and the emergency GPS thingy that is miraculously still velcroed to the dashboard despite the moisture. The main idea is to make it to Marrakesh in one piece.

We had a brief stop before leaving the motorway to replenish the fuel and take a piss at a service area, although it's a motorway service station the man who administers the fuel whose fat wife is probably one of the fatty's herding the sheep and goats on the motorway verges insists that you pay cash. This being our first stop and knowing no better you oblige and say OK, fill her up please. It was thirty liters and it came to 480 dihrams, we gave him a 500 note and he proffered no change, fucking thieving wanker, I could have filled it up myself, I've done it before you know you cunt.

The roadbook tells you where the petrol stations are as they are few and far between and Svetty needs a drink every 300 to 350 kilometers so we'll be topping up whenever we can, likewise I think it's about time the wife reached into the back and passed me an IPA to refuel the pilot.

We are now heading off road, at long last, there's a gathering of vehicles parked up having a conflab, these are the ones that came past us on the AutoRoute, Peugeot 205's' and 305's, Citroën C5 and AX, a newer model of the Fiat Panda and Renault Twingo's to name but a few. The issue for these chaps was that the route was boggy wet sand with very deep tire ruts full of water, obviously the ruts were full of water as it was still as you might have guessed still pissing it down, it looked boggy as fuck but this is where Svetty is going to come in to her element.

Svetty has good ground clearance, doesn't weigh much over 1000 kilograms when empty and has a bullet proof suspension. So we tooted flashed our lights and went past everyone at some speed, not at great speed as I was just checking the traction in third gear but we are fairly motoring, fairly motoring off road is about 30 kilometers an hour. What the équipes that were standing looking at the track didn't seem to fathom was that even if you have a low slung road car you can easily pass rutted sections by straddling the track with one wheel on the center non rutted bit and the other on the verge, this works until you encounter trees or other obstacles on the verge then you might get stuck. Anyway we'll let them find that out for themselves. Fortunately for us I've driven Svetty on enough tracks to know when the ruts are too deep and these looked passable and even if they were too deep the sump guard would trim the muddy sand off the middle of the track like a snow plow.

My confidence is gaining, Svetty is loving this and so am I, the copilot wife was less impressed as we were cruising in fifth gear at 50 kilometers an hour following a straight track for about 10 kilometers and there was water everywhere. There were many tracks heading off hither and thiver but we were following the road book that was amazingly intuitive and we kept the electricity pylons we were following to the right as it told us to do.

The track had become much less rutted but had massive puddles across it. I opted for the straight line approach which I suppose was a tad on the foolish side as you have no idea how deep they are, there was a Fiat Panda about 500 meters or so in front of us zig zagging around the mini ponds. We soon caught up with it and as the raid rules state, if someone is blocking your route, toot your horn and flash your main beam and they have to let you past, the little Panda did so and we passed at speed covering it in wet sandy shit. During all this excitement Svetty's suspension did bottom out a couple of times but this is what she was built for and she was lapping it up. It was fucking epic, I was living the dream even if it was a rainy, sandy and muddy one, there was wave after wave of sandy muddy water coming over the windscreen and finding it's way into the car, the windscreen wipers were working overtime.

After ten kilometers or so of a straight line following the pylons the track became much more interesting. We were now weaving along a snaking track up and down small hills between trees and scrub, it was good that there were trees and scrub to give an idea where the track was heading otherwise you could have ended up anywhere, that was good news as even following the roadbook it now felt as if we were in the middle of nowhere and we hadn't seen another vehicle for some time, were we going the right direction? We're just following tire tracks as there are no land marks to refer to. The road book said we were going the correct way and after a few kilometers of weaving around having fun on the track we found a few of the other équipes, they were stuck up to their chassis in ruts.

The stuck équipes had obviously gone hell for leather on the AutoRoute and had gained some distance on the rest of us or hadn't needed to stop to refuel or have a piss as no one had passed us since we started the off road section and we were motoring faster than most of the other équipes. There was a Renault Traffic van and our adopted friend with bad teeth in his Peugeot 206 stuck, both were grounded one behind the other in ruts. We stopped and offered to help and winch them out but a support Land-Rover had already pulled up in front of them and much to my amazement fixed a tow strap to the van that was in front, then another strap from the van to Mr bad teeth's Peugeot. There was much protestation from bad tooth man as they were stuck so deep that just dragging them out could possibly rip something important off their vehicles, something like the exhaust or the whole bottom of the car depending on how sturdy it was and how far the rust mites had invaded it. Anyway, I offer a massive respect to the Land Rover as it did succeed in its endeavor and managed although I say rather violently pull both vehicles at the same time in tandem free of the ruts and there didn't appear to be any damage or casualties so we started Svetty up and got on our way while they were discombobulating their tow straps. As some of the other équipes had also stopped to help I was going to get going as I'm having too much fun to get stuck behind them.

There are three vehicles in front of us and they are going for it, up front in first place was a Toyota Land Cruiser, arguably and irrelevant of the age or model they are the toughest and most reliable off road vehicle ever designed and built. The Taliban use them so they must be tough. Next in line was a short wheelbase Nissan Patrol, possibly the second best 4x4 ever manufactured but much cheaper than a Land Cruiser, next in line a good old Land-Rover Disco. Then here we are in fourth place with good old 46 year old Svetty.

I am really, really, really enjoying this, driving way too fast off road, weaving around, the four wheel drive drifting in the corners. This is creating winky man semi-on inducing excitement or dare I say it I'm veering towards it being a full hard-on inducing driving experience. I don't think that I have felt like this driving a car since taking my fathers VW Passat GT on the M65 motorway past Burnley the day after I passed my driving test which was at least 35 years ago. Obviously at that time I was what they now refer to as a young driver, admittedly I was only 17 and had only had my license for less than 24 hours but I had an inquisitive mind and was intrigued to know if the manufacturers brochure's stated top speed of 130 miles per hour of a VW Passat GT was actually correct, obviously I had to find out. This question I cannot fully answer as I only got up to 125 miles an hour before the M65 ran out of road at Nelson. The motorway now extends a further few miles to Colne so if I had tried a few years later 130 miles an hour might have been possible.

Third place Disco is holding me up, I gave him a toot and flash of main beam and he indicated for me to pass. We are on the tail of the Mr Wong trucks and loving every second of it, I asked the copilot if she wanted to swap places but she was knackered and we agreed that we would swap places tomorrow. Onwards I went in a Dukes of Hazard style, in hot pursuit of the two Wong trucks in front. We had dispensed with taking any notice of the roadbook as we were following équipes that looked like they knew what they were doing, that was until I looked to my left and saw quite a distance away most of the other équipes except for us and the 2 Wong trucks in front going in a different direction. Co pilot wife is back on it and we are in fact following the two Wong équipes in completely the wrong fucking direction. We were still having fun though. I turned on the mental Nat Nav and took the most direct route to join the other équipes who we assumed were apparently going in the correct direction. This detour route involved driving straight through a forest and driving over many fallen trees and branches, Svetty bless her, as ever she took it all in her stride and we rejoined the group losing our fourth place.

Mental note and reminder to self, this isn't a race, it's 3000 kilometers of endurance so I don't need to be at the front or if I am at the front at least follow the copilots instructions unless she falls asleep and try and go the right way, dickhead! Driving haphazardly through the forest there was a big clunk, we or should I say I had bashed the roof rack into a tree. I got out, the roof rack was still affixed to the roof albeit it is now fixed 6 inches further back on the roof than it originally was.

The twisting trails ended and we were now driving up a big wide open area with pretty much all of the other 48 equipes. This is lush as we are racing for fun in a straight line. According to the road book this section is timed and will be about 5 kilometers long before we arrive at the next road section where the timed section will end and the off road fun for today will finish. We will then follow the road book and will eventually arrive at our first overnight stop at a the hotel somewhere near Azrou, I'm really looking forward to arriving and putting my feet up as I haven't really had any sleep for the last 48 hours.

This last section before going back on tarmac was as wide as a football pitch and dead straight as far as you could see. As I said, we were racing for fun, no danger just enjoying ourselves. Super Mario man in his Renault 5 was going great guns considering it was a 1 liter 30 odd year old rust bucket. We for some reason had picked a race with a Toyota RAV 4, it was a fair scrap as it's about the same size and engine capacity as Svetty. The sandy mud was getting more and more sandy and Svetty was loosing traction. I wanted to stop and engage the differential lock so all four wheels were playing in unison but I didn't want the little Toyota to pass us and as we are on a timed section every second counts. We are nearing the end of the timed section and the electronic road book tells us we have 100 meters to go until we need to stop racing. There's now only another 200 meters after that before we are back on the road. Seeing the road ahead and knowing we were going to turn left on to it I again ignored the roadbook or even the tire tracks in front of us and decided to take the shortest route to the road. The down side of this was having to drive up a banking, possibly 40 or 45 degrees steep and then trying to peer over the top to see if any vehicles were approaching before joining the road. On the plus side the Toyota we had been tussling with had in sheep fashion as we had done before hand followed us and got themselves stuck on the banking, I smiled to myself, tooted and headed off in what was hopefully the direction of Azrou.

We are back on a tarmac road and according to the roadbook we are soon going to boringly join an AutoRoute that will take us to within 20 kilometers of the hotel. Now we are back on the road my penile erectile excitement has subsided and I'm back to having an aging mans mangina. In retrospect, as we're on honeymoon I should have notified the wife of the winky arousal and you never know if I had asked I might have received a driving gobble or a quick tug job but hey ho, hindsight is a wonderful thing as they say, whoever 'they' are, I've never really understood that phrase but I use it a lot.

Now we are away from the coast road I have noticed there is a lot less rubbish dumped on every available banking or riverside. I have a theory which is that, as the coast road is the main tourist route the rubbish is strategically placed so tourists and there are many of them driving down the coast road in their campervans is to make them think what a shit hole this place is and turn round and fuck off back home. I refer here to campervans as they don't provide much to fund the local economy. They don't support the hospitality industry as they don't need a room, they carry enough canned food to survive the apocalypse so don't need to fund the local retail economy. They do however keep the petroleum industry going but probably not as much as Svetty does and to top it off most of them that I have seen in Morocco are Dutch or Belgian's, who as we all know are wankers! I can make that last statement in confidence as we have lovely next door but four neighbors who are a Dutch couple and their sentiments are the same, they hate the Dutch.

We arrive as directed by the road book at the entry to the AutoRoute. It's a peage again, lets see if we can keep form and fuck it up again. Proper job, we selected the correct lane and the machine administered us with a ticket, 56 kilometers on the motorway then there is about 20 more kilometers to the hotel. The roadbook tells me there is a service station just before we leave the AutoRoute and Svetty's getting thirsty so we'll stop and give her a drink of petrol. We arrived at said service station and there were a few of the other équipes already there enjoying a brew and whatever shit service station food was available. At least in Morocco everything appears to be relatively cheap so you don't feel butt fucked for buying a sarnie at the AutoRoute service stations. This didn't worry us as we still had much of our stash of nibbles from Morribobs in Gibraltar left over, stashed somewhere in the back of Svetty and there was no chance of them going off due to the Moroccan heat. So we had a piss, chatted to a couple of the équipe's about the day so far, refueled and carried on in the direction of somewhere near Azrou. There was only a few kilometers left on the AutoRoute. When we arrived at the toll pay booth, I handed over the ticket and payment card, much to the disgust of the person in the booth as it appears they like you to pay in folding money and like the wankers at the petrol pumps proffer no change and pop that in their pocket.

Svetty just didn't feel or sound right, her engine revs were all over the place and her engine was pinking, this usually happens when she's being hammered up hill due to lack of fuel going from the carburettor into the engine. Something was definitely wrong but in the lashing rain and with only 20 kilometers to go I decided to soldier on to the hotel. We had been warned that the petrol can be a tad shite and that these issues could possibly occur.

A few kilometers further on Svetty was now running ok but not quite right. She was fine if we kept our speed up which is where some local twat hindered things. We're stuck behind what on my little experience of Moroccan vehicles is quite a smart 4x4 pick up, I knew it was Moroccan as the number plate had illegible squiggles on it instead of letters and numbers. It was racing along at almost 30 kilometers an hour wandering all over the road. I assumed it was owned and driven by a man who worked at a petrol station who had accumulated enough money by not giving any change to non locals and had therefore accumulated enough ill earned cash to buy himself a half decent ride. I surmised he was texting his wife who was currently herding their flock on the AutoRoute embankments and asking her to select a sheep or goat to kill for dinner, obviously that's dinner after night fall as we are in Ramadan. He would pick her and dinner up in half an hour.

At last we are on a downhill section of road and we managed to overtake the assumed petrol station attendee wanker. My mistake, it was a woman driving. I should have fucking known!

We are now on a long, long snaking down hill road and apparently we have only two more kilometers to go before arriving at our first Moroccan destination, I'm really looking forward to getting in the bar and sinking a cold one or three. It was getting dark and I thought we would at least be able to see some street lights or anything ahead in Azrou but even through the rain there was nothing. We were still in the middle of nowhere and it was bleak looking. At last a petrol station came into sight on the left and in a further 300 meters we will apparently arrive at the hotel.

Boom, a right turning and we are driving into the hotel car park. This place might be in the middle of nowhere but its fucking huge, it's hidden as you come down the hill. We abandoned Svetty as near to the entrance as we could in a great big puddle that was on a par with the ones at the port in Algesiers but I didn't care, that was where Svetty was sleeping for the night. As the other équipes started to arrive the hotel owners put the exterior lighting on, tacky color changing lights I assume they had purchased from Temu Morocco if it exists, they were vibrantly illuminating the entrance. Once upon a time this would have been a luxury hotel and by Moroccan standards I guess it still is.

We waited in line with the other equipes to check in, that's us back to the joy of our favorite British pass time. The French don't seem that interested in queuing and prefer to loiter around and witter to each other in groups. There didn't appear to be any other customers at the hotel other than the 49 équipes to check in plus the support crew. The reception was working overtime, it looked like the family, I assumed it was a family that were working on reception and I also assumed they owned the hotel and had pulled out all the stops for staff numbers, there was at least 4 generations working in complete disharmony. The disharmony mainly occurred with the gentleman who was at least in his 90's who was making copies of everyone's passport or ID card. Normally this would be a quick whizz through the photocopier procedure but alas, like the general impression of the hotel thus far the method was somewhat antiquated. He had an all in one printer, scanner and FAX machine of the type we were introduced to at school in the new as they had just been discovered at that time in the 1980's the 'computer science' lesson. This was taking ages.

Meanwhile, while waiting in line one thing was very obvious. As shit, wet and windy as it was outside it was colder inside the reception. One would have thought that if you were expecting more than 100 people checking into your hotel you might have bothered to put the heating on. On the plus side I had my SuperDry and SuperWarm coat on which I had on the off chance as it might be needed cleverly inserted a Wooly hat into the massive internal pocket. The Wooly hat was quickly administered to my head.

There must have been complaints about the cold as to much applause a rather smart looking pyramid shaped gas heater was wheeled into the reception area and eventually the bloke who had left his post on reception thus causing more check in delays to bring the heater in eventually managed to light it.

The queue was going down slowly so I sloped off to find where the bar was, I found a restaurant area, smoking salon and boom shakaloom a bar! Irritatingly the bar area didn't appear to contain any beverages of any sort, just a few dusty cocktail glasses. This situation I feel will create much disgust from the other 48 French équipes as whether they are drinkers or not, having an aperitif before lunch or before their evening dinner is the law. Luckily we still had plenty of stocks in our mobile bar. Planning ahead always pays off, 'up there for thinking down there for dancing'.

Eventually we were allocated a room. Room number 212. Upstairs floor 2 I asked? No, ground floor just turn round and take the first left. Okeydokey, strange room numbering system but thank you very much. The corridor was unnecessarily wide with big rugs on the floor featuring weird patterns on them. It reminded me of a combination of the acid induced swirling carpets in 'Fear And Loathing In Las Vegas' and the Bates hotel in the film 'The Shining'. Room 212 was inevitably as cold as the reception and despite being huge it was very hostel like. I won't bore you with a description but suffice to say it was better than having to put a tent up at the originally planned overnight camp. We didn't know the name of the hotel as it was probably something written in squiggly Arabic so we named it the 'Cold Bates Hotel'.

Firstly we set up the room 212 bar, we are only having a kip over here but on the basis that there is not a stocked bar in the hotel, a makeshift bar is better than nothing. I appear to have forgotten the issue we encountered en route with Svetty but to be honest, having been on the go since 4 this morning I really can't be arsed to do anything about it until tomorrow morning. I did however have a quick peep under the bonnet trying not to get too soaked and couldn't see anything untoward so went back to the bar in room 212.

Dinner is provided this evening at the Cold Bates Hotel. As no-one bothered mustering for a briefing at the port in Tangier we don't know the times of anything that is happening this evening. Back off we went to the reception area where almost everyone was loitering and gabbing to each other about their experiences on etape 1 while huddled around the pyramid heater. Apparently dinner will be served at 8, why do people eat so late? In my world 8 is supper sandwich time, 8.30 is book time and 9 is sleep. One thing we had failed to understand or just didn't listen to yesterday at the registration was that we needed to give our tablet to one of the support team after each etape so they can check the roadbook has been working correctly and extract some information or other off it. The instructions we had understood were that at the end of each etape we were to delete the route of the previous one so there is no confusion which days road book you are following, the last thing you want to do is go back the same way you had just come. What we didn't understand is that you do this after your tablet has been reviewed. We received a frowning look from the support team chap so replied with a sorry were a bit fucking thick shrug of the shoulders.

While in administration land or should I now say vehicle issue land I described Svetty's problem to one of the support team. The consensus was that it could be iffy fuel, possibly everything electrical firing the engine is wet from vigorous water crossings, who can say. There is a compressor in the support wagon that can be used to blast any moisture out and a pump to suck the iffy fuel out if that's what the problem is out of the fuel tank. It's late, dinner is starting to be served so we'll have a group look at Svetty in the morning. We made a quick pop to bar 212 for a swig of wine, I'm not taking anything into the dining room as everyone who didn't plan ahead would start pestering us for a drink.

Where to sit for dinner? The tables are of the big round banquet type each one seating eight. We were on the hunt for a table where partial English speaking people that we have already conversed with have already taken their seats and sat themselves down.

Normally I would very much enjoy having a meal with French people to improve my language skills but I really can’t be arsed today. We gave up hunting and just plonked ourselves down where there were two chairs next to each other. Normally at a meal we would in principle sit at opposite sides or ends of the table so we can engage in conversation with different people. This is something you do when you live and work with the same person day in day out. This evening however it was safety in numbers, well a number of the two of us in case no one else at the table wanted to engage in conversation with us. Although all the conversation was in French it was actually very enjoyable. Our fellow diners were interested to know about where we lived, how the wedding was etc and it was a level of conversation that even being in a very fatigued mental state we could understand, participate and enjoyably engage in.

Dinner arrived at the table along with beverages, a nice Moroccan bottle of wine or two? Although Morocco is a dry country they do produce a lot of wine. The wine production is a continuation of generating income from when Morocco was ruled by the French. So we had bottles of water served to the tables, wankers! We're in Morocco so stereotypically tagines arrive on the table. I'm grateful for the heat they are giving off. I'm sat next to a window and like everyone else we are all still wearing our coats. There's thick condensation running down the window. I did remove my wooly hat for the meal though as it's the done thing for etiquette and to avoid looking like a thug. There were 3 tagines placed on the table each one containing a meagre piece of chicken thigh for each person and some couscous mixed with veg. I could have eaten a whole tagine to myself no problem but unfortunately I have to share. The hotel, catering predominantly today for a French crowd thoughtfully deposited many baskets of bread on the table. Normally bread is a side thing to go with your main dish but today I think we might have been expected to make sandwiches.

The mention of bread leads me on to the way the French treat their bread at the dining table, it is a thing that has always been a mystery to me, it's not something I have an issue with as long as they don't do it at my house. There are several baskets of bread on the table and everyone has a side plate to put said bread on, what the French do however is choose to dispose of their side plate, maybe on account of saving on the washing up and instead choose to shred their bread into pieces on the table. After 13 years of living in France this procedure still bewilders me. Anyway, it was a good job there was lots of bread because as mean and stingy as the meat and veg serving per person there was plenty of oily goo to be mopped up.

Before the dessert arrived I popped to bar 212 for a piss. When it arrived that was also a let down, it consisted of a small bowl of yoghurt and a biscuit of some description. I think, no I know I have now lost the will to live and I'm ready for bed.

Asier gave a little talk after dinner, meagre as it was, the dinner that is not Asiers speech. I didn't really understand much of it but the gist of it was that breakfast would be served between 6.30 and 7.30 and etape 2 would start at 8.00. Maybe he was also apologizing on behalf of the raid organizers for choosing such a wank freezing cold hotel, the patrons of which have no idea how much food French people like to consume after driving all day and didn't even have the courtesy to have a fucking bar or at the very least a glass of wine on the table for the still hungry diners.

We went outside for a pre sleep smoke. There is a smoking salon in the hotel but on the principle of the health of others

we take our lung cancer inducing threat outdoors, we do the same at home and also in other peoples homes and venues where they encourage lung cancer inducement indoors, we will always insist on doing it outside. I might be a cunt but I have no intention of infecting people in my immediate surroundings with a potential life threatening lung disease.

Anyway we went out of the reception entrance to enjoy the swirling Temu lights and were joined by the co pilot of the old Fiat Panda with the 'In Rust We Trust' sticker on the back of it. She retrieved a bottle of Cognac or Armagnac from her coat pocket and asked if we wanted a swig. I said thanks but no thanks, unusual for me but unfortunately it will give me heartburn and I won't be able to sleep. The wife also said thanks but I only drink beer, the lady then reached in her large handbag and offered the wife a bottle of Corona which she refused. Thanks to the makeshift bar in room 212 and nearly non existent portions of food at dinner I'm already reasonably wankered. We had a smoke and a random conversation about something I can't really remember but was along the lines that she had left her children with her mother and come on the raid with a random boyfriend. We said goodnight and went off down the Cold Bates Hotel corridor to room 212, it was now a room as the wife had said the bar was now closed for the night, miserable fucking bitch wife! Anyway it was much needed sleep time, the hotel obviously had the mentality that blankets are better than heating as there were loads of them. There was no need for background sleep noise tonight, I just needed to open the window a touch, wrap myself in blankets and drifted off to sleep to the sound of the wind and rain. Sweet dreams. Tomorrow is stage 2.

# 11 Stage 2 Azrou – Kerrandou

Repeating klaxon sounds wake me above the sound of the natural white noise filtering through the open window generated by the wind and rain outside. That is a stupid sentence, of course the wind and rain is outside. If it was raining inside the glorious Cold Bates Hotel it would be even shitter than it already is. I had set the alarm on my phone for 5.30 to give me time to have another recky under Svetty's bonnet hopefully in the dry before people were up for breakfast at 6.30. Obviously it wasn't dry so I wrapped up to keep SuperDry and left room 212 to see what I could see. Not a fucking lot, I pressed the light button and the Bates corridor illuminated. When I reached the reception area there were no light switches, the only light was coming from the still burning pyramid heater, sofas had been moved close to it and in the gloom I could make out that the hotel staff were sleeping on the sofas. The smell was like a 3 in the morning taxi office with either a butane or propane bottle gas heater blazing away. Maybe the staff were dead from carbon monoxide poisoning, I didn't bother to check but no one moved.

I walked towards the lights that were still swirling outside the reception. I felt like someone who is dead or dying walking towards the light.

Before having a look at Svetty I need to smoke my customary couple of morning cancer sticks. After the first one my bowels said good morning and what fucking time of day do you think this is. Quickly I returned to room 212 for my morning shit. This didn't impress the wife much at all as my rattling of the key in the crappy lock on the room door woke her from her slumbers. I quietly had a shit, there wasn't much action as there wasn't much in the way of food to excrete so it was a fairly calm affair. With that procedure successfully accomplished I headed off back in the direction of the swirling lights of death for cancer stick number two.

I don't know what I was trying to achieve right now that I had failed to achieve last night by rummaging in Svetty's engine bay but I'm here now so I might as well do it. I rummaged in the boot and found the torch, I then just managed to open the bonnet without it blowing inside out and inserted my trusty bonnet stay stick in before the bonnet decapitated me or set off in whatever direction the gale force wind was heading. Would you fucking believe it? Everything looked just the same as last night!

I started the old bird up to see how she sounded this morning. This involved the usual Svetty starting procedure. Press the accelerator pedal a few times to prime the carburettor, turn the key, BOOM she started first time, then you have to wait a few minutes before giving her any revs. The reason for this is that the 46 year old dashboard is falling to bits and where the choke cable goes through the dashboard it is fucked and falling to bits so the choke doesn't work hence you just need to let her warm up slowly in her own time. It's very similar to getting a wife going in the morning. A little blip of the throttle and she stalls. Quick turn of the key and she's running again. Patience, give her another few minutes, it's very cold and so is the fuel and air going into the engine. After a few more minutes we're on it, she's revving and sounds as OK as Svetty ever does. In celebration I returned to room 212 to roll another cancer stick.

The wife was out of her pit and doing her morning ablutions in the bathroom when I returned to room 212. I sneaked a quick mouthwash to set me up until lunch and we headed hand in hand to the restaurant area. We did go to the restaurant but definitely not hand in hand. I think we might have done that once in the dim and distant past. I don't do breakfast and I'm sure they don't have sizzling bacon and pork sausage sandwiches so I just went for a luke warm cup of coffee with enough sugar in it to last me the day. I didn't loiter around as I wanted to double check on Svetty.

I went back out into the wind and rain and sheltered in Svetty. I turned the key and proper job she restarted without a problem, good old Svetty, a few revs later and she was unfortunately back to what she was like last night sounding like a bag of spanners. Oh fuck are the words that spring to mind. It's now 7 and we are due to depart at 8. I don't think this is moisture or bad fuel that is causing the problem otherwise she wouldn't have run so well earlier. Mr bad teeth arrived and started garbling something to me that I didn't really understand about Svetty's engine. What I did however understand was that his copilot who was his nephew had received a phone call during the night saying his mother had died. He was at a loss as he would be without a co pilot as his nephew was going to take the nearest public transport link and then a direct flight back to France.

A few revs later and, STOP! Svetty just stopped, there was nothing. I kept turning the key and still nothing. Dashboard lights were illuminated on the crumbling dashboard, she was running fine a few minutes ago so the battery should be ok. The other équipes had started mingling outside getting their vehicles ready for etape 2, checking tire pressures, oil and coolant levels, all the things you would do before a long off road desert car journey.

The wife arrived to retrieve the wedding outfits from Svetty, firstly as she wanted to get ahead in the raids fancy dress points scoring tally and also the other équipes who had seen the wedding photos wanted to see us in person in the outfits. Secondly they were fairly layered outfits and would keep us warm without donning ski pants and thermal underwear neither of which we had packed. I thought with the current Svetty situation she was being over enthusiastic and I had a gut feeling Svetty would need some medical attention before we were going to go anywhere soon, however as previously, leave the wife to it, she knows best and if it makes her happy it keeps her quiet. The wife returned a few minutes later not in wedding attire but in her greasy overalls and work gloves ready to lend a hand under the bonnet.

There was a small crowd gathering around Svetty, with much discussion about what might be wrong. Mr Mercorocco and his boyfriend were currently being of the most help. I say boyfriend, I cannot be totally sure but their voices even in French and their mannerisms did shout that they would be frequent visitors to whatever the French equivalent of cANAL sTREET in Manchester is. They were mechanics or engineers of some sort and obviously knew a fair amount about getting cars going that don't want to get back up and running. This next sentence is a totally meaningless statement but if you drew a profile picture of the head of Mr Mercorocco it would be an exact match for the profile picture printed on my hair clippers. You haven't met Mr Mercorocco nor my hair clippers so it is a meaningless statement but I thought it was worth mentioning.

Mr Mercorocco and his boyfriend set too taking the spark plugs out and many other thing's that with my reasonable knowledge of engines appeared to be totally fucking useless and pointless but like with the wife, if it makes them happy and feel useful and important then let them let them carry on with it. Eventually the diagnosis was 'moteur bloqué'. This needs no translation and yes the engine is blocked, that's why it's not turning over.

Mr Mercorocco had a plan to unblock the engine that he briefly explained and we decided that we would go for it. The raid provides two mechanics at all times but the idea is comaradery between the équipes and Mr Mercorocco was doing this in spades.

I should explain who Mr Mercorocco is as I never knew his name or bothered to ask as I would have forgotten it immediately. This équipes car as you might have guessed is a Mercedes that is going to or should I say is now in Morocco. This was clearly displayed on the LED message bar mounted on the back of the roof rack on their car. This wasn't just any old Mercedes, it was a four door boring family saloon, the similarities ended there. Firstly, this beast had wheels and tyres bigger than a monster truck, well not quite the size of a monster truck but they were all the same massive compared to the size of the car. Secondly it was the body work, essentially the wheel arches had been cut away to allow for the monster tyres and they had installed blue LED lights in the wheel arches which were probably from TEMU and tacky as they were actually looked pretty cool, also the front and back aprons had been cut back and anything else that might in extreme circumstances catch on the ground or a banking had been cut off. Svetty has had this done but not to this extent. Thirdly it had height adjustable suspension and could sit with its chassis ground clearance as high as a Land Rover on steroids. What I liked most was the fourth modification, the air intake to the engine was on a huge manifold sticking out of a hole in the bonnet, it looked like something off an American hot rod and it sounded like one. There were jerry cans strapped to the sides, spare wheels on the roof and boot lid, high lift jack, rock sliders, the bumpers had been replaced with steel girders, you get the idea, there was pretty much everything you might need for off roading and all in some way fixed to the outside. Like many of the other équipes it had lots of sponsors stickers plastered all over it, the massive wheels and tyres had indeed been donated by one of their sponsors. Mercorocco really was an awesome looking and performing beast both on and off road considering it was a modified version of what started life as essentially a granddad car. Robust as Svetty is I was starting to feel rather inadequate and ill equipped.

Anyway Mr Mercorocco asked if we had a tow strap? Of course we have it's one of the essential bits of kit we brought that we needed to show at the technical inspection yesterday. The massive car park of the equally massive Cold Bates Hotel had once featured a very pretty but now defunct or frozen fountain in the centre of it. All the équipes had thoughtfully parked at the edges of the car park in an orderly fashion usefully leaving the defunct fountain as a makeshift roundabout in the middle.

Mr Mercorocco's plan was to tow Svetty round and round the defunct fountain while I left her in second gear lifting the clutch every now and then to hopefully unblock the engine. I was far from convinced that this would help but out of politeness went along with it. We fixed the tow strap to Svetty and to the Mercorocco. He fired up his beast and it roared, sucking in air and sounding menacing, hopefully if Mr Mercorocco was correct in his quick non mechanical fix of Svetty we would be roaring again soon. Off we went, I was expecting a little tow around the fountain roundabout but he was flooring the Mercorocco, I has holding onto Svetty's steering wheel for dear life. As it was nearly departure time and the other équipes were enjoying the wind and rain we had an audience of over 100 people watching the misery of Svetty not doing anything but being dragged round and round in circles. Svettys engine wasn't budging.

This is fucking shit! Day two of the raid and Svetty needs some serious medical attention. Mr Mercorocco abandoned us at the far end of the car park and wished us bon courage.

The support crew rang a local garage that they have apparently used many times in the last 10 years of organizing raids and arranged for a tow truck to take Svetty down in to Azrou to see the doctor. Apparently the Moroccan spanner men are very good and we would be fixed today and would be able to rejoin the raid tomorrow. I had my doubts!

All of the other équipes lined up and prepared for the departure on etape number 2. Meanwhile we checked back into Cold Bates Hotel for another night or at least paying to stay there during today, it was very expensive, a whole 300 Dirhams for the night. It is Sunday and it's Ramadan so despite the support crew's optimism I'm fairly certain that nothing is going to be done to Svetty today. We waved the remaining 48 equipes off. As ever they were enjoying flashing their lights and tooting their horns and off they all went on an adventure to have fun and leaving just my beloved Svetty looking very sad and abandoned at the far end of the carpark.

Just before the last support vehicle departed we waved them down. We had charity donation items to give them. We gave them to them now just in case we didn't rejoin the raid tomorrow as I wasn't taking any of it back home. I suppose we could have kept it for now and just dumped it on a river bank when we passed one. Anyway we rummaged in the back of Svetty and gave the support crew all the stuff from the church in Gibraltar and a box containing the bits and pieces that are required to make the god forsaken fucking wheelchair function. At least if we didn't make it any further the poor and needy of Morocco would receive their charitable donations. Off the support truck went and we just stood there in the wind and rain for a moment feeling very despondent then we went back to room 212.

Back in the hotel we passed a group of fat Moroccan women doing some light cleaning work, where do they appear from? Back in room 212 the first job when I arrived was to revert room 212 back into bar 212. My instincts tell me one or more of Svetty's inlet or exhaust valves has broken and is sat on top of the corresponding piston thus stopping the engine from turning. This if I am correct in my assumption is not a ten minute fix and won't be fixed today so, fuck it.

IPA or John Smiths for breakfast darling wife? It's still only 8.30 but bollocks to it, we're stuck at Cold Bates Hotel waiting for Svetty to be picked up on a recovery truck and don't forget we are on our honeymoon. Fucking miserable as it currently is.

I'll have an IPA thankyou darling husband ta muchly. I downed a John Smith's and out of boredom I went for a wander around the hotel. The fat cleaners had gone somewhere, I assume they were kept in the basement or the attic as no vehicles had arrived or left and fat Moroccan ladies need to be housed somewhere. I know that no vehicles had arrived or left for certain as one of us had been constantly on recovery truck arrival watch from the window of bar 212, the fatty's must be somewhere. There is no one here, I mean absolutely fucking no one, during my wanderings I took myself through the kitchens and random store rooms, took a look outside at the massive empty Olympic size swimming pool that some dick had missed a trick here as with all this rain it would be full by now but they had forgotten to put the plug in so it remained empty and unloved.

Back to the reception and there isn't even anyone manning or fat womaning the reception, They might have at least been napping on a sofa in the reception as that is what they appear to do most of the time so I could give them a nudge and wake them from their slumbers but nothing, there was no one. If this was my hotel I would be on standby should a passing tourist see your tacky color changing lights illuminating the entrance that you had obviously forgotten to turn off last night wish to check in and they might walk in and think, this looks a bit bleak, fuck this for a game of soldiers and go somewhere more accommodating, welcoming and warm. This slap dash tardiness might mean they miss out on an extra 300 Dirhams of income today, that is if someone happens to be passing the hotel.

I was starting to feel hungry but was thinking that there's fat chance when someone does eventually appear at the reception of asking for a menu for lunch or dinner as I'm sure the reply would be sorry the kitchens are closed or you can have a scabby bit of chicken in a tagine if we can be arsed to cook it for you. I think we might starve!

We are both now totally fucking bored waiting for the tow truck and IPA stocks are going down fast. I put a message on the raid's WhatsApp group saying, is there any chance on a Sunday during Ramadan that the recovery truck would actually arrive today? The consensus of replies was unfortunately 'probably not'. There were many updates from Asier to all the raids équipes, apparently the mountain pass we should be taking was closed due to snow but when everyone arrived at the police stop point there would be a police escort in convoy over the pass. This all sounded rather exciting but we are sat here watching out for a tow truck and watching the news in Arabic. What I liked abut the Moroccan news is that they actually show people being shot or blown up.

We decided to take a walk down to Azrou to pass the time and possibly get a spot of lunch, what better than a proper leg stretch after spending so much time in Svetty or loitering about for the past few days. We decided the best course of action was to put everything back in Svetty that we didn't need. She was going to a reputable garage according to the raid team and if we needed to make alternative plans at least everything would be locked up safely in Svetty. We put everything in apart from a ruck sack each with clothes and toiletries and the remaining snacks from Morribobs and most importantly the remaining contents of bar 212 back in to Svetty.

The rain has stopped and the clouds were lifting, snow capped proper looking rugged mountains instead of barren hills were now coming into view from my epic desert adventurers vantage point while I stood heroically having a fag outside the reception of the hotel with the backdrop of the never ending swirl of the coloured lights that no one has yet managed to turn off, maybe if there was anyone about I would have told them to switch them off and reduce their carbon footprint, there was however still no one about, not even a lacky sleeping on the sofas in the reception. Now I can see the snow capped mountains I understand why it has been and still is so fucking freezing.

The wind was still howling but at least the rain has buggered off so we went for it and set off down the valley following the road, it was the same route the raid had taken a few hours before but we probably wouldn't get as far as them. According to the directions on the phone Azrou was about five kilometers away. It didn't look that far but maybe looking down the valley towards it was deceptive. Anyway, we had fuck all else to do so we set off down to Azrou but not before leaving Svetty's keys at the hotel reception should the recovery truck turn up. Easier said than done as there is still no one to be seen at the reception so we thought, fuck it, we will just leave the keys in Svetty and go for a wander. It's not as if you can hop in and drive off in her and there are no other vehicles in the carpark so the recovery truck would assume Svetty was the intended patient or call the raid team who had arranged the recovery to confirm they were collecting the correct vehicle.

Before continuing I would like to inform you that the town of Azrou sits at 1250 meters above sea level on the edge of the Atlas mountains and now we can see down the valley to the town I reckon we are at least a good couple of hundread meters if not more above that. I believe the general requirements for a hill to become a mountain is that it must be in excess of 1000 meters above sea level so we are currently residing at approximately 1450 metres above sea level therefore we are nearly a mountain and a half above sea level.

Based on the previous paragraph I can make this one sound more heroic than it actually is. We set off in a howling gale down the mountain in the direction of Azrou, the wind battering our faces but we soldiered on with a stiff British upper lip. We approached what I thought was the outskirts of Azrou as it was where we could see many buildings down the valley from Cold Bates Hotel car park. When we had walked that far it was only what appeared to be a small village which hosted amongst fuck all else a middle school called Bensmim, a delinquent school next to it and behind it what Google maps listed as 'The Local Prison of Bazaro' this would explain the very high walls and watch towers. I'm really not starting to warm to this place. I would like to offer you another one of my ridiculous unfounded theories. I think the kids are educated at the middle school to prime them to be thieving, robbing terrorists. After education they are let out as ill educated petti criminals in the making to work on their skills. They will then return following their initial criminal activities only if they are careless and encounter their first arrest and will then take their place at the delinquent school to be re-educated in crime. After further training they are released again and are then free to carry out acts of robbery and terrorism at their leisure thus serving the purpose that they were educated for twice until that is they are arrested for the second time. Following the second arrest I surmise that as failed criminals, not failures as criminals or terrorists but they were caught for their misdemeanors and therefore would provide no income to the underground Moroccan economy and as such they are then put in the prison section and left to rot as no hope losers. It's just a theory, based on no factual evidence.

After the next corner we then saw where Azrou actually was, it's another 3 kilometers down into the valley and it looked like a sprawling mountain oasis. We should have known that we were nowhere near yet as we had only come 2 kilometers using the walking route on the phone. There was only one road to follow and it was too cold to take the phone out of my pocket to take a look at where we were. The road down to town was now visible, it was like a mountain pass, obviously it was as we are walking down a mountain. The road was twisting and turning like a twisty turney thing and looked like a long route to where we wanted to go, fuck, this is going to be a tedious 3 kilometers to cover about 2 kilometers or less as the bird flies in actual distance to the town.

I managed to get the courage to briefly take my hands out of my pockets and take a look at the map. There is a track going straight ahead at the next bend in a straight line into Azrou. We left the road and followed the track. This was our first experience of how third world Morocco still is. We passed a few houses, I say houses, our winter firewood is stored in a better looking shelter. There were random galvanized wriggley tin clad enclosures masquerading as houses, these were obviously inhabited as there were stove chimneys sticking through the tin roofs bellowing out smoke and next to them the obligatory satellite dish. I assume they were inhabited by humans as you don't generally give goats, sheep and hens heating or satellite television.

We continued heading down on the track, we were passing more shacks, goats, hens and stray dogs until we came to a river. This is the first river that I've seen that it's banks weren't covered in rubbish, there was plenty of rubbish dumped here there and everywhere but this time not on the river banks. Fortunately for us, the locals who obviously used this track as a route into town had placed stepping stones in the river to facilitate your crossing, they must go everywhere on foot or motorbike as you couldn't even get a Svetty down here.

We are back on the main road, it's a long straight boulevard type of road. Well you would call it a boulevard if anyone had bothered to finish it or do anything at the sides of it but obviously they couldn't be arsed. It was a lovely looking road and it was a shame no one had bothered to finish it. We were walking into what I assume is the upmarket suburb of Azrou. The area is possibly a work in progress or is more likely to be a, well, fuck it we've built the road, that'll do. Some of the houses were spectacular in size and design compared to the tin shacks 500 meters back up the road but nothing was finished. Maybe we are in a ghost town as we haven't seen anyone and it looks like nobody has tended to anything for sometime.

As we continued down the 'boulevard' something weird and at the time slightly scary happened.

A black BMW 535 arrived at speed and pulled up at the side of the unfinished boulevard right next to us. As I just mentioned we haven't seen anyone except for goats, dogs and hens or any vehicles on our walk thus far, probably as it's Sunday so the arrival of this BMW at speed that looked like it had encountered a ram raid or two and possibly a shoot out was a touch worrying. Out of the BMW strolled this wide boy! I felt a tad worried. He had an accomplice in the passenger seat who might for all I know be packing an AK47 or just a plain old pistol and they are out and about preying on tourists on a Sunday lunch time while no-one else is around to witness their behavior.

I will point out that I have no fucking intention of being here as a tourist, I'm just stuck here. We should not be here, we should be blasting our way through the desert but alas we are here at the side of the unfinished boulevard being approached by this Moroccan wide boy. When I say wide boy this is just a figure of speech. He was a tall stick thin chap but did have the swagger of a wide boy. I don't really know what a wide boy is or should look like to really understand the concept but I've watched enough shit television to form a mental image.

Wide boy approached us and I think he tried to introduce himself but I couldn't be sure. He was speaking in a mixture of French and Arabic. What little I could understand were the words, hotel, raid, NIVA, rescue, repair and garage. We were ushered into the BMW, it was even worse on the inside than it looked on the outside, it felt like we were being kidnapped but at least it had the heater working so I was happy to sit in the warmth.

Wide boy drove off at speed heading back up the road in the direction of Cold Bates Hotel. I doubted we would get back up the mountain road to the hotel without crashing on account that he had no comprehension of which side of the road he should be driving on or he had just chosen to take the most direct route, the other option was that as the car stank of fuel it might explode in a ball of flames at any point en route. This vehicle wasn't even worthy of being referred to as scrap and had seen very better days. I looked at the odometer and it read 475500 ish kilometers on it! This heap of shit was held together by nothing other than the will of Allah and little else. While talking off the will of Allah, we buckled up our seat belts in the back as you do. It appeared to me that the use of seat belts was an option based on the preference of the individual occupant. Possibly they didn't wear seat belts so they could bail out quickly should the fuel fumes ignite and we burst into flames. We drove in silence back up to the hotel. When we arrived we were introduced to the passenger riding shot gun. When he got out he didn't have a shot gun, AK47 or an ex army pistol. It was apparently wide boys rather elderly father who was the proprietor of the garage and the man who would be able to fix Svetty.

Instead of brandishing a firearm the old man brandished a very old, greasy tow rope. I said that we were expecting a tow truck, a small low loader with ramps on the back, bright yellow straps to secure Svettys wheels to the truck bed and orange flashing lights! No we had a fucked old BMW that had barely made it back up the mountain to Bates cold Hotel to rescue Svetty. Fair enough the return journey for them would be all downhill but without her engine running Svettys brakes will be even shitter than usual as the engine won't provide the brake servo with the much needed extra pressure it requires to make the brakes work at least a bit, I suppose Allah will yet again be with them.

I still wasn't sure or even remotely confident that these two clowns weren't a two man dodgy Azrou petty mafia or maybe there were other members of their mafia down in Azrou, they looked dodgy as fuck. I surmised that they were somehow in cahoots with the 'no one' at the hotel and were going to steal my beloved Svetty and leave us abandoned at Cold Bates Hotel. They would then sell Svetty on the black market or swap her at a local market for a camel. I'm stereotyping here again, I've only seen one camel so far and it didn't look worth swapping for anything. It is possible however that all the camels have already been swapped for stolen cars and then to hide the bounty the thieving mafia cunts have already had all the camels boiled down to make glue or Morocco's version of corned beef.

The wife and I were looking at each other with the unspoken words of, this a bit fucking weird and dodgy. I proceeded in this interaction with some caution. The old man had a look under the bonnet and like everyone who had done so previously today re-emerged shrugging his shoulders and none the wiser. They wanted to drag Svetty down the mountain to their workshop. They would let us know later what they found. I did think that Svetty even if she was freewheeling down the mountain road would probably overtake their shit old BMW. They started fixing the greasy, frayed old tow rope to Svetty and their heap of shit.

Not so fast amigos! You aren't taking Svetty anywhere without me knowing where she is going. We hesitantly agreed to accompany them to their workshop. We would find our way back to the hotel later even if it meant trudging back up the mountain road on foot. Old man was going to steer and try to brake Svetty while being towed by wide boy. I was gestured to ride shot gun and hesitantly climbed in, the wife sat behind me. I reached for the seat belt and there wasn't one! That's obviously why it was not worn.

We set off with a big jolt, wide boy appeared to have already forgotten he was towing another vehicle. Wide boy drove as recklessly on the way down as he did on the way up, oblivious on blind bends while driving on the wrong side of the road as to what might be coming uphill on the same side. I should have sat in the back, at least the flaking leather on the front seat head rests would have partially obscured the view ahead. I could see Svetty in the rear view mirror weaving all over the place being pulled side to side by the tow rope. After what seemed like a life time of terror we arrived at the unfinished boulevard where we were previously kidnapped. Although we're not Muslim, Allah must have been with us on the journey to get us down the mountain road in one piece with this wide boy lunatic at the wheel. We turned off the boulevard and looked to be joining an unfinished ring road, presumably to an industrial area with a nice big workshop waiting there for Svetty. I was trying not to look at anything until we arrive which is difficult without putting your hands over your eyes and peeping between your fingers.

Away from the relative pleasantness of the boulevard Azrou was now starting to look like Baghdad or some similar place you might see on televised news reports that has just been or is about to be bombed. Half finished or falling down concrete buildings, most of them with nothing more than the concrete frame in progress or not yet old and crumbling enough to have fallen down. We entered a built up area, I say built up, it was the same concrete structures just built closer together, some of the buildings looked like they were actually finished and inhabited. After what felt like going round in circles for a few minutes, I don't think we were but everything looked the same, we came to a halt. We were ushered out of the death trap and led to what I can only describe as a roller shuttered market stall. It was no bigger than a market stall inside, not even big enough to fit the smallest of cars in. Outside there was a concrete area just big enough to fit one car on and accessed from a yet again unfinished road via an unfeasibly high kerb.

We were told to wait there and wide boy set off again dragging Svetty and old man in tow. A few moments later they arrived a couple of hundread meters further up the road from their market stall workshop. They were doing something, wide boy drove down and parked up their piece of shit just down the hill past the market stall workshop. Obviously they had been discombobulating the tow rope. Next the old man freewheeled Svetty down the hill gaining enough speed to mount the massive kerb and came to a sudden halt in front of the market stall shutter.

Without any further conversation the old man set to work but not before me insisting that I install my trusty bonnet support stick to prevent him from being decapitated. Wide boy invited us into the market stall, proffered the wife the only rickety chair and for that matter the only piece of furniture in there and lit a little gas heater for us to warm our hands on which was most kind of him. Despite my early and as you will have just read not totally unfounded impression of this father and son duo, I was beginning to warm to them which is more than I can say for my hands.

The old man came inside to briefly warm his hands and came back from somewhere with a screwdriver and a collection of spanners. I've seen better quality tools supplied for free in an unfathomable box of flat pack furniture. I offered him the contents of our well stocked semi professional tool kit in the back of Svetty but I just got a look you could only describe as 'are you trying to tell me how to suck eggs white man' so I let him crack on. Firstly he removed the ancillary shizzle from around the engine to give him some access to where he needed to get at. Svetty's ace to work on as unlike modern cars where you can't see where anything is beyond all the plastic covers, Svetty has more space in the engine bay than the engine itself takes up. Some parts however are still very difficult to get access to unless you have three small very hands. At this point the old man actually climbed inside the engine bay to give himself better access. We were fascinated watching how he worked and his dexterity. Finally the top engine cover was off, without being technical it's the bit where you put the engine oil in, it's a tedious job to remove it even when the engine's not in the car. He started prodding about inside with his fingers then he found the problem and it didn't look good.

I'll explain the problem with Svetty in as simple a way as is possible on the basis that you dear reader probably own a car but have no idea and no intention of understanding how the 'internal confusion' engine works. Basically the bit at the top has a shaft in it. This top bit is where the fuel goes in and the exhaust fumes go out. The fuel is ignited by a spark to make an explosion. The explosion of fuel pushes the pistons down, the pistons are connected to another shaft in the bottom bit of the engine and make the engine go round. With me so far, if not don't worry. The top and bottom oily shafts must go round in unison for the engine to work. It's a bit like a group of homosexuals shafts working in unison when engaging in a circle of tadgertourous. Anyway, both shafts are connected to each other by a chain to keep them in perfect harmony. Like anything mechanical a chain will wear and stretch over time, in order to keep everything in rotating harmony there is a 'chain tensioner', this basically pushes on the chain to keep it tight and extends as the chain stretches to keep it tensioned. Understood? Probably not but we will carry on.

Old man pushed his finger on the visible bit of chain and it moved, it didn't just move it was slacker than a fat Burnley whores, well you can guess. In a process of elimination he took the chain tensioner out. Another brief explanation for your information and education, the chain tensioner has a serrated shaft on it that as the chain stretches it moves out onto the next tooth and engages to keep it in place and the chain is kept nice and tensioned as it should be. Unfortunately it looked like an alligator with metal teeth had been chewing on it. The chain tensioner was fucked and so are we as he didn't have one in his market stall but would be able to obtain one tomorrow.

I'm feeling really fucked off as the chain tensioner along with 90 percent of the engine was brand new or refurbished only 18000 kilometers ago and was like new. Old man I think wanted to check on the condition of the chain and the sprockets and associated items attached to the oily shafts and proceeded to remove the front engine cover. To remove said cover you need to remove the radiator.

In the Moroccan environmentally friendly way he pulled the bottom hose of the radiator and let the coolant run down the street. He obviously didn't have a tub to put under it to keep it for reuse or dispose of it responsibly. His shit spanners were struggling to grip two of the bolts on the front engine cover so he went to warm his hands and came back with a hacksaw and proceeded to saw the bolt heads off. I asked why he was doing this and as far as I could understand he said the bolts were just spinning, I begged to differ but couldn't be arsed saying anything. When the cover was removed we could see how badly the chain had been flapping around, tensioned, un tensioned and repeat for some time as the sprockets were worn and tinged blue from the heat stress. This is getting worse by the minute, I'm in two minds as to whether this would be a simple tensioner change tomorrow and we will make a do with the sprockets and chain in the condition they are in so we can catch up on the most direct road route to rejoin and carry on with the raid or if there is some more serious internal organ failure to operate on.

We're both feeling really fucked off, tired and cold, there's been flakes of snow wafting around while we've been stood here, welcome to sunny Morocco. We've now been loitering around here for a few hours and decided it was time to wander back up to Bates Cold Hotel or find a taxi as there would be no chain tensioner available until tomorrow and there was not a lot we could do.

Wide boy reappeared, he'd been coming and going all afternoon, possibly doing car rescue or running drugs or trading ammunition, who can say. As he spoke more clearly than his father we started to tell him that we were going to fuck off back up to Bates Cold Hotel and would come back tomorrow. Wide boy appeared to have gone into Arabic mode again and wasn't understanding French or decided not to. His father continued pulling bits of Svetty making a nice heap of bits while still kneeling in the engine bay, I'll be amazed with his haphazard non arrangement of nuts, bolts, washers and springs etc if he ever gets Svetty back together the way she came apart.

To converse with wide boy we initiated emergency google speaking translate, this was a one way street as he couldn't work it out on his phone. Fortunately a knight in shining armour, well in a shining purple pimped up old Honda pulled up further down the street. That's my friend said wide boy, he speaks very good English. Wide boy shouted or just yelled at him, it's difficult to tell in Arabic, it's like the German language, everything sounds aggressive or could be a potential threat. Wide boys friend sauntered up the street treading carefully not to get his smart looking trainers covered in the coolant the old man had discharged from Svetty. I love the word discharge, don't you? Discharge is on a par with moist to utilize in conversation without using obscenities such as fuck, cunt and twat which by now you are well aware are some of my favorites.

Mr Honda or should we call him Mr Purple? I'm going ahead with the advice of the wife here and we are going one shade of color down from purple to name him. Hence forth we will call him Mr Pink Honda, Mr Pink, as in Mr pink from the film Reservoir Dogs, seems appropriate or did so at the time.

Mr Pink introduced himself, obviously not as Mr Pink, I have no idea what he said his name was, he did tell us several times but there comes a point in the day, especially one like this when you are in need of IPA and you just nod, agree and really don't give a flying fuck what anyone's saying. Mr Pink was very helpful in translation and said if we exchange numbers he would keep us updated on Svetty's progress via the WhatsApp thing. The bonus of this is that the updates would be in English.

Now we are acquainted with Mr Pink we asked him to tell old man and wide boy that we were off and we will go and find a taxi to take us back up to Bates Cold Hotel, we would come back tomorrow when we receive news from you on the repair progress. This is where I started to like the Moroccans, obviously not the fat women sexually, nor their disregard for the environment or lack of heating in their hotels it is just their attitude towards complete strangers. The old man said, no you cannot get a taxi, he insisted that he would give us a lift back up to Bates Cold Hotel if we gave him a few minutes to finish what he was doing on Svetty. Old man would then go and get his car and give us a lift back up the mountain. Bless him as he did also offer that we could go and stay at his house but we had already paid for a cold room up at Bates so we politely turned down this offer. At the hotel we could at least have some peace and raid the ever dwindling contents of our makeshift Bar 212.

Old man walked off to get his car, he said via Mr Pink's translation skills that he was going to carry on with the work on Svetty later tonight after sundown following today's break of Ramadan when he would be allowed by Allah to have something to eat, drink and have a smoke. He was old and tired and following all of his religions rules of not consuming anything during daylight had apparently fairly sensibly in my mind decided to spend Ramadan sleeping during the daylight hours and working during the night when he could do whatever the fuck he liked.

We were waiting ages in the cold for the old man to return with his car. I was feeling scared about the upcoming 5 kilometer journey back up the mountain based on the state of his sons car and I was wondering what sort of a heap of shit deathtrap the old man might arrive in to provide his free taxi service. While we're waiting I will recount one of the things the old man had told us during the long boring cold afternoon. Apparently he used to work for FIAT, not just in a normal garage but traveling all over the globe as a race car mechanic. This was back in the day in the 1970's when race car engines were not the computerized nonsense that they are today. Anyway the Fiat engines he worked on were apparently the basis of and essentially identical to what became the engine that the Russians put in the first Svetty in 1976 and still to this day they use the same engine albeit with a few modifications to keep up with modern times such as fuel injection instead of a carburettor and other shite unnecessary electric things that inevitably fuck up because they were made and assembled by vodka pickled Ruskies.

I think the old man might be arriving soon, I could hear vehicle noise approaching in the opposite direction of which he had set off on foot twenty minutes earlier and it was now audibly heading in our direction.

A vehicle came round a corner at speed further up the road from the market stall workshop and literally came to a skid stop where we were waiting. I wasn't expecting this, the old man was driving a MINI Cooper S Turbo! The more astute of you will know that a MINI Cooper S is not fitted with a turbo but the old man had bolted one onto his engine. Old man got out and came round to open the passenger door like a gentleman to let us in. Old man obviously loved his MINI as it was spotless inside and out. We climbed in, well I should say that I shoehorned the wife's arse into the back seat and I climbed into the passenger seat to ride shotgun. Old man obviously loved his car so I was happy to sit next to him and chew the cud. Hopefully aside from his arriving at the market stall showing off his pristine car he would revert to old man Sunday driver and potter us back up to Cold Bates Hotel at an annoyingly slow pace avoiding pot holes on the way and respecting his side of the road. The wife had already buckled up in the back. I reached for my seatbelt that was tangled somewhere in the back but at least there was one. The old man said apropo the seatbelt that I was fumbling for 'that is not necessary'.

Old man fired up the MINI and set off, Fuck me! This little thing shifts like shit off a shovel, he was changing gears like a rally driver, gear lever in motion even before he had touched his foot on the clutch pedal. We approached a roundabout and he just used it as a chicane, next we were back on the unfinished potholed road we had been on previously that led to the unfinished boulevard and then on to the road back up the mountain. I think the old man's theory was that on an unfinished potholed road driving in a lightweight car over powered by the turbo that you just go as fast as you can and the car will become like a flat stone skimming across water.

I have to say, unlike the wank old BMW, solid and pristine as this little MINI was, on account of the driver I was yet again fearing for my life!

The old man suddenly put his foot on the brakes, slowing us down to an acceptable or legal speed. If I had managed to access the seat belt I would have used it and avoided nearly knocking my remaining teeth out on the dashboard when he did this. What's the problem old man I asked? Police ahead in the distance doing speed checks the old man replied. We left the unfinished potholed road at the next roundabout, this time he did not use it as a chicane and we joined the unfinished boulevard heading uphill in the mountain road direction. We turned right and followed the road up to where the police were waiting at the bottom of the mountain road. We are now travelling at Sunday driver speed and the old man doesn't appear to be at all bothered by the presence of the police, they are probably his brothers but I suppose you need to keep up appearances. We passed the police and immediately the old man Schumacher is giving it all on the go pedal again! He's shifting up and down gears in the corners and is basically driving at full throttle all the time, just using the gears to keep his speed and engine revs at the maximum. I think he was very much enjoying himself. On the plus side unlike his son the old man is keeping more or less to his designated side of the road and despite driving like a rally driver smacked up on speed I actually felt safe even without the comfort of being safely strapped in to the rather plush bucket seat. In no time at all we arrived back at the Bates Cold Hotel, we prised ourselves out of the car, said thankyou, shook hands, said see you tomorrow and bon courage with your work tonight on my beloved Svetty.

A crowd had arrived at Cold Bates Hotel. When I say a crowd, there was a Belgium plated minibus parked outside with a trailer on it. On the trailer were eight off road touring motorbikes. The bikes looked lush, mean and purposeful, they were obviously en route to a raid somewhere and had stopped off here en route. There were only the eight Belgian people wandering about and the two of us at the Bates Cold Hotel. I tried to engage in conversation with the passing Belgian's in the reception and corridor but being Belgian they are the most ignorant and arrogant race in the world, that is apart from Americans who are just ignorant, arrogant, selfish and sheep mentality fat fuckers.

I was standing outside the reception having a smoke and a pretty young lass asked me for a light. She really was a pretty looking little fitty. We got chatting and it turned out that she wasn't Belgian but was actually Lithuanian and it just happened that she was traveling with the arrogant ones as a group to go an a raid somewhere that I cannot remember the name of so lets just say somewhere in the desert. She showed me her motorbike and all I could think of was, if I was 25 years younger the best throbbing thing you could have between your thighs you Lithuanian little fitty is my throbbing cock. Obviously I left this thought in my head, said good evening and retreated back into Bar 212.

Food supplies were running low and not wanting a shit tagine again, that is if any food was available but as ever there was no one about to ask, we opted that dinner would be the last of the Morribobs snacks, the sausage rolls were becoming decidedly soggy and a little pungent but the crisps and sweets were good. With fuck all else to do I had a catch up on the raids WhatsApp group to see what fun they had been having today while we have been at misery level 3. Apparently they were having lots of fun, fucking wankers! It's still early but it's been a long stressful day and we should be in Kertandou tonight not still stranded near Azrou. I put some white noise on the phone and drifted off to sleep.

# 12 Stage 3 Kerrandou – Hassilabied

Wakey wakey rise and shine, hands off cocks, on with socks. It's only 5am but I can't sleep. I'm excited about picking up Svetty and driving to Sidi Ali to spend the night with the other équipes ready to hit the desert on stage 4, at least we would have only missed stages 2 and 3. I unplugged the phone and turned off the white noise. Left room 212, Bar 212 is unfortunately closed at this hour, I walked through the reception where as usual someone was sleeping on one of the sofas, if only the staff were as present if not remotely as attentive during the day.

I ventured outside and fuck me will this rain ever end, I administered my two breakfast cancer sticks. I hoped the Lithuanian fitty might have ventured out for an early morning smoke in some sexy underwear or skimpy biking leathers or preferably a combination of the two secretly hidden in a provocative nature under a long silk dressing gown. Alas I stood smoking sheltering from the rain all on my own.

Back in room 212 I did a check on WhatsApp to see how Svetty's surgery went. I didn't need to read the words, the photos Mr Pink had sent told the story or more specifically the disaster that had occurred. In a nutshell and without being too technical I'll try to explain.

As you know the chain that synchronizes the top and bottom oily shafts of the engine has been flapping about for some time on account of the alligator chewed chain tensioner. The reason the engine would not turn is that the valves in the top bit of the engine that open and close to let the fuel in and the exhaust fumes out had collided with the pistons that go up and down in the bottom part of the engine. The result was 2 broken valves. Normally a failure like this would be totally catastrophic as one would smash into the other and destroy the engine. Good news though if it can be described as that.

Back in the 1970's some Russian engineer at AutoVAZ (AutoVAZ was the Russian Communist owners of what is now known as LADA and nowadays DACIA in western Europe) cleverly installed a little thing on AutoVAZ engines that will stop the timing chain moving too much or jumping. The short story is we don't have a totally fucked engine but we have 2 broken valves and 4 bent ones but at least they haven't smashed a hole through the pistons.

The top bit of the engine has apparently been passed on to one of the old man's friends who will rebuild it today, they said they won't have the exact parts but will modify or manufacture something to do the job and get Svetty up and running. Old man would then put Svetty back together either tonight or tomorrow when he gets the top bit of the engine back. Fucking great we are stuck here at Cold Bates Hotel and not going anywhere today. I had a John Smiths mouthwash and went for a cancer stick in pursuit of the Lithuanian hottie. Unfortunately they had left, there goes my fantasy.

Quick recky, if we don't get Svetty back until tomorrow that will leave us, depending on what time she is ready for us to pick her up we will have to drive about 600 kilometers probably through the night to catch up with the raid and then rejoin it at Sidi Ali for etape 5. Knowing garages, let alone market stall workshop garages, tomorrow could be tomorrow, or tomorrow or tomorrow after that. There was no way I was staying at this fucking miserable place for another day so I sat down and started to hatch plan B.

Right then, let's have a look where can you travel to via public transport from Azrou? Thanks to Google the answer is Casablanca. There is a coach leaving Azrou at 2 o'clock this afternoon arriving in Casablanca at 8 o'clock in the evening. CTM is the coach company and a one way ticket is the equivalent of 13 euros each so we thought, fuck it, we are on honeymoon and it saves us sitting around here watching the rain and me occasionally fantasising about the Lithuanian little hottie who was now probably enjoying a pulsating motorbike engine between her thighs somewhere in the Moroccan desert instead of enjoying my ageing but still just at a push hard pulsating cock.

The coach tickets are booked. We had planned to visit Casablanca after the raid anyway as a stop over on the way back up north from Marrakesh so we were just doing the same journey in reverse using public transport, we already had a hotel booked in Casablanca albeit not until next week. I rang the hotel, it was a Hotel Campanile and after explaining our situation they said yes no problem, we will rearrange your booking so you can arrive tonight instead of next week. I messaged Mr Pink to say we would pop in at the market stall workshop at about 10 to see Svettys internal organ damage for ourselves and would then find ourselves somewhere to have a spot of lunch before having a six hour nap on the bus.

We need to get a taxi back down to Azrou. I roused the only person still in the hotel from his slumber who was as usual residing on one of the sofas in the reception. He was obviously knackered after having the chore of checking out the arrogant Belgian's and the Lithuanian hottie. Normally at a hotel you just ask at the reception and in minute or so a taxi arrives. I politely asked if he would ring for a taxi for us. No the reception man said, I will not arrange for a taxi. What the fuck, why not you lazy bespectacled Moroccan cunt? I politely asked if he had a telephone number of a local taxi company so I could arrange one myself.

There was obviously some misunderstanding. Bespectacled man actually wanted to drive us back down to Azrou himself as he clearly had fuck all else better to do. Off we went then, piling ourselves with our rucksacks into the back of his Citroen Berlingo bus, it would have been easier to put the rucksacks in the boot but apparently the boot door was broken. Important question from Mr Bespectacled, where are we going?

Good question, I have no fucking idea, I do however have a photo on my phone of the market stall workshop, I showed it to Mr Bespectacled and he said, my friend knows that place he will come with us.

We arrived at the market stall workshop in one piece, Mr Bespectacled was a very safe driver, possibly because he was blind as a bat and couldn't see where he was going so he took it steady. When we arrived the old man, wide boy and Mr Pink were at the market stall workshop waiting for us. The old man proffered me a gift, it was the two broken valves, ta muchly that has really brightened my day. I said do you have any strong glue to fix them back together? The joke was lost on him. Next the old man showed me the pistons, the two where the valves had broken and had bashed into the pistons were looking a tad sorry for themselves. Thanks to Russian engineering the pistons were at least still in one piece. Old man was going to resurface the piston heads by hand and make them all shiny and flat again ready for the top part of the engine arriving back later today or possibly tomorrow so he can put Svetty's beating heart back together and fingers crossed and obviously with the will of Allah get her back up and running.

We are now going on our alternative Moroccan adventure, not the one that we had anticipated but here we are and stiff upper lip and all that we are going to make the most of it, stiff upper lip is the only stiff thing about me right now after the departure of my fantasy Lithuanian biker.

We explained to old man via Mr Pink that we would be going away traveling for a few days and will return to collect Svetty when she is out of surgery. The old man asked where we were going, Casablanca on the bus at 2 o'clock. Old man kindly offered to give a us a lift to the bus, based on his Schumacher driving from yesterday I politely refused. The bus station is only a kilometer or so away and we have plenty of time to find the bus station, where the bus departs from and then find somewhere to have something to eat.

So now we are back packing like university drop outs, I would have much preferred to be off-roading in the desert but on the plus side I won't have to pay to put fuel in the bus. We marched off, rucksacks on our backs in the direction of the bus station. Azrou on a Monday is quite a bustling place, there were people everywhere. After half an hour we arrived at the bus station, I needed a piss so headed to the toilets.

Fucking filthy Moroccan bastards! Obviously in this part of the world the toilet is of the squatting type and some people or possibly just one person has obviously not squatted and just leant against the wall instead of over the hole in the floor and done a stinking runny shit. My shit at times can be explosive but I've never managed to shit up a fucking wall. There was no flushing apparatus just a bucket of water on the floor. I stood pissing someone's shit off the wall, I was doing this to provide a public service to the future users of the public conveniences all the while trying not to breathe in and holding back my increasing need to start gagging and gipping at the stench of shit.

Piss over and done with which I somehow managed to achieve without coughing up a mouthful of bile. I advised the wife to hang on for a piss for now unless she was really desperate. The wife said "If I hadn't left my SheeWee in Svetty I could have pissed some more of the shit off the wall" Now you are wondering what a SheeWee is? It basically a silicone funnel shaped to fit around what some call the mans munching chin rest pelvic area allowing women to have a stand up piss like a man. I've seen it in action and the wife can piss allover the place with it.

I had a cancer stick to clear my nostrils of Moroccan wall smeared poo particles then we went to look at the departure boards to check where we were going to be setting off from, best to be prepared, I really didn't want to miss the bus and spend another night at Cold Bates Hotel. There were no departure boards as you would know them, there were just bits of paper stuck on the walls and columns none of which indicated a bus going to Casablanca. I asked a greasy looking man in a booth where the CTM bus to Casablanca was leaving from? Not here 500 meters that way pointing with his greasy finger. We exited the bus station and walked approximately 500 metres in the direction of the greasy finger. Nothing! We mooched around the general area looking for somewhere that a bus might stop. I'll ask someone if they know where it is, 'just at the end of this street and turn right', still nothing, I asked another person, 'its on the main boulevard, 200 meters after the next left'. We appeared to be walking round in circles looking for a non existent bus stop. There was a second hand washing machine shop with a man stood outside, I asked him if he knew where our destination was and he said follow me. 100 meters down the road there it was, the CTM office, not a bus stop at all. We had walked past this place four fucking times. Much to the delight of the wife there was a clean sit on toilet so she very much enjoyed relieving herself, I contemplated having a poo before the bus journey but I didn't really need one so I didn't bother.

CTM appears to be more of a postal or courier service rather than a passenger service as the office come waiting area was filled with boxes and parcels that would soon be loaded into the luggage compartments of the bus when it arrives. Just time to get a spot of lunch before the bus. No such luck, there were many eateries in sight but being Ramadan nothing was open.

The bus arrived, we got on and so did many parcels and boxes. This was quite a plush bus, leatherette seats, not the usual carpet like itch your bum to fuck seats normally found on a bus, there were USB chargers, air conditioning not that it was needed, all the mod cons. We are quite used to bus travel following our 50th birthday trip to Barcelona and Montpellier where incidentally the wife's Rupert Renault overheated and the engine was fucked before we even left home so instead of a road trip we took the train and bus instead. There were only a few passengers on the bus so we got ourselves separate seats and reclined to watch the scenery. The scenery was boring and I nodded off, normally on a bus we would indulge in a few tinnies or prepare a bottle of vodka and coke in advance but respecting the Muslim country we abstained.

We stopped somewhere and I woke up. Time for a piss and smoke break. A man in a uniform of the CTM livery came on the bus and was passing to each passenger what looked like a Maccy'd Crappy Meal box but finished in royal blue with gold lettering on it. Ohh free gift? I looked around and no one was opening their box, they just left them on the seat or placed them in their lap. I rejoined the snoozing wife on our allocated seats and continued to watch the boring scenery.

It was just going dark and some random woman started wandering up and down the aisle of the bus chanting or wailing something or other and proffering pieces of some sort of cake to the passengers. I assumed the daily fast was over, the passengers with pack ups got their food out of their bags, everyone including us ate the wailing woman's cake and the Crappy Meal esque boxes were opened. Now, I'm not in any way religious apart than believing that I am a God of some description, I must be as my body is a temple with an ever increasing slightly wobbly dome growing on it, just like a mosque. Anyway, in the box was cake, a bottle of water and a tub of nuts and dates. It was lush that as clearly non Muslims we were being included in their religious ritual.

The bus sauntered into Casablanca, my fingers were sticky, not from fingering a Moroccan fatty in the dim light on the bus or god forbid the wife but from handling the dates in the goody box. Should my fantasy Lithuanian hottie have decided to stalk me and follow me onto the bus I would have been more than happy to engage in dimly lit mutual maturation resulting in sticky fingers all round.

I put the hotels address in the phone and we set off following the walking route in the direction of Hotel Campanile City Centre. The phone wasn't keeping up with us but I thought we were going in vaguely the right direction. After about 15 minutes I realized I was holding the phone upside down. We turned round and walked back past the bus station. Now we are on the correct route, we are only twenty minutes walk from the hotel and a bar! That is twenty minutes if I didn't like a dick think that I know better than the sat nav and decide to follow my nose. Forty minute's later we finally arrived at the hotel, delayed thanks to my arrogance and ignorance.

At the reception the very kind man said unfortunately we can't change your reservation from next week to today. The booking was made through a reputable internet booking site and would be automatically debited on the day of the original reservation. The receptionist said give me your card and I'll put your payment through but I'll cancel the transaction. You will receive an email saying there is a payment problem so just ignore it, you won't be charged. Good customer service, anyway we booked in and paid for two nights accommodation. Off up to the room we went and without hesitation set up our now rather meagre mobile bar. The room was clean, modern and warm, very much unlike Cold Bates Hotel, we are however staying in a room at an international chain of hotels so I expect it to be amicable. Following a quick couple of lukewarm John Smiths, we dressed for dinner and down to the bar we went. I say dress for dinner, I put my boots back on but didn't bother to lace them up, going for dinner in socks isn't even in my slap dash dress code book anywhere near appropriate.

Cold beer! Proper job! We sat at the bar and perused the menu before choosing a table in the restaurant. The menu was the normal generic hotel chain wank that tries to cater for everyone. There was a band playing in the restaurant, I say a band as there were four people making a fucking racket with some instruments. I don't know the genre of Muslim noise to refer to it as but it was intolerably loud and shit. The woman wailing on the bus earlier would have fitted in a treat as their lead singer. We selected a table as far away from the noise as possible, in the hotel next door would have been preferable. Some of the diners were actually enjoying this fucking racket and actively clapping along encouraging them, tourist cunts, I can call the other residents tourist cunts as the reason for me being here is that I'm not really a tourist but this is the better alternative to topping myself due to depression in Azrou.

A waiter arrived and asked if we would like to order a drink, the wife went for a beer, I went for the cheapest bottle of red on the wine list, we don't have any of that one, can I suggest this one, it's locally produced and very good. How would you know young man you are Muslim and don't drink? I could hardly hear him due to the continuing racket of the band and I don't think he could hear me either. The waiter kept on insisting that I buy the local wine as they don't have any others in stock, this was a half bottle priced at 360 Dirhams, I was getting annoyed, I walked him to the bar and showed him the wine rack behind the bar and said which bottles of wine that are on list are stored there? Eventually I got a 260 Dirham bottle of wine. Next to try and order food over the increasingly irritating noise. I needed sustenance so went for a pasta thing, the wife went for a beef tagine. We ate the mediocre hotel food and took our beer and wine back up to the room away from the noise. I nodded off to some news channel on the television as comforting white noise.

# 13 Etape 4 Hassilabied – Sidi Ali

The joys of staying in a city centre hotel and sleeping with the window open. Way before Dawn's crack the traffic outside was creating as much noise as the wankers attempting to play noise in the restaurant last night but the traffic noise was much more acceptable, traffic has to do it's thing, noisy wankers don't.

Morning ritual, off outside for a couple of cancer sticks but not before a glug of wine mouthwash, there's just a dribble left in the white box, I would have preferred one but there's no IPA or John Smiths left and the bars probably not open yet. Now we're back on the coast it's windy as fuck again. Even though it was only about 6 there was a suited man at the hotel door stood there waiting to open it for me, I assume you should give him some coins for this service but I didn't have any so I went for a walk around the block.

During my wander around the block I passed the underground carpark where in different circumstances we would have been parking Svetty in safety and comfort some time next week, I shed a little tear, wiped my eye and carried on around the block. I was on cancer stick number two and needed to pick up speed as it was necessary to hastily retreat back to the room for my morning shit before there would be a requirement to use the hotels laundry service or find a shop selling cheap undies.

We had our tourist heads on today. The place name Casablanca screams romance and sandy beaches to you does it not? According to the internet there's not that much to see in Casablanca but the must see place is King Hassan II mosque. We planned a route on foot on the phone and En route to the mosque our route would take us close to Rick's Café, this is the actual place that was recreated in Hollywood for the filming of Casablanca the movie way back in 1942. We set off on a romantic walk along the coast road to see the mosque. There were no sandy beaches or sights to be seen, only docks, ship yards, out of town shopping centres and heavy industry and a huge amount of traffic. We veered off the route to check out the menu at Rick's Café, it looked a bit pompous, over priced and wank so we decided we wouldn't be going there for lunch. Phone sat nav said we were still two kilometers from the mosque but it looked very close. As we continued our walk the mosque just got bigger. When we eventually arrived I thought fuck me, who had the bonkers idea of building a mosque instead of a football stadium, this place is off the scale on massive architectural achievements.

When I visit places, especially of an architectural nature I like to mooch about and have a look at my own leisure, I hate guided tours with twats, usually American's asking pointless questions to the guide so they appear interested but are actually just highlighting themselves as uneducated thick fuckers. Alas, access to the mosque is only possible on a guided tour so we bought our tickets and waited for our slot at 11.15. We mustered with our group and walked across the concourse to the mosque, even the concourse was massive, I still had my phone sat nav on and it said there was still half a kilometer to the entrance. I won't dwell too long on describing the mosque as you can easily Google it if you feel the need but suffice to say, barring magnificent high rise buildings like the Chrysler building in New York this place is second on scale and magnificence to Gaudi's wonderful and awe inspiring Sagrada Familia in Barcelona.

Despite my detest of guided tours I actually quite enjoyed it. We walked back across the concourse enjoying the salty taste on our lips of the sea spray being blown in by the gale force wind to regroup have a smoke and plan where we would visit next.

There wasn't as I had already ascertained from my Google searching not much else to see in Casablanca so we decided to head in the direction of the city centre to see what sights could be seen and find somewhere for lunch. Every eatery we passed was closed, thanks Allah for Ramadan. If nothing else we could always eat at the hotel. The city centre was just shops, traffic and concrete buildings, there wasn't anything else to see, I was bored and in need of refreshments so we just headed in the direction of the hotel.

Last night on my self imposed convoluted route to the hotel we walked down a street near the hotel that was lined with the sort of big camper van type things that you associate with film sets in the movies.

We did by chance arrive at the same street as last night and indeed it was full of nose to tail vans, all connected with electrical cables, there was clearly a television show or film being shot in the vicinity. There was what I presumed were the actors and actresses being escorted out of the vans by men in black suits holding umbrellas over them heading up the street in the direction we were heading. When we arrived at the end of the street there were many people spectating and crowd barriers everywhere. There were film cameras on trolleys and lots of presumably film crew scurrying about. We stopped to watch for a few minutes. There were cars traveling up the street at speed followed by gun shots and screaming, it was probably an action movie being filmed or a staged gang land shooting had just taken place in front of a crowd. Surprise surprise it was pissing it down again so we headed on through the crowds of spectators back to the hotel.

Quick check on WhatsApp to see if there was any news from Mr Pink on Svetty's surgery. Good news, there are photographs of the top bit of Svetty's engine looking all shiny and new. Apparently the old man would put the engine back together when he arsed to get out of bed, presumably that would be after sundown. Anyway, boom, progress, we went down to the bar for a celebratory cold one or three. Asier had also messaged to check if we were OK and I said we wouldn't be rejoining the raid but would possibly see everyone in Marrakesh.

We're sat at the bar and rolled a smoke to take outside, the barman said, stay there and passed us an ashtray, unusual to be openly encouraged to smoke indoors but on this occasion we obliged. Three beers later and I thought at this price we will be out of Dirhams before tea time so I decided I would go in search of a shop. Before leaving the bar I asked if they would be serving food all day as no restaurants appeared to be open. That's Ramadan for you he replied and yes food will be available all day.

Obviously in a Muslim country you don't just go out willy nilly in search of a Spar shop or such like to buy beer and wine otherwise you will inevitably return empty handed, thirsty and disappointed so I went to the room to do some research. I had previously done some research apropo buying alcohol in Morocco and it is apparently available at the larger supermarkets, namely the Carrefour supermarkets which is incidentally a French chain of supermarket. I understand that even then it might be necessary to ask where the 'cave' is as it will usually be in the back corner of the store behind a closed non descript door. Being in the city center there were no big supermarkets so it was necessary to initiate beer and wine acquisition plan B. According to Google maps there was a place called the 'Wine Shop' just 200 meters from the hotel, I pin pointed the location on my phone and set off in earnest. When I arrived minutes later there was a man selling oranges from the window. I could see inside past the orange seller and there was what looked like bottle shelving but all empty and long since used. I asked Mr Orange if this was the wine shop and he replied, no more, closed for long time. I returned despondent to the hotel.

Attempt number two, the wife had found another place 500 meters away from the hotel near where the action movie or whatever filming was taking place. This shop was called 'The Bottle Store'. Yet again I set off in earnest. I had to fight my way through the crowds still watching the filming or waiting for something to happen in the cordoned off street and the traffic that was all jammed up on account of one of the main city streets being closed while actors ponce around doing whatever they were doing.

When I arrived the shop was all closed up and looked like it had been for many years. Next door but one was a grubby looking general store, there was next to no illumination in there so I thought I would go in and have a look about. The back half of the store was totally dark so possibly this is where 'The Bottle Store' is and it's kept out of sight. Using the power of the illuminated screen on my phone I had a look around, I'm sure my phone has a torch built in to it somewhere but I'll be buggered if I know how to find or operate it. Alas, the unlit area at the back of the store was just filled with cleaning products, presumably unlit because to the Moroccans cleanliness isn't high on their list of priorities and no-one bothers to use that part of the store. Not wanting to return to the hotel feeling once again despondent I thought fuck it I'll ask the totally disinterested man behind the counter if he knew anything about 'The Bottle Store' next door but one.

'No more, closed for long time' was the reply just like Mr Orange had said, this was obviously the standard reply. I thought this place looks dodgy as fuck so I'm going to risk it for a biscuit. Are you sure it's permanently closed I asked, yes was the reply, are you sure I asked again. Yes, closed was the same reply. I love engaging in what could become a moderately heated conversation in French after a few beers. Anyway Mr Disinterested wasn't budging so I politely asked him if he knew where I could buy wine and beer as it was very expensive at the hotel. There was a long pause, he sighed a bit and then gestured towards a man who had silently appeared at the far corner of the L shaped counter. Mr Disinterested said follow him. I thought this place looked dodgy but I wasn't quite expecting that response. Being a good boy I followed Mr Silent around the back of the counter and through a door into a dimly lit corridor. Mr Silent kept gesturing with his hand and a nod of his head for me to follow him. We turned a corner in the corridor and came to another door, Mr Silent opened the door and fumbled around for a light switch, light switch found the room was illuminated, we are in a fairly empty room with two doors. Is this a choose the door escape room thing I've inadvertently walked into? Mr silent chose the door we would use, he opened it, fumbled for the light switch again and boom there it was, an illegal offlicence! I selected two whites and two reds and as many cans of beer as I thought I could physically carry. Incidentally the red wine I had chosen was the same as I had been stung for in the hotel last night but was a mere 90 Dihrams, a saving of about 60 percent. I was silently ushered back into the shop where Mr Silent and I quickly put my bounty under the counter. Each item was wrapped in newspaper and put in a black bin bag.

I assume this was as a disguise so I would look like someone taking their bins out on my way back to the hotel or a bin man who had lost sight of his bin wagon. Mr Disinterested totted up what was owed on his calculator and showed me, it was a whole 360 Dihrams, about the same as the half bottle of local wine the annoying twat in the hotel last night was trying to get me to buy. I proffered Mr Disinterested my debit card and he shook his head. I am a dick sometimes, I knew this would be a dodgy transaction so why did I ever think I could pay by card?

Back in the day I wouldn't have expected to buy cocaine, speed or ecstasy tablets from some dodgy place in Burnley with a swipe card so why did I expect to here. I left, found a cash machine and returned with folding money. I gave Mr Disinterested 400 Dihrams and said to keep the change. He actually smiled and I left in the direction of the hotel feeling triumphant at what I had achieved. The moral of this paragraph is, where there is a will there is a way.

Lets face it, in this shit modern world we now live in, if you want or have the need to you can seek out and buy anything from a teenage Filipino bride who might turn out to be a lady boy to a nuclear weapon and everything else in between, everything is available to buy if you look for it.

En route to the hotel I had to take a moment and marvel at the stupidity of the vehicle drivers in Casablanca. The filming down the road and subsequent road closures were causing traffic mayhem. There were two tram tracks running down the middle of the road serving the city's metro system. With the car lanes blocked many drivers had decided to use the tram route to get to where they were going. Dangerous but a good idea I suppose until you have trams coming in opposite directions with cars in front and behind of them. With no traffic moving on the road either side of the tram tracks and the trams stuck because of cars on their tracks everyone just sat there tooting their horns in anger. I chuckled to myself and continued my journey with my bin bag of contraband.

We reclined in the room sipping our illegally obtained beer and planned our next move. There were two options available. Option one was to see if the old man had got Svetty up and running tonight and then get the bus back to Azrou tomorrow or possibly the day after and spend another day in Casablanca getting pissed here as it's better than returning to Cold Bates Hotel for an extra night. Option two was to get the bus down to Marrakesh tomorrow and meet up with the équipes on the raid the day after tomorrow for the finish of the raid at Mogador Aqua Fun Hotel. We have already paid via the raid for the hotel on the night the raid finishes and it seemed a shame to have travelled more than 2000 kilometers south from home not to go a couple of hundread kilometers further south and enjoy the delights of Marrakesh. The bus journey was only four hours so we decided on going to Marrakesh.

We booked tickets for the 8.30am bus and this time we checked where it would be setting off from. Checking where it was departing from was a sensible thing to do as it was departing from the CTM office somewhere in Casablanca and not the bus station where we were dropped off, we would get a taxi there in the morning to save any Hasselhoff! I rang the Mogador Aqua Fun Hotel to check they had availability for tomorrow night, they said yes so all was good.

Bugger all left to do so we went down to the restaurant for dinner. Although we now had bar supplies in the room it's always nice to sit in the bar for a pre dinner drink and we can also smoke in the bar. You will remember we asked earlier if food was served all day. We perused the limited menu again and went to chose a table. Fortunately there was no band playing but they were set up and probably waiting for some unsuspecting diners to arrive so they could annoy the fuck out of them. There was a fat man in a shiny black suit loitering around, I recognised him from last night as he appeared to be the guest wailer of the intolerable noise making band.

Just in case the noise makers decided to start fucking everyone off while we were enjoying our generic hotel dinner we selected a table as far away as possible from the imminent noise and waited for a waiter to arrive. Mr Fat Wailer waddled over and said we couldn't sit where we were sat.

Why? There is a function occurring soon, could you take a table over there beyond where the band is set up? No fucking problem Mr Fat Wailer, behind the speakers would be a blessing. We relocated with our beers and seated ourselves in what was the restaurant's smoking area, I assumed it was that as there were ash trays on the tables. For the health benefits of the other hotel occupants this area was separated from the surrounding areas by some plastic plants, I don't think they would be a brilliant barrier against passive smoke inhalation.

After a few minutes a smart young gentleman arrived to take our food order. We both ordered a starter and main course. The starter we decided on was the universal hotel favorite of Caesar salad, you can't go wrong with it, the main course I can't recall but that will become irrelevant. Five minutes later the young gentleman returned, he said, due to the event in the main restaurant you can have your cold salad starter but your cooked main course you will have to wait for until 8 o'clock. What the flying fuck! It's only 6 o'clock, I'm used to the French long lunches and dinner's but I'll have either drunk or smoked myself to death with a two hour break between courses. I politely asked why we couldn't have our main course for two hours. Mr Fat Wailer arrived to explain. Apparently the main restaurant area and associated kitchens were being used to prepare a break of fast Ramadan feast. Apparently Mr Fat Wailer was the hotel manager. OK fair enough, I accept and respect your obligations during Ramadan. I have however seen every creed and color of guest in this hotel but definitely not any Muslims other than the staff.

Right on time with my thought, four minibuses arrived outside and out piled what I assume were Mr Fat Wailer's family, extended family and friends. He greeted them all with hugs and they all filed in line jabbering all the way to a buffet that had appeared in the restaurant. So this is what is really fucking me off right here, right now as Fat Boy Slim once mixed in to a tune on Brighton beach.

We are in a worldwide chain hotel and the manager has decided that the paying guests have to wait while his bessie mates who have just been bussed in have their meal while we paying customers at the hotel sit and wait. The greasy fingered non resident cunts were tucking into their meal and eventually our salad starter arrived. I was glad we were moved as the fucking racket started up again from the band. Clearly hungry Muslims don't wish to engage in conversation during their meal. Anyway we ate the salad and walked off without paying for the food or drinks. I felt I had a good argument for not paying and would express it vocally should I be challenged.

Just eating a mediocre salad wasn't digging it for me on the needing food front but on principle I wasn't going back to the restaurant for the main course in two hours which would have only been some generic hotel shit anyway, it would not be the feast Mr Fat Wailer and his friends were currently enjoying. I spied over the road from the hotel a food place that now after the sun down was open so went to have a look. It wasn't very appealing looking, in fact it was appalling looking, they made some sort of sandwich but I have no fucking idea out of what. Time for Google maps and ask find 'fast food near me'. Proper job there was a Papa John's pizza takeaway just a few minutes walk away from the hotel down a couple of zig zagging streets. Google reliably informed me it was open. I assume without copyright issues the establishment would have been called Papa Joe's but in Morocco it was called Papa John's. I asked the wife what she wanted. We could have both walked there and eaten in but there's something deliciously naughty about paying for a hotel room and leaving a pizza box or two on the melamine surfaced desk that nobody ever uses. The wife decided she would opt for her go to pepperoni and if they do it a cheesy garlic pizza bread. I would normally go for something tuna based but thought I would see what was on offer.

Off I troddled again, down the lift and through the reception leaving behind the fucking wailing noise emanating from the restaurant and Mr Fat Wailer's possy who were still sat eating with their sticky fingers preventing legitimate paying guests from sitting and enjoying a peaceful dinner. Why people can't or haven't been trained at an early age to use a knife and fork is beyond me. Unlike my previous outings this afternoon this one to buy food was totally legal and above board, that is unless buying a carry out pizza will in some way anger Allah.

I arrived at Papa John's and there it was on the menu board, my holy grail of a food combination. Carbanora topped pizza, I assumed the bacon element would be lookalike bacon but hey ho I ordered it, waited, paid a mere 80 Dihrams for everything and took the pizza boxes back to the hotel. There were unhappy residents of the hotel in the lift complaining about the Muslim wankers who had overtaken the restaurant as they also wanted to eat. I think they felt more hungry after sniffing the delicious aromas that were emanating from my three boxes of Papa John's deliciousness.

Back in the room we did what hotel residents do who are pissed off with the likes of Mr Fat Wailer manager and put the greasy boxes on the bed and tucked in to eat, I don't know why we did this as we need to sleep in the bed. The pizzas and cheesy garlic bread were delicious, we ate up and left the empty greasy boxes on the afore mentioned little used writing desk. One does this when annoyed by one cunts actions, that is to reiterate Mr Fat Wailer, I would actually have folded the pizza boxes up and put them in the bin but we had already filled the bin with beer cans and wine bottles.

I had to give myself a kick, this was for having a total disregard for how you leave your room as it is not actually fair that it will be a fat non sexual Moroccan bitch that has to clean up after us and not Mr Fat Wailer so I did make an effort to make the room look presentable ready for the morning.

I opened the window to allow the sound of vehicles and the wind in to provide white noise comfort and also to let the smell of the garlic pizza out. I drifted off to sleep. Tomorrow we are going to Marrakesh, how exciting and interesting I'm sure it will be.

# 14 Etape 5 Sidi Ali – Tansikht

We are up and on it like a car bonnet, metaphorically speaking as the car bonnet along with the rest of Svetty was still in Azrou. Firstly this morning lets start with some good news. Mr Pink at some ungodly hour of the morning had sent us via WhatsApp some videos of him riding shotgun in Svetty with either wide boy or old man at the wheel. I think it might have been old man Schumacher driving as they weren't hanging around and were also from what I could see as they were driving at night they were rallying off road. Anyway Svetty was up and running and whoever was driving Svetty they were clearly enjoying themselves and Svetty would be enjoying herself too doing what she was designed and built to do.

We have a bus to catch at 8.30, there's a petite taxi out in the carpark, I went down to see if he would wait for ten minutes while we collected our rucksacks and if he would take us to the CTM office to catch the bus. No problem he said, he thought he knew where we wanted him to take us. We left the room cards at the reception and left. There was no mention of not paying for half a meal last night, shame really as I could have done with an argument to get the day going.

We got in the petite taxi and the driver set off at slow speed hopefully in the direction of the CTM office, I don't know how old or how many passengers this little Dacia had hosted during it's life but the seats were thread bare. While we're sat in the taxi with time to kill I will explain what the petite taxi is. All the petite taxis are little Dacia hatchbacks. In Casablanca they are all painted red, in Azrou they were all beige and green. Being a small car they all have off road style roof racks with high sides on them so you can just throw your luggage on the roof and hope for the best and with the will of Allah that the luggage didn't fall off at speed, fat chance of that in Casablanca as it's only just after 7 and we are crawling along in traffic. It's a long time since I've been in a taxi, in France they are too expensive to even consider using one unless you have a prescription from your doctor for a taxi to transport you to a clinic or hospital in which case they are paid for by your health insurance so you don't really care how extortionate it might be.

We chewed the cud with the driver en route about the normal shizzle, where are you from, have you been busy, does it always rain in Morocco, the usual shit. When we arrived at the CTM office I asked if he would wait a minute while I checked we were at the right place. I got out, took my life in my own hands and crossed four lanes of morning traffic mayhem. The man in the CTM office looked at his passenger list and indeed we were at the correct place and booked on the 8.30 bus to Marrakesh. I gave a thumbs up to the wife who was still sat in the petite taxi and risking life and limb again crossed the road to retrieve said wife and my rucksack. The taxi fare was 150 Dirham's so the wife gave the driver 200 and said keep the change. The driver got out with a big smile on his face and hugged us like he had just won the lottery. Taxi drivers obviously don't often receive tips in Casablanca.

We sat outside the office waiting for the bus so we could have a smoke. What happened next is one of the highlights of this trip thus far. Above where we were sat there was a ledge with pigeons wandering about on it. You have probably already guessed it, one of the pigeons shat on the wife, proper job pigeon. My joy was short lived as another one or maybe the same one shat on my man bag. We went to sit elsewhere.

The bus arrived, parcels and passengers were taken off and on. There was time during the journey to Marrakesh to reflect on our thoughts about the romantic sounding city of Casablanca. This reflection didn't take long, just two words 'shit hole'!

We sat back and enjoyed the rubbish littered scenery. One thing that amazes me and I thought that this only appeared on television program's or in films is how much stuff can be piled on top of a wagon, pick up truck or on the roof rack of a standard car not to mention the number of people. Some of the sights we passed of vehicles dragging themselves along nearly doing a wheelie with so much stuff piled on the back or teetering on the point of tipping over was very comical. In most westernized country's they would be pulled over by the rozza-z's and arrested or at least cautioned for reckless driving and endangering the lives of the occupants and others in overtaking vehicles should your four storey pick up truck catch a gust of wind and blow over. We did indeed pass a few shed loads en route, it appeared to be an everyday fact of life. Call me sensible but if it was me I would take three trips loaded up in safety.

When I'm bored on a bus I like to see where we are using the OSM& application on my phone. We were not far from Marrakesh and as if by magic the rubbish strewn banking's, random goat and sheep farmers on the verges disappeared and everywhere started to look plush and clean. The bus pulled into the station, we alighted into what was a very welcome I won't say heat but we'll settle for warmth in relation to what we have endured thus far. According to Mr Pink there is a meteorological line just north of Marrakesh where the weather changes from wank in the north to amicable in the south. I doubt there is any scientific basis to this idea but he told me so I'm telling you.

Taxi to Mogador Aqua Fun Hotel please. For your information the petite taxis in Marrakesh are yellow. The driver asked, which one? Which one what? I don't know!

Apparently there are two hotels with the same name, one is 2 kilometers away from the bus station the other is 20 kilometers! I had previously taken the liberty via the raids WhatsApp group of asking for the details of the hotel that was included as part of the raid as our original plan was that after we finished the raid we would stay for an extra night so we would have a day to explore Marrakesh before heading north up to Casablanca.

When we arrived at the hotel we explained to the lass on reception that we were due to stay tomorrow night with the Feraille Raid group and had telephoned ahead to check that it was OK to stay tonight. She looked through many papers and couldn't find any reference to 100 plus French people arriving tomorrow. Looking around the reception she was possibly correct, this place was a world away from the shit hole that is the Bates Cold Hotel, there were ornate coffered ceilings, mosaics on the floors and walls, a fountain in the reception and ornate reproduction baroque furniture. Possibly we had got the wrong Mogador Aqua Fun Hotel? Anyway we're here now so we checked in and paid for tonight's accommodation.

A man in a smart white jacket arrived and escorted us to our room, it was a good job he did as otherwise we would never have found the room. Unlike city center hotels that go upwards this place was a two storey sprawling maze of interlinked buildings and manicured gardens and as the name suggests it was all set around a massive swimming pool complex. I should have packed my swimming knickers. After what seemed like several kilometers we arrived at the room and Mr White jacket opened the door with a flourish. Fuck me, I can hardly see far enough to the patio doors at the distant end of the room. The room was huge on an epic scale, Mr White dutifully opened the patio doors and placed 2 reproduction baroque chairs the same type as the ones in the reception and a coffee table out on the patio. Mr White left before we had time to think that we should have offered him a note or some coins, we would do that later.

We filled the refrigerator with the tins procured yesterday and sat for a while enjoying the view of the pool. Before getting too comfy we had a couple of tasks to achieve, firstly, I wanted to take a photograph of the outside of the hotel and send it to Asier just to check we were at the right hotel. Secondly and more importantly we needed to procure some food. The hotel restaurant was only open in the evening for a buffet but not to worry, according to Google maps there was a Carrefour supermarket just up the road from the hotel so we went off in pursuit of snacks to go with our refreshments. While walking back through the main part of the hotel yet another hotel disappointment occurred, instead of a bar they had a fucking tea room. Not to worry, we had supplies.

Nat NAV is usually pretty good however the same issue occurred as when we were leaving the bus station in Casablanca we set off to the supermarket in completely the wrong direction. I hadn't put directions into the phone but I reckoned as it was at most a kilometer away we would surely see it as on the map as it was the first place next to the hotel complex. Where my theory fell down was that for some reason I thought the hotel was on the southern outskirts of Marrakesh but it was actually on the northern outskirts so in my mind everything was the wrong way up?

Anyway we got to a point where there was nothing to see ahead other than barren land so we sauntered to the nearest main looking road and headed in the opposite direction. Joyously this took us back up the opposite side of the hotel and there was a big sign saying Carrefour 500 meters.

This place must be where all the inhabitants of Marrakesh shop, it isn't just a supermarket, there is every shop here that you could ever desire apart from possibly a DIY store, there was even a greasy KFC amongst other eateries that were actually open. I suppose as Marrakesh is more cosmopolitan and tourist infested than Casablanca the rules of Ramadan are somewhat ignored as the greed for tourist money is god. Anyway, we went into the Carrefour, you might recall my research into alcohol shopping in supermarkets where the 'cave' is hidden away. Not here, the first thing you see when you go into the store and look down the line of tills is at the far end of the line of tills is the word 'CAVE' in metre high bright red letters. Proper job, we'll get a few more supplies while we are here. The wife procured some snacks, I procured some deodorant, I had lost mine somewhere, and we went for a mooch in the cave.

There was a security man at the shutter, I assume security rather than police as he wasn't as far as I could see packing any firearm. Passport please. I didn't ask why and handed it over, Mr Security scribbled something on his clip board and gestured us to enter in a manner that said Allah will bring fire and brimstone on your soul for buying alcohol. Let Allah do his best at least we'll die happy you miserable Muslim cunt. He was probably gagging for a beer but religion didn't allow.

We sauntered back to the hotel on a different route and passed a nice looking little kebab, salad, basic food eatery. We would return later. Back at the hotel Asier had replied that yes it was the correct hotel and he was looking forward to seeing us tomorrow. I felt it was a good public service to advise the équipes on the raid of the lack of a bar at the hotel but the bounty of booze available at the nearby supermarket.

We are missing a trick here. We have technically won the raid! We are the first to arrive at the final destination in Marrakesh. We're a day early and haven't even got a fucking vehicle! Mr White jacket was stood at the reception door so we asked him to take photo of us, he happily obliged. We struck a pose like we were the winners of the world formula one championship but without the champagne. I gave Mr White jacket a few coins and thanked him. Time to share our victory photograph on the raids WhatsApp group with no other explanation other than 'GAGNER'!

Time to be touristy for a few hours. I asked Google where there were places of interest near me. There was a mausoleum, a fort and some street in a walled part of the city that was apparently of interest. We were in no rush so went into honeymoon mode, we sat in our fake baroque arm chairs on the terrace, drank, nibbled and smoked. This didn't last long, we get easily bored sitting around so we wandered off sightseeing.

Stop one was the mausoleum, this was about a kilometre from the hotel in the direction of the barren land we had mistakenly taken to be the direction of the supermarket earlier.

Being a good well prepared husband I had this time put all the destinations into the phone and we would follow the walking route between the three destinations before ending up back at the kebab shop we had passed earlier near the supermarket for dinner. We are walking across a barren patch of land that might at some time have been proposed as a massive car park for something that was never built. Up ahead was a white building, not much bigger than a large garden shed but taller and circular with a domed roof. This was obviously the mausoleum. When we got to it, well it could have been anything, there was a niche in the south side of it with a tramp living in it fast asleep. I was expecting that what you could see on the ground was just a marker and there would be a labyrinth of marvels below ground to explore but no, that was it.

Stop two was a fort, to get to this the footpath route took us through what I can only describe as a rubbish tip for building materials. There was a very high wall to one side of us where the rubbish had been piled up but it was obviously used as a through route as a sturdy path had been carved through the mounds of rubbish. we came across a track and the phone eventually said turn left. To the right of us there was a pair of very tall metal gates that were fixed to the wall that all the shit was piled up against that we had just followed. Behind the gates there were two men in army uniform with machine guns flopping around on their straps over their shoulders. Turning left was obviously the correct direction. The Fort wasn't anything special to look at, we perused the deteriorated information board and it had something written on it that in 1800 or something, lets just say sometime in the distant past it was built to protect what we had now learned was an army base behind us, hence the men with guns at the gates. We walked on.

Stop three. This supposedly was some sort of special street located in the edges of the walled city, We followed the phone and went through a non grand looking archway into the ancient walled city of Marrakesh. We continued following the phone turning left and right down identical narrow streets and passage ways and arrived at destination number three. It looked no different to anywhere else we had passed since entering the area through the non grand archway. Possibly there was some historical significance but I didn't really care, in my tourist mindset I like to see things magnificent and awe inspiring, this was neither. Fuck this, I'm bored and hungry it's time for stop number four, kebab shop.

I couldn't believe how far we had walked until we started back in the opposite direction, in the happy direction of the bob shop, this put a spring in my step, I would have broken into a run but I remembered I haven't run for at least twenty years and I was currently puffing on a lung cancer stick. The bob was pretty good, not the usual elephants foot deliciousness shaved off with an old set of hair clippers but the flavor was there and it was none the less delicious. The young lass at the bob shop appeared to be doing everything herself, she was both waitressing and cooking so the service was inevitably slow, but who cares we weren't in a rush, I checked my mental diary and it was pretty much empty for the rest of the day.

A couple arrived and sat at the table opposite, they were very touristy looking, obviously they were and today so are we. They were obviously English so as we do in situations like this and being in a country where French is the second language the wife and I conversed in French. The lady was rather large, a ginger and looked very sun burnt.

As since leaving le Bost nearly two weeks ago and this was the first sunny day we have encountered I wanted to ask her where she got her epic sunburn from, maybe she was Scottish and had burned at the mere thought of being exposed to sunlight. Second thoughts, that would involve engaging in conversation so I didn't bother. Sun burnt ginger's boyfriend, husband or escort whoever he was went next door to the pharmacy and after some translation help from the poor lass who was waitressing, cooking and now translating bless her, he returned with what I assume was after sun.

If the fat ginger lass had any respect for Muslim culture she would have been covered up anyway and not be suffering from sunburn. Her family sized pizza arrived and she tucked in, oddly he didn't have anything to eat, I'm now thinking I could have done with a pizza but hey ho the bob was good, ginger ate her pizza with gusto with greasy fingers while the man massaged greasy after sun cream into her red raw skin.

Dinner over we ambled back to the hotel to plan our mooch around downtown Marrakesh tomorrow, drink beer and find some shit on the television to stare at. See you in the morning.

# 15 Stage 6 Tansikht – Ouarzazate – Marrakesh

What a beautiful morning, perhaps it is going to be a nice, sunny, hot day as there was a man watering the plants and grass around the pool complex and I doubt he would be wasting his time and water if it was going to rain. We had our walking itinerary for today planned on the phone, we had looked up places of interest, just to see and marvel at while passing by them, the route would take us through the famous Marrakesh markets so fingers crossed it will be a good outing and will be more entertaining and interesting than yesterday's.

The first sight see location we were due to pass was apparently an ecclesiastical marvel, it was just a church, we ignored it and carried on walking towards the world famous spice market, it was smaller than I expected, just a square in the middle of the maze of general market.

My favorite mother in law had asked that if we came across any could we buy some vanilla pods as the local spices are very cheap in the market. We asked at a couple of stalls and they said sorry, no, we only sell local spices. The wife asked one last stall holder or he might have been a random man and he guided her to all his friends or families different market stalls to see if they had any but alas there were none to be found. The wife was gone on this search for so long I thought she had been kidnapped. When the wife returned she gave the gentleman a few coins for his time and effort.

Vanilla pods are grown in Indonesia, that is quite a distance away even as the crow flies or whatever the Moroccan equivalent of a crow is for locally produced or should I say locally grown spices you stupid woman.

Vanilla pod acquisition failed we had a mooch about the market. Once upon a time the residents of Marrakesh would have bought everything here from a button, to a mutton to a side of beef. Nowadays its full of stalls selling not much more than slippers, belts, handbags, leather jackets, knock off fakes of anything you desire and souvenir tat shops selling refrigerator magnets, snow globes and t shirts emblazoned with the words 'I heart Marrakesh'. Considering the limited availability of goods on offer in the market and the number of stalls there must be either significant competition between stall holders or they are all owned by the same family, extended family or cousins. We did however buy some very nice but overpriced dog collars that were probably made by Mr Wong and not hand crafted locally as stated by the seller. The wife also bought me some nice leather chicken dippers.

We carried on following the phone for directions as there was no other way of getting out of the market without walking round in circles for hours and we headed in the direction of the next must see monument. We were heading for a city entrance archway, I had in mind something on the scale of the Arc De Triomphe in Paris. The route took us along a very long straight street that was a sight in itself to behold. Along the street in little groups of workshops were, joiners, cabinet makers, forgers of the metal variety not money, welders wearing at the most a pair of sunglasses for eye protection, fabricators, upholsterers. This street had every trade you can think of all in order and it looked like they all worked together to manufacture the myriad of stuff they were individually producing potential bits and pieces for.

We stopped to photograph a group of men hammering a piece of red hot metal fresh out of their forge on a huge anvil. One of them shouted at us 'money', as if you want royalties for having your photograph taken by a tourist you sweaty arrogant cunt. The wife gave him some coins, I told him to fuck off and we carried on to what promised would be the Marrakesh equivalent of the Arc De Triumph In Paris. When we arrived it was as wank and uninspiring as the arch we had passed through yesterday evening while visiting the uninteresting non descript street. There was a small white painted sort of castle thing next to it but nothing that you would bother to print on a postcard.

I took the executive decision that as there wasn't much up this end of town to see we would retrace our steps back to the market. I would have circumnavigated the market but it was the most direct route to the south side of this thus far shitty city. When we walked through the market earlier it was quiet and calm, all the tourists were still tucking into their hotel breakfasts but not now.

The market was heaving. If you haven't been and I recommend as free travel advice you don't fucking bother to then I will inform you that the alleyways are about 6 feet wide or lets say in modern money about 2 meters wide. These narrow passages work well if everyone adheres to my old high school rules, my high school was St Wilfred's very religious high school in Blackburn. At the school there was a rigorously imposed rule that you walk on the left at all times and you do not under any circumstances even if it's a rucksack that as you well know is designed to be carried on your back or shoulder, your bag must however be carried at your side in the way a businessman carries his briefcase. Possibly the school had high expectations that we would all one day file left carrying a briefcase to our mundane office job, they obviously had high hopes that few of us lived up to.

There was one teacher at the school who was a tiny little man who i think was a science teacher but was also obviously a martial arts aficionado, he used to walk down the corridor and judo kick your bag off your shoulder if you weren't carrying it correctly. I think these days he would be arrested for child cruelty.

Back to the misery of the market and specifically the transportation of luggage by tourists. We are stuck, well nearly stuck, we are traveling at less than shuffling pace held up by fucking cunts who are walking three a breast dragging suitcases and stopping every ten shuffles to admire the overpriced tat at each market stall they shuffle to. This would be all well and good if there was a one way pedestrian system in operation but there was not and there were suitcase brandishing cunts coming the other way. It was suitcase gridlock! I have a method for navigating such gridlock situations that I find to be fairly effective, as I'm six feet and a bit tall and of a generous but not too fat of a build so I just keep on walking, if people don't move I'll barge past them or walk over them, it doesn't matter if I offend anyone, its not as if I will ever see them again in my life apart from possibly in court.

Now we appeared to be going round in circles, I didn't recognize anything from when we walked through earlier in the opposite direction, probably because all the stalls were selling the same limited range of shit and everything looked the same.

I don't know if you have ever watched the classic comedy series Father Ted from the 1990's? If you haven't then I suggest you educate yourself and watch it. Anyway, there is a scene in the Christmas special where Father Ted, Father Doogle, Father Jack and Mrs Doyle the house keeper leave Craggy Island for a day trip to go Christmas shopping on the mainland. Long story short they all go to a department store and the three priests take a wrong turning and end up in the lingerie department and can't find their way out, they then meet up accidentally with five other priests who were in the lingerie department fondling women's knickers. They had to engage in a military style operation quickly to avoid embarrassment and to escape from what was purportedly the biggest lingerie department in Ireland. That is how I felt stuck in this never ending godforsaken market.

Eventually we found an exit and out we went onto a narrow alleyway devoid of people, I'd had enough, the wife and I had a very brief conflab and with little hesitation we both decided to fuck the sight seeing off, it's not as if there's anything interesting to see anyway. The plan was to walk back to the hotel, watch telly and get mildly pissed all afternoon until the remaining équipes from the raid arrived at the hotel.

Back at the hotel we looked at the équipe tracking on the raids website and everyone had finished the raid at Ouarzazate and were now making their way to Marrakesh in time for dinner and the awards ceremony. I do hope we get a special award for arriving first without a car. I thought that everyone would arrive in convoy but the équipes were arriving in dribs and drabs, some stopping off for food but mainly popping into the cave at Carrefour for supplies so we gave up waiting outside to clap. The people from the raid we did see were all wearing their finishers medals around their necks that had been presented in the desert at Ouarzazate. The medals were really smart looking, round, possibly polished slate hung on a red ribbon and with the Feraille Raid emblem and 2025 etched on them. I wanted one of those.

Before moving from beer on to the wine supplies there was some essential administration to take care of. That was arranging for us to get back to Azrou to pick Svetty up. We weren't in a mad rush to get back as originally we were going to spend tomorrow in Marrakesh and the following day in Casablanca but we had already, seen it, done it, and got bored of it.

As luck would have it there is a direct bus from Marrakesh to Azrou run by the same bus company that we arrived with. Tickets are now booked for tomorrow leaving at 12 midday and arriving in Azrou at 8 in the evening, that will be a numb bum eight hours on the bus but it's better than going back the way we came. We would pick Svetty up tomorrow night, endure another night at Bates Cold Hotel, drive up to Tangier for the ferry the morning after and be back in Gibraltar for a limp carry out curry for dinner. We could even as we would be ahead of our original itinerary spend an extra day in Gibraltar to take the time to go up the rock and see the monkeys before heading home. I'll message Mr Pink to say we would pick Svetty up at about 8 o'clock tomorrow.

You might recall from earlier that I hate Gibraltar. Well I still do hate Gibraltar but it has been moved down on my most hated places to visit list to the number two slot. Morocco has now shot up there to the number one spot pop pickers. The only good thing about Morocco are the locals who cannot do enough to help you when you are in need. I'm not dissing the whole of Morocco as I have seen friends pictures of lovely idyllic holidays on the beach or by a pool but that's just not my cup of tea and lets face it, unless you try hard you aren't going to get anything other than a cup of tea.

We are reclining in our palatial room and rather than Asier mustering everyone to tell them what time dinner and the prize giving ceremony would be held we all received a WhatsApp message advising us that dinner would be at 8 o'-clock. Bugger, that's 3 hours away, we haven't eaten anything since the bob shop last night and we are pursuing a hearty liquid diet this afternoon.

What I did next was the most romantic thing I've done in the last fourteen years with the now wife. I hatched a plan. I said to the wife I was hungry so we would have a walk up to the supermarket complex to find us something to eat to put us on before dinner which although Asier had said 8 o'clock It could easily be 10 o'clock by which time I would be wankered and tucked up in bed. Also as we are now going back to Bates Cold Hotel again tomorrow with zero chance of refreshments or food we need to take some more supplies with us. After three trips from the hotel to or past the supermarket complex we arrived only fifteen minutes later and five of those were getting from our room to the hotel reception.

I directed the wife straight into the KFC!

Romantic? That's what you are thinking isn't it. Well believe me it is. I have a pathological hatred of anything fast food other than a well made bob or a nice chippy tea. My distaste isn't particularly based on the processed shite they feed you and have the audacity to charge you for but it is more concentrated around the litter that is created by the patrons of the eatery who can't be bothered to either find a bin or take their rubbish home so choose instead to chuck it out of the car window or drop it if traveling on foot just on the street. Where we live there is or was very little litter, in fact none, that is until a fast food chain whose bags, paper cups and food boxes have a yellow M printed on them opened in La Souterainne a few years ago. Now there is litter, mainly on the motorway slip roads all with an M emblazoned on it. One of my proudest achievements in my 52 years on this planet is that I have never set foot in a fast food outlet with an M on the sign.

When it comes to fast food KFC is the wife's favourite. As a child on a Saturday evening when my parents were going out to a pampas grass keys in the bowl party or whatever they got up to we would have two treats, firstly father would drive us to the Paki sweet shop in Padiham, before you get on your high horse, saying I'm being racist I will point out that when we were taken to the Paki shop it was in the era of Alf Garnett in the situation comedy's 'In Sickness and In Health' and 'Till Death Us Do Part' when the phrase 'That bloody Paki' was widely used on television. We would arrive at the Paki shop armed with 50 pence each to spend on jarred sweets, I always bought a combination of midget gems, poor Ben's and a stick of really hard liquorice, then we would go to KFC for a carry out chicken sandwich before calling on Mrs Utley who was our baby sitter. I have no idea how my parents had come to know this woman, I think from vague recollection she was somehow associated with the Niff Naffs at the spastic home. My father didn't give Mrs Utley a lift to our house she drove herself there in one of those 1970's powder blue three wheel disabled cars. It was however necessary to rouse Mrs Utley in person on two accounts, firstly she didn't have a telephone and secondly she was deaf, hence she had no requirement for a telephone. We would then sit at home eating our KFC and our bags of sweets while Mrs Utley watched the wrestling on television.

Back to where we were apropo romance. For fourteen years, every time we passed a KFC the wife will start with 'can we just please' before she gets any further I would always interrupt with NO! So I thought that as we are on honeymoon, fuck it, today I'll treat the bitch, it should stand me in good stead for another fourteen years. We ordered a selection off the menu and ate many different chicken based items, whether it was actually real chicken or something reformed I don't know. What I do know is that it was greasy enough that tomorrow's morning shit would inevitably slide out effortlessly and unaided leaving me with the pleasure of a one wipe clean sweep. The food if it was natural chicken or reformed processed shit did actually taste pretty good. Back to the hotel.

Time for dinner and the prize giving ceremony. It was a buffet which was good as it meant it would be on time and after the KFC I could just treat myself to a plate of salad so I could feel healthy in a food offsetting sort of way. As there was no bar at the hotel no one had gone for a drink and mingled, it appeared that everyone had just drunk their bounty from Carrefour in their rooms. I suppose apart from us the other équipes had been mingling over the last 6 days, I guessed they all just wanted some food and an early night before a trip into Marrakesh or heading north back in the direction of France tomorrow morning.

We exchanged pleasantries with a few people but they had obviously formed their bonds and had created their little groups that had been formed by their camaraderie during the raid, towing each other out of sand dunes and fixing each others cars and the like in the desert. Dining tables were being moved so they could sit in their clusters. We decided rather than imposing ourselves on anyone we would have a table for two in between the dining area where the équipes had been allocated and the rest of the hotels guests.

I felt like an imposter being here, I ate my salad and decided to call it a night. We went outside for a smoke and whoopey doo it was raining again. We decided that after all we would stick around for the prize giving but not before taking the long hike back to the room for liquid refreshment.

When we got back to the restaurant everyone was chewing the cud exchanging stories of their adventures.

Mrs Always Tipsy and copilot of the 'In Rust We Trust' Fiat Panda asked us to sit with her as she was interested to hear about our alternative adventure. We ended up with quite a group listening to our tale and politely correcting us on our French. I was feeling less of an outsider now. Asier announced that the prize giving ceremony would be starting in twenty minutes in a room somewhere else in the hotel the whereabouts of I didn't understand but I think there will be enough people milling about to get into sheep mentality mode again and follow everyone else. I made a quick trip back to the room to use the toilet, that is code to say consume more wine.

Quick smoke on the way back to reception where all the équipes were now milling about. Clearly no-one had understood where the prize giving ceremony would be held. After what was clearly more than twenty minutes allowing for the refreshment trip everyone filed off down a corridor.

Following behind everyone else we found where the room was. It was a smart looking room, probably for weddings or banquets but with the tables removed. There was plush bench seating around the perimeter and two rows of seating in the middle, elaborately draped curtains and chandeliers. Everyone found a seat, in the corner of the room a slide show was playing of photographs the support crew had taken during the raid. There was a shelf in between the center rows of seating where the trophies were lined up ready for presentation, best fancy dress costumes, best decorated vehicle, who got lost the most, who helped équipes in need the most, oldest vehicle to finish, fastest équipe on the timed sections and the équipe that was voted the best overall egg on the raid. If Svetty was here with us and hence we had finished the raid we would have had a chance of bagging at least two of the trophies, but alas Svetty is waiting patiently for us back in Azrou. The trophies were similar to the medals everyone except us were still proudly wearing, the trophies were of the same polished slate or something similar but instead of a round medal they were carved into the shape of a map of Morocco, they looked very smart indeed. The raid support team were all lined up ready to congratulate the trophy winners and Asier started his farewell Ferraille's speech, he spoke so fast that I could only understand the odd word. He appeared to be doing a resume of the raid with the aid of the slide show.

What I did understand however was that the presentation of the trophies was about to start. What happened next we were not expecting.

First award goes to équipe 666. What the fuck, had we misheard? Obviously not as we were ushered up and raucously applauded. Asier was waiting for us with something in his hands. He said a few words so fast that as usual I couldn't understand a word of it and presented us with our finishers medals, in true Olympic achievement style he put them over our heads. We were thrilled to have a medal, even though we got here by a slightly different route and means of transport to the other équipes we had arrived first.

We shook hands, hugged and thanked everyone and feeling happy we gestured to go back to where we were sitting. It then got even better. Asier said no, no, wait here. One of the support team walked over to where the trophies were lined up and came back with one of the trophies. Asier said this is a special trophy for the newly weds and presented it to us. They had obviously invented a new category as it was etched with the words 'Ferraille Raid' 'Just Married 06/03/2025', this we had written in cardboard letters on Svetty's back window at the registration and during etape 1 which lasted until the cardboard lost it's battle against the rain and fell off somewhere in a soggy mess to add to Morroco's rubbish issue.

I'm not an emotional person but this gesture of the medals and a specially made trophy brought a tear to my eye. Asier wasn't finished yet. One of the support team stepped in to translate as it was important that we understood what Asier was going to say. Asier already knew we were going to pick

Svetty up from Azrou tomorrow night. We were asked the question, 'are you rushing back to France after picking Svetty up or do you have a few days spare'? Leading question I think. We have a few days spare as we have already done the total waste of time that is sightseeing in Marrakesh and Casablanca.

Asier explained that there is another raid arriving in Morocco tomorrow that they have organized but instead of a tour like the Feraille Raid this raid would be based around one desert camp and involved circular routes for five days starting and ending each day at the same place. This was more of a tare arse around the desert in whatever vehicle you like rather than a tour in an old banger. Asier thought that after seeing Svetty in action on etape one before she broke and our rally driving style that both we and Svetty would very much like to join this raid. OK then where's the catch?

There wasn't one, he would send us the coordinates of the camp and we could go and join them for as many days as we wanted if we wanted to or had the time to do so, the raid support and food would be included, there would be no cost to us apart from fuel and refreshments. We hugged everyone, well not everyone that would have taken ages and sat back down proudly cradling our trophy while the rest of the now inconsequential trophies were given out. After the prize giving had finished we had various photographs taken with our trophy in front of the lush draped curtains and took the long hike to our room.

We had a small celebration and got stuck into tomorrow's refreshments, it's OK we can buy some more in the morning. The priority was to post this evening's events on social media as you do. We discussed the offer Asier had made and the logistics of doing it. We would discuss it further on the bus back to Azrou tomorrow. We laid ourselves on the massive bed and passed out.

RAID
2025
Ferraille Raid
Just married
06/03/25
RAID
RAID

# 16 Back to Azrou

Today will be a long day, I'm not really looking forward to eight hours on the bus but needs must and I'm missing Svetty. Busses are great for saving on fuel but there is little interaction with your journey. There is little chance of food today so we enjoyed the buffet breakfast and stuffed ourselves. It's quite amazing how zero pork content sausages and something baconesque also devoid of pork can taste quite acceptable and even dare I say it pleasantly palatable. Thinking I probably wouldn't get a meal until the day after tomorrow I enjoyed three plates full of non pork based breakfast delights.

Breakfast over and it was time for a quick trip back up to Carrefour, refreshments, snacks and sweets were on my brief shopping list. Back at the hotel and there was little else to do for an hour or so.

As there was a plush bathroom I decided to have a bath, I didn't need one, it wasn't even Sunday but it wasn't my water I was using so I thought fuck it, lets waste some water, it's not as if the Moroccans need water, yesterday was the only dry day since we arrived six days ago and then it still pissed it down in the evening. On the odd occasion I indulge in having a bath I get bored waiting for a bath to fill so I like to get in while it's still running. The bath was so big that by the time it had filled to the level of my winky I was bored and got out.

I didn't clean myself in the bath, I never do, that's what showers were invented for, in a shower you wash yourself and the dirt goes down the drain. When sat in a bath you sit in the filth that consists of your own knob and toe cheese mingled with the clinkers of your own shit that might be loitering following a false clean wipe. I got out, drained the bath and soiled the lovely white hotel towel with the remnants on my filth.

We left the hotel and hopped into a yellow petite taxi that was conveniently waiting outside and asked him to take us to the bus station. We were an hour early but better to be early based on past experience, just in case this bus was not leaving from the same place that we had arrived at or outside some random CTM office. We were blessed with sunshine getting into the taxi but as ever on this trip a monsoon started as soon as we closed the doors. In Moroccan tradition we didn't bother with putting our seat belts on. The wife asked the driver if it always rains in Morocco, the driver replied that nowadays yes, it was something to do with global warming.

We sat around for an hour waiting for the bus, the wife went to a shop over the road to procure some sandwiches as she hadn't put them on my brief shopping list earlier. Meanwhile, unsure of the number of stops the bus would make and for how long each stop would be I inhaled as much nicotine into my system as I could manage.

The wheels on the bus go round and round, round and round, round and round. Svetty here we come, we are on the bus to rescue you my ageing Russian tractor. The wife and I had a conflab on the bus apropo the logistics of joining the second raid. Today is Friday the 14th of March. We need to be back home in Le Bost on Friday the 21st, therefore we have a week to play with from now, that is from where we are today sat on the bus.

We need to arrive back home in Le Bost next Friday so that we will arrive at least one day before the baby sitters need to leave chez nous and head back in the direction of Welsh Wales, it's polite is it not after a three week trip away that we spend at least one day with the babysitters rather than returning home, saying thanking you ta muchly, thanks for not doing any housework for three weeks, fuck off back to Wales and we'll see you at Christmas. The wife and I agreed that there were two options available to us and that before deciding we would see how well Svetty had been fixed before planning whether we would go north back to Gibraltar or south to the coordinates Asier had sent us to join the second raid and run wild in the Moroccan desert and have some fun at last.

The bus stopped at a bus station somewhere or other in the late afternoon, we got off for a smoke and a much needed piss. I found the toilets, well I found a hole in the ground in a small room. Unlike the hole in the floor cubicle in Azrou there was no shit smeared up the wall so I just went ahead and pissed down the hole. When I had finished I left the cubicle, obviously I did, I wasn't going to take up residence there like a tramp. I walked back to the bus and a fat Moroccan non sexual woman approached me. Money! Money! She grabbed my arm and repeated herself. I politely told her to fuck off. She didn't have a high vis jacket on and clearly wasn't an employee of the bus station so I didn't feel guilty for telling her to fuck off. Possibly she was too fat for an XXXL high vis jacket and was actually employed at the bus station in which case she would receive a salary, meagre as it maybe but there is no reason to manhandle or should I say womanhandle innocent users of the public conveniences.

This bus station must have been a major stopping point as there was a CTM office, you see one when you don't need to find one! Out from the office came a man in uniform brandishing the same Ramadan passenger happy meal boxes that we had been gifted with on the journey from Azrou to Casablanca, we thankfully accepted ours. The wife went for a piss before the bus departed, I warned her about the fat woman demanding money. The wife returned, bladder relieved and said she had followed my lead and told the fat woman to fuck off.

Bus journey nap time. It was getting dark and there was not much to see other than the winding road ahead illuminated by the bus's headlights. I did look ahead for a while but we were obviously on a mountain pass and it was a tad scary, the driver obviously knew the route very well. I nodded off for a while and was awoken from my slumber when we stopped somewhere and half of the passengers got off the bus.

I checked the time, it was 7 o'clock, I then checked my phone to see how far we were from Azrou, according to the

OSM& app there was one hour of journey time to go, we will arrive in Azrou on time at 8 o'clock and after a short walk we will arrive at the garage shortly after, that is if we can remember where the garage is, I did save the vague location on my phone. This bus stop is clearly some sort of end of Ramadan feast time affair, the passengers who were still on the bus were tucking into their Ramadan Happy Snack boxes. The driver left the bus and opened the luggage compartment. I assumed that some of the passengers must be leaving the bus in the middle of nowhere to wait for another bus or to be picked up by a loved one and taken home.

I went into the services for a piss. I say services it was more of a truck stop. Inside there was a bar, without any alcohol, a thread bare pool table and a clean hole in the floor to piss in. Piss accomplished I returned to the bus, it wasn't necessary this time post piss to tell a fat lady or anyone else to fuck off. When I returned to the bus the driver had dispensed with his uniform and had changed into a Muslim thwarb and flip-flops. The driver then left the bus and walked over to what looked like a car wash or once upon a time had been a car wash. The driver obviously knew the place as he found and turned on a tap and started to wash his feet, ready presumably for prayer time.

We waited on the bus for the driver to pray to Allah and hopefully with Allah's blessing the driver would take us safely to Azrou. Non Muslim religion moment coming up, apropo what I am about to tell you, what the fuck is going on outside?

You will recall from the Campanile hotel in Casablanca that during the Ramadan feast everyone non Muslim can go fuck themselves while the Muslims enjoy their feast. At this truck stop or whatever it was it was no different. There was a covered verandah in front of the truck stop where we had stood smoking sheltering from the rain, further inducing our increasing risk of lung cancer. At the far end of the veranda a barbecue was lit and there were many people queuing up presumably for food or possibly it was just a fire to warm their hands, I assumed it was a barbecue as human hands warming over a fire doesn't in my experience smell like barbecued chicken.

The bus driver came back out of the truck stop with his prayer mat under his arm so had obviously gained Allah's blessing that the bus would get us to Azrou and proceeded not to take us to Azrou but to join the queue at the barbecue for his feast. I wanted to say 'OY dickhead, bus timetable to adhere to' but I thought better of it. It's now 7.30 and they are all just sitting down to eat, it appears that the bus timetable like the restaurant schedule at the Campanile in Casablanca goes out of the fucking window during Ramadan. Yet again locals must have been shipped in to enjoy the feast as there were more people gorging themselves on barbecued chicken and couscous than there were passengers on the bus and vehicles in the car park. It's now 8 o'clock and we should be in Azrou. The driver finished his meal got changed back into his uniform and put his shoes on and we were back underway.

I only have three words to say right now 'inconsiderate fucking wankers'. Don't misunderstand me, as I've mentioned before I have no religious beliefs myself but if you have, please don't inflict them on the rest of us, let alone on a bus timetable. I'm sure there must be non Muslim or non practicing Muslim bus drivers in Morocco who could drive this bus.

We're back in Azrou and only an hour or so late, we alighted the bus at the CTM office where we left from a week earlier, I didn't tip the driver as he was a selfish religious cunt. Fortunately we had taken the liberty when we left Svetty at the market stall workshop last week of taking the umbrella that we had strapped to the roof with us on our alternative adventure and it has bless it seen some action since. Tonight though, it should have been 'this evening' but its now 'tonight' thanks to the Ramadan adhering cunt of a bus driver. The umbrella offered no refuge to the elements, the wind blowing the rain made it totally fucking useless. Either by luck or instinct we managed to take a direct route from the CTM bus stop to the market stall garage where Svetty was impatiently waiting for her papa to get in and start her up.

Old man, wide boy and Mr Pink were loitering around waiting for us at the market stall workshop when we arrived, tired and soaking wet, apart from our upper bodies that were still SuperDry. We exchanged pleasantries and old man started Svetty up and opened the bonnet. Old man had now got to grips with the bonnet stick which was great news as without it Svetty's bonnet would have been blown into a mangled mess or someone might have lost a limb or even worse been decapitated while we were peering in the engine bay. We could see fuck all in the dark so I retrieved a torch from Svetty's boot and commenced a disinterested inspection of the engine bay. I'm not sure what I was supposed to see, all the damage had been inside the engine and Mr pink had already sent me photographs to show how shiny and new'ish it looked before they put Svetty's beating heart back together.

Anyway I looked. Excuse me old man, where is the breather pipe that goes from the bottom bit of the engine up to the air filter to allow excess hot oil fumes to be collected and filtered? The reply via Mr Pink was, we replaced it with a pipe going directly to the back of the car as there was a lot of fumes coming out of the exhaust that must be from the oil breather pipe.

Do they think I'm a fucking retard? Fifty years ago or even more the best Russian engineers designed the Auto VAZ 2121 engine and put the oil breather pipe there for a reason, that reason I guarantee is not to be replaced by a length of garden hose worryingly lashed to the exhaust pipe. What kind of dick straps something plastic next to a hot metal exhaust pipe? There is shit coming out of the exhaust because something is not quite tickety boo with the engine. In the light of day, a few days later I would find a whole host of other missing or bodged bits and bobs but just now they are unimportant.

Mr Pink asked if we would like to take a test drive to see if we were happy with Svetty. I said no, it's pointless, I'm never happy, never will be, it's a life choice in the same way that since Covid I've continued social distancing and volunteered self isolation as a life choice during my general day to day life, basically I took this life choice to avoid interaction with other people.

I said to Mr Pink, you lead the way up the mountain to Bates Cold Hotel and we will follow in Svetty, I'll let you know what I think when we arrive at the hotel.

The wife paid the sum of 7000 Dirhams for the repairs which considering the work they had done I thought was fairly reasonable, it would have been at least 3000 euros in France. Wide boy accepted the payment in folding money, that was the last of our Dirhams gone and with a slight of hand that even a card magician would be jealous of wide boy secreted the stack of bank notes somewhere about his person before the old man could see them.

We were going to follow wide boys fucked old BMW back up to Bates Cold Hotel and Mr Pink would be riding shotgun with him. It took wide boy some time to get his heap of shit going. It was good to be back in Svetty but after her catastrophe and now I'm sat in the drivers seat someone reappeared who had been absent for the last week. Yes, it was that fucking miserable cunt Mr Anxiety. We set off and Svetty sounded and felt ok. When we started the climb up to Bates Cold Hotel Svetty's beating heart sounded a tad rattly. I assumed old man hadn't adjusted the tappets correctly, the tappets are the things that open and close the valves in the top bit of the engine to let the fuel in and the exhaust fumes out. When the oily shaft in the top bit of the engine goes round it opens and closes the valves. When a valve is closed there are very specific tolerances of the gap between the tappet and the oily shaft, 0.1 millimeters is the gap on the fuel inlet and 0.15 millimeters on the exhaust. Should the gap be incorrect the valves will either not open fully or not close properly. If the gap is too big the valve will not open far enough and won't let enough fuel in and the exhaust fumes out properly or on the other hand if the gap is too small the valves won't close so when the fuel explosion occurs in the piston in the bottom bit of the engine instead of the power of the explosion pushing the piston down to turn the engine some of the explosion goes back through the valves and you have less power. Engineering lesson on tappets and valves over we will continue, I hope you understood that, if not don't loose any sleep it's not that important.

We arrived at the hotel to enjoy again the never ending whirling lights illuminating the entrance to the reception, we had arrived which was a result and although Svetty wasn't perfect I felt she would do for now, possibly not good enough to join the next raid but at least good enough to get us back to mainland Europe. Mr Pink asked if I thought the engine was ok, I said it was ok but not perfect but I wasn't going to stand around in the rain discussing what I thought the minor issues were, Svetty was running, she had got up a steep hill without too much effort albeit sounding a bit rattly. Mr Pink said if there are any problems don't hesitate to let me know. Believe me sunshine, if there are any problems you will be the first to know.

We had booked in to the hotel but still had to rouse a man sleeping on one of the sofas in the reception. It was now 10.30 so they had probably thought that their only guests for tonight are going to be a no show. The person who was snoozing was the very nice man that had insisted on giving us a lift to the market stall workshop seven days earlier. He showed us back to room 212, the wife asked if we could have one of the rooms with a balcony so we didn't have to go outside for a smoke. He said it's ok you can smoke in your room, no thanks, we'll have a room with a balcony pretty please. Off he scurried back to the reception to get another room key.

We settled in, set up a mini bar and snack shop but not before asking for the room heating to be put on. The wife and I discussed the options available. I didn't think my Svetty anxiety would cope with heading back south. We decided we would go back to Gibraltar tomorrow to clean up mother in laws apartment that we had left in a post wedding shit hole of a state and if Svetty was behaving possibly return to Morocco the day after. We planned to get the 16.00 ferry tomorrow from Tangier to Algesiers, opting for this ferry would give us plenty of time to dawdle from Azrou up to Tangier. Makeshift bar more or less emptied, snacks and sweets consumed it was time to deploy the white noise and hope that Svetty anxiety apropo tomorrow's journey would stay away for the night.

# Congratulations

I have put this little section in as an in between chapter interlude in for two reasons.

Firstly, you will remember from chapter one that there are requirements of creating what will be classed as a novel, not that this is a novel but there is no category for a real life ClusterFuck event book so I was aiming to make a novel. You will also recall that the requirements are a minimum of 60,000 words. I didn't think that many words were possible so I was going to make a novella or even a short story but here we are today and the word count is in the region of 68000 words and there is still a long way to go. I congratulate myself on this achievement.

Secondly, I congratulate you for having the patience to have read my ramblings this far, personally by now I would have been bored as fuck and would have used the pages of this book as slightly rough shit paper.

Congratulations to everyone then, well done we should all be very proud of ourselves. Now that the interlude is over lets continue on our journey, there is a limp curry carryout with my name on it waiting for me in Gibraltar tomorrow.

# 17 Azrou to Gibraltar

Svetty started up first time, bless her. One thing I hadn't noticed last night was that the fuel light was on and the needle was all the way to the left, that is to say empty. The fuel gauges on Niva's are notoriously shit so you tend to clock your kilometerage and refuel after every 300 kilometers instead of relying on the gauge. I know that old man and Mr Pink had test driven Svetty but she had a full tank of fuel only 20 kilometers before she broke and I doubt she had been test driven for 280 kilometers.

We set off following the sat nav which was going to take us on the reverse route that we took to get to Bates Cold Hotel on etape 1 back to Tangier but unfortunately without the off road section.

We could have used the paper roadbook in reverse and taken the exact same route but my anxiety didn't fancy being stuck somewhere off road without a support crew so we would just stay on the road route. First stop, we need to get some fuel. We stopped at the Shell station just up the mountain road from the hotel. 40 liters later, 40 fucking liters, she must have been running on fumes last night, some thieving cunt must have drained the tank! We paid in cash with the last of our Dihram's, if we do return to Morocco the day after tomorrow we will acquire some more at the ferry port.

We're now out of Dirham's but full of fuel and should have enough to get us back to Tangier, if not we still have 40 liters in jerry cans in the boot. Svetty trundled over the mountain pass in the rain and mist and then, what's that, there's something flapping and making a noise, it was the bib numbers stuck on the doors that were about to unstick themselves, I wanted to pull over and remove them to keep them as a souvenir but before I could do so they went flying off into the rear distance to add to Morocco's ever increasing rubbish pile.

As we've experienced nothing but wind and rain on this whole trip now that we're heading towards Tangier to leave

Morocco on the other side of the mountain there was lush bright sunshine. We freewheeled Svetty down the other side of the mountain and arrived in a small town. I have no idea of the name of it but suffice to say it looked as miserable as Azrou. There was a tanker wagon parked at the side of the road so I slowed down made sure nothing was coming the other way and passed it.

200 meters further down the road there was what looked like a policeman in a long coat the likes of which we had seen previously, he put his hand up to gesture us to stop. He was definitely a policeman, an old wrinkled one but none the less a policeman, an enforcer of the law.

I wound the window down and didn't say anything, I waited for him to engage in conversation. Living in France you learn that when you get pulled over by a Gendarme you don't say hello, hey how you doing, isn't it a nice day or anything. You just sit there while they walk around your vehicle, you get your papers out ready, identity card, passport, insurance document, carte grise and driving license for inspection. After a few circuits of Svetty Mr Policeman plod said, are you French? No we are British, unfortunately. Do you speak French? Yes we live there, I was thinking that what he was about to say would however be beyond my understanding of the French language.

Apparently we had ignored an orange light and stop sign. I had no recollection of seeing or passing either. Mr Plod said 400 dirham fine! I honestly had no idea what I had done wrong but old and wrinkly as he was he had a gun which in my world means you oblige and don't argue. We had just used the last of our folding money to replace the robbed petrol and had no Dihrams left. The wife opened the purse to show him. He saw a 50 Euro note and said Euros are ok. We gave him the 50 Euro note and he said park over there, I will go and do the paperwork. We took the opportunity to top Svettys fuel up from one of the jerry cans and top up the engine oil. A few minutes later Mr Policeman returned with a form that made no sense whatsoever but I signed it and he gave me a 10 dirham note in exchange for our 50 Euro note. That's a pretty shit exchange rate and I very much doubt the 50 Euros would get anywhere near the coffers of the Moroccan government but would more likely be used for a lavish break of Ramadan meal for his family and friends tonight.

We carried on our merry way, there's only a few kilometers to go before we join the motorway north to Tangier. We got our ticket onto the motorway using the correct lane and feeling confident in Svetty's wellbeing we got up to a steady 90 kilometers an hour, all is going well, it's about lunch time so I said darling bitch wife, please pass me a refreshment please ta muchly.

Is it just me or has it just got really fucking hot in here? I looked at Svetty's temperature gauge and it was nearly in the red, she normally runs at between 80 and 90 degrees and she was at just over a hundread degrees. I put the hazard lights on and slowed down to a troddle while we found a gap in the roadside barriers so we could pull safely off the motorway. We found a spot, turned the engine off and had a look under the bonnet. Oh fuckerdy fuck fuck fuck! There was steam coming out of the vent on the radiator cap and out of the radiator expansion tank that was bubbling away. This is not good. We put our high vis jackets on and put the we are fucked warning triangle on the hard shoulder behind Svetty.

When I had got my wits back together I immediately found the problem. There was actually no problem, the problem was that some fucking dick of a cunting arsehole at the market stall workshop and I guess it was wide boy wanker had filled the cooling system with water and not as the term cooling system might suggest it requires coolant you Moroccan dick. If the old man had thought or bothered to collect the coolant rather than contaminating the streets of Azrou with it he could have reused it.

Just for your information, engines get very hot and need to be cooled by a radiator and a fan. Engines are usually at a temperature running at in the region of 90 degrees. If you have ever boiled a kettle and I'm sure you have and if you paid any attention during your physics lessons at school you will know that water boils at 100 degrees. So if the engine is running at 90 degrees, if there is just water circulating and cooling it the water will at the least be suitable for simmering a boiled egg but not cooling an engine. Coolant however boils at about 130 degrees, this is why you put coolant in and not fucking rain water.

Fortunately we had 5 litres of coolant in the back of Svetty should we have needed to top her coolant levels up. I did not however expect to refill the whole system at the side of a motorway in Morocco. Svetty in the same way that she likes to consume fuel and oil is thirsty when it comes to coolant, it takes ten litres of coolant to fill her up. We only have five litres but it will have to do, we made the rest up with water until her radiator was full. My worry as is any drivers after an overheating episode is what else in the engine has it affected. Only driving off again would tell. We left the high vis jackets and the 'we are fucked' warning triangle within reach should we need them again. I returned to where we were before the boiling an egg episode and sipped on a tinny.

I kept checking the temperature gauge constantly for the next 10 minutes or so, after that Svetty would have overheated if she was going to. All was good in engine temperature land, the wife rolled us a smoke and we enjoyed the litter strewn scenery. A few minutes later what sounded like a very big motorbike, probably a Harley Davidson or the likes was approaching from behind us. Everyone behind us on the motorway was approaching from behind us as I was just tootling along until my confidence in Svetty returned, even the fat women herding their sheep and goats were gaining on us!

Next thing there's a toot, toot, tooting! It was the 'In Rust We Trust' Fiat Panda inching past us. Driver and always tipsy co pilot waving and giving us the thumbs up. The reason for the noise was obvious. Most of their exhaust was not under their car as is normal but was strapped to their roof rack.

We continued without stopping towards the ferry port in Tangier and will hopefully arrive, fingers crossed without any further incidents in plenty of time for the 16.00 ferry. This will be lush as with the hour time difference between Morocco and Spain we will be in Algesiers by 16.30 and in Gibraltar by 17.00 ready for tea time.

Boom shakaloom, we've made it to the port. Well done Svetty. We passed over our return IOU ticket and Svettys visa and followed the signs to the big green boat where we joined one of the lines of vehicles waiting to depart. There were quite a number of the Feraille Raid équipes waiting and many other vehicles from different raids. One thing that made me feel good was that after a wander around to pass the time I walked passed a Porsche Cayenne and a Mitsubishi Land Cruiser that were umbilicaly connected to the vehicles in front of them and were going to be dragged by their umbilical tow straps onto the big green boat, at least Svetty had made it back under her own steam, literally!

I think the Porsche repairs however minor they might be will be a tad more than Svettys 7000 dihram open heart surgery. Mrs 'In Rust We Trust' sauntered over and we had an incomprehensible conversation about something or other, even with the aid of Google translate I didn't have a clue. I rechecked Svetty's oil and sat in the sun enjoying a tinny while we waited to board the big green boat.

The big green boat had been sat there for ages and all the vehicles had disembarked ready for their occupants to experience the misery of Morocco and what little it has to offer. Here we are again just sat here waiting and waiting, its 15 minutes until we are due to set sail and there are a lot more vehicles to put on than when we came the other way. At long fucking last, the first line of vehicles is waved forwards to embark, maybe the stated time on the schedule is when they can be arsed to do something and not a sailing time. They can't even blame Ramadan variations as I think the big green boat is Spanish owned and there is still three hours until sundown.

We were waved forward, we are in the last line and there's only a campervan and two cars behind us so when we're on we should be setting sail soon. We were directed to the far end of the big green boat where yet again considering it's size is completely unnecessary as it is not even half full and we were directed to turn round which I did and then reversed to somewhere near the campervan that was behind us. Some fat man in greasy high vis overalls started waving his hands at me, gesturing me to do something but I had fuck all idea what. I reversed back a little more but apparently that was incorrect, I think he was gesturing right hand down so I did, obviously his right hand not mine, I couldn't see where I could move to so I moved forwards, and stopped putting my head out of the window and shouted in my politest English 'where the fuck do you want me to park'? He banged his greasy fists on Svetty's bonnet, waved his arms around randomly again, I reversed back to where I originally was, turned Svetty's engine off, got out and left her where she was.

We went up the many stairs to the upper level. The return journey would be different to the outbound one, there was no paperwork to do, the bar and restaurant were open and you could even buy duty free fags and alcohol in the shop. We were heading to Gibraltar so there was no need for us to bother ourselves with duty free. We had a mediocre carry out curry planned for tea so there was no need for the restaurant but the bar would provide a nice cold beer. We sat and drank our beer, we should be in Algesiers soon. Beers finished we went outside for a smoke. What the fuck we are still here, we've not even set off and it's nearly 17.30.

We could see that the fat cunt in greasy high vis was now down on the outside part of the deck waving his arms like someone having an epileptic fit and brandishing a whistle. Blowing his whistle and trying to direct 40 tonne articulated wagons to perform a 10 point turn on the open deck before reversing into the whatever you call the bit where all the vehicles sit for their journey on the big green boat. Doing all this while having an epileptic fit must be difficult, especially when you are an arrogant greasy cunt. The comedy value of watching this cunts ineptitude at trying to direct wagon drivers to u turn their wagons and reverse them to somewhere on the big green boat using only a whistle and epilepsy was all the same priceless.

Some of the drivers were obviously regulars, they knew the routine, others stopped got out of their cabs and waved their arms at the fat cunt as a reply to his epilepsy as if to say what the fuck does this epileptic arm shit mean or are you just trying to invent a new spastic arm dance with your 1980's rave whistle in your mouth. Some of the wagon drivers gave up and reversed back down off the boat turned around and reversed onto the boat. I've never driven a 40 tonne wagon but this latter solution would appear to be the quickest and least stressful way of boarding wagons onto a big green boat with a door at only one end.

Fuck me, the line of wagons waiting on the dock side was growing and so were the camper vans and cars. The big green boat is now two hours late. Would you believe it they are obviously boarding the vehicles for the 7 o'clock crossing onto the 4 o'clock boat. I can see the logic of this, why send two big green boats from Tangier to Algesiers when you can delay by three hours half the passengers on the 4 o'clock ferry and as you now have the restaurant and bar open you can make more money while saving however much fuel it takes to power a big green boat 20 kilometers across the straights of Gibraltar to Algesiers. Seven o'clock on the dot the big green boat set sail.

I wish I wasn't driving, Mrs 'In Rust We Trust' had her bottle of duty free whiskey on a table and was sat with a few other people and had successfully already made a severe dent in it. I would make up for it when we arrive back at whatever it is called terrace in Gibraltar.

I noticed when went back down to the vehicle deck, ah yes that's what it's called, I couldn't remember a couple of paragraphs earlier, that there was a reasonable puddle of oil underneath Svetty, either that or the big green boat had sprung a minor leak in the same location. We only had about 25 kilometers back to Gibraltar so I decided, fuck it, Svetty will get us there or she won't. We did much toot, toot, tooting with Mrs 'In Rust We Trust' as we left the big green boat, we left the port and just like One Direction we went our separate ways, probably to never see them again.

We are back in mainland Europe, Svetty can happily suffer from another major heart failure now and we'll just ring the assurance and get her and us taken home without having to cross the sea. We tootled our way from Algesiers to the border crossing into Gibraltar. This time at the border crossing I was a very good boy. I drove very slowly, in fact annoyingly slowly for the car behind us. Said vehicle was so close behind us that his headlights gave me a miserable glimpse in my wing mirror of the shall we say rather dark smoke that was belching out of Svetty's exhaust. I'll worry about that tomorrow, the priority right now is to pop into Morribobs for refreshments, tuck Svetty up in the underground carpark at something or other terrace and have a curry. We would have a proper recky of Svetty tomorrow.

I couldn't wait until tomorrow so had a look under Svetty and drip, drip, drip of the oil messing up the nice floor of the underground carpark. A quick look under the bonnet and the oil was hemorrhaging from the timing chain cover. As I have previously educated you the timing chain connects the oily shafts in the top and bottom bit of the engine. The cover of the timing chain and associated shizzle is made of metal and so is the engine that the cover is bolted to. There was and should still be a paper gasket between the two metal components to stop the hot oil that is circulating inside the engine from depositing itself on the floor outside of the engine. We actually saw the old man remove the gasket and hang it up to dry for reuse during our first visit to the market stall workshop, he was thoughtfully keeping it for reuse, although not ideal to reuse a gasket he wouldn't have been able to find another one so it was better than nothing or he said alternatively he would use some gasket gobber as a temporary fix. I don't think they had bothered to use either.

I was a little annoyed, I consumed some of the mother in laws vodka, got my angry head on and sent Mr Pink a rather scathing message to inform the old man and wide boy that they had firstly forgotten to put any coolant in the cooling system, secondly they had forgotten to put a gasket or any gasket gobber on the timing chain cover and thirdly that some robbing cunt had syphoned all but a dribble of petrol out of the fuel tank. I invited them to take a trip to Gibraltar. They declined.

Today is apartment cleaning day, when I say cleaning it's more ranger, to ranger in French means to tidy, not specifically to clean. You get rid of the rubbish, do the recycling of which there was plenty but you don't clean up the dirt and grime that was already there when you arrived. The favorite mother in law isn't the cleanest or most house proud person I've ever met which is odd considering the number of steam cleaners she owns, perhaps she should take one of them out of it's box. Anyways ranger over the apartment looks better than when we arrived so we went out for a walk and some lunch.

With much regret and thanks to the slapdashness of the old man and wide boy it was necessary to message Asier to say thank you for your kind offer of a free pass on the next raid but unfortunately we won't be joining you, we can afford the fuel for the trip but not the oil the amount Svetty is hemorrhaging! I told Asier not to use the market stall workshop ever again. I advised Mr Pink of the same.

We are a day in hand so we might or might not head north towards home stopping somewhere in Spain tomorrow. I'll see how my mood is in the morning.

Morning all! It's wet and it's miserable and I have no enthusiasm to go anywhere or do anything. We decided we would have a toss it off day in the apartment to recharge and we would head home tomorrow morning bright and early, if nothing else the meteo says it will be sunny tomorrow so if Svetty does go tits up again at least we can work on our tan while waiting for a recovery vehicle to arrive.

# 18 Gibraltar to Salamanca

Svettys oil is topped up, we are packed up so lets go for it and see how far we can get. We don't have anywhere booked to stay tonight, we hadn't booked anything too far in advance should the inevitable ClusterFuck happen, which obviously it did. We left Gibraltar and headed up through Spain stopping every 150 kilometers to top up the ever leaking engine oil.

Despite tootling along behind slow wagons we are making good progress, we've been on the road for five hours and the signs say Salamanca is 90 kilometers away. We have stayed in Salamanca some years before but only briefly for an evening meal and an overnight stop, it is a very beautiful city and I would like to explore more of it. It's only early afternoon so I ordered the wife to firstly pass me an IPA and secondly look up a hotel for us preferably with secure parking in Salamanca.

In a wifely fashion the wife found us an IBIS City Center hotel, there were rooms available but she couldn't book it on the phone. I wasn't overly enthralled about driving Svetty into the city center but if we wanted to go sightseeing it's obviously the best place to be. The route from the motorway to the city center was pretty straight forward, it was just a long straight road with these occasional weird green or red lights positioned along it. I remember from studying my highway code some 35 years previously that red means stop and green means go. That might seem an odd thing to you for me to say but when you have lived in the middle of nowhere for 14 years you forget what these lights are for as you don't have to encounter their hindrance on your daily journeys.

We dumped Svetty outside the hotel, went to the reception and asked if we could book a room for the night. No problem but all the rooms facing the park at the front are taken it will have to be a room overlooking the street at the back of the hotel. Fine with me Mrs Receptionist I'm not planning on sightseeing from the hotel window. After checking in we drove

Svetty round the block into the underground car park. There was a man next to where we had parked feeding his dog in the back of his car, while we were getting our bags out of Svetty he said in perfect English, do you know your car is leaking oil? Yes thankyou very much I am more than aware of that fact, by the way you have a very beautiful looking dog.

Thanks to the trip to Morribobs in Gibraltar we set up a good bar in the room, well we didn't really, we got a few cans out and a box of wine, we were only on a stopover and would unlike in Morocco be able to procure refreshments with our dinner or even as we are still on honeymoon just say fuck it and pop into a bar for a beverage or two.

Tourist hats on we took a city map from the reception desk and bimbled off, I won't bore you with the sights of Salamanca as this is the tale of Clusterfuck and not a travel guide, however within the ten minutes walk to the magnificent central square with it's arched walkways and Romanesque pillars I had seen more glory in architecture in one small part of a small Spanish city than I had seen in Morocco visiting Casablanca and Marrakesh that is apart from King Hassan II's mosque, if you are ever in that part of Spain I highly recommend that you visit Salamanca.

As usual I'm getting hungry and I had totally forgotten we are in Spain, eat at lunch or wait until stupid o'clock for dinner. At least we could have eaten at lunch if we had been here at that time. The hotel does food so fuck it, we'll eat at the hotel, at least we can then have an early night ready for our anxiety inducing journey up north hopefully arriving somewhere in the south of France tomorrow afternoon.

We perused the menu at the hotel, it was either pasta or pizza. The young lass who was on reception explained that she was the only member of staff on duty so the menu was what was already prepared and would just be heated up. That's ok, thanks for your honesty, I wasn't going to expect a three starred Michelin pizza in a hotel or for that matter anything cooked by an actual chef. We ordered refreshments and the lass brought us our delicious if slightly soggy pizzas. We ate up, drunk up, went for a smoke and then went to bed. Long drive tomorrow. Night night.

# 19 Salamanca To Le Bost 2 Ways

Today is Wednesday 19th march, we have an overnight stop tonight somewhere as yet undecided and unplanned in the north of Spain or southern France then tomorrow will be the final leg home to arrive in Le Bost on Friday late afternoon, hopefully.

We're up nice and early and not feeling very eager. Considering the Spanish don't eat until 10 o'clock at night they don't half get up early for work. It's 7am and on my morning stroll around the block trying to disengage and hopefully on my return to our room unleash last night's pizza from my bowels there is traffic everywhere. This is probably normal but I'm not used to cities. A tractor passing at 7am, that's normal for me.

Bowels emptied we handed our room cards in at the reception, packed our shizzle into Svetty, topped up the oil as I forgot to do it yesterday afternoon, said a little prayer and exited the underground car park into the joys of the Salamanca rush hour.

We've traveled about a kilometer from the hotel and I can smell oil, hot oil, oh no for fuck sake, we can't only smell oil we can fucking see it! Oily smoke was wafting into the interior. This is not good, this is very, very bad indeed. We pulled off the three lanes each way major city center road in to a taxi waiting area. I would have taken a deep breath before moving from the drivers seat but I may have died of asphyxiation if I did.

FUCK FUCK FUCK is all I was going to and could say. The wife told me to calm down. We opened the bonnet up and there was oil all over the fucking place and I mean fucking everywhere. There wasn't a surface, pipe or cable in the engine bay that wasn't covered in engine oil.

There was no oil filler cap in place any more, hence the oil was being spurted out of the top of the engine and was burning on the exhaust manifold and anywhere else that was hot, the filler cap had done one and vanished. I don't like to finger point in situations like this but the finger was firmly pointed at me. It was me who only fifteen minutes earlier had taken the cap off to top the ever dripping oil supply up and with my lets get on the road as soon as possible anxiety levels at about 100 out of 10 I either didn't put it back on properly and it had come off or I just didn't put it back on at all and left it on a ledge in the engine bay to fall into the road as soon as we set off. With the routine of topping up the oil every 150 kilometers I put it down to the fact that I had just not put the cap back on properly. Anyway, we're in a situation and we need to do something, I or should I say my anxiety was to blame so one way or another I would however somehow resolve the situation.

I retraced our route on foot back to the hotel which was easy as I just followed the oil slick on the road. We had been in the kerbside lane for the kilometer or so that we had driven so hopefully I would find the filler cap at the side of the road or I was more hopeful it would be sat waiting for me in the underground car park at the hotel. I didn't see anything on my route back to the hotel nor did I in the car park so clutching at straws I asked at the hotel reception if anyone had found and handed in an oil filler cap from a 1979 LADA NIVA?

The receptionist looked at me like I was a moron which at this moment in my life I was. Although I had checked the car park area I had another thought, what if someone had seen it and out of courtesy and cleanliness popped it in one of the bins in the car park. I went and rummaged in the bins near to or on the exit route but it was to no avail, I still had no oil filler cap.

I retraced the route back to Svetty and the wife all the time still hoping I would stumble upon it but alas I did not. When I got back at Svetty the wife could see I had clearly lost the will to live.

All we need to do is find something to seal the hole where the filler cap was and should be. We tried a disposable rubber glove tied on with a zip tie. I started Svetty up and comical as it was watching some of the fingers inflate with oil that solution wasn't going to work. Next we went for a plastic bag, yet again sealed with a cable tie, oil started to ooze out from under the cable tie so that was also a non starter. We needed something more sturdy. The wife suggested a drinks can cut in half and secured with sturdy wire, both items we have and it appeared to be a good idea. We measured up an IPA can and it was a bit too big so the wife wandered off up the road to purchase some canned drinks in a smaller diameter tin. When said wife returned she had a can of some non descript pop and a thin can containing an energy drink. The pop drink looked like it was about the correct diameter so we opened it poured the contents down a drain and cut the can in half. It was quite a snug fit so hopefully with some sturdy wire twisted around the bottom to make a seal we would be up and on our way in no time. We got the pliers out of the tool box and twisted the wire as tightly as we could. I restarted Svetty for the third time and good idea as it was to use a drinks can the oil was still pouring out. I'm amazed there is still any oil left in Svetty's engine.

My turn to improvise now, according to the wife there is a hardware type store just up the road that she had passed while obtaining the pop cans. I wandered up and had a browse to see if I could find anything useful. Bingo, silicone cup cake things could be the solution to our problem, the serrated if that's the correct word to describe the shape of their sides might be an issue but I reckoned being silicone and with a good pull on a cable tie we might just get a seal, i pontificated for a while as to which colour to buy, pink or blue, I decided on blue to match Svetty's paintwork.

I marched back down to Svetty and the wife confident that I would rectify the situation that I had put us in. We installed a silicone cup cake thing on top of the engine, secured it with a cable tie pulled as tight as I could and started Svetty up for the fourth attempt sat in the taxi stop where taxi drivers were becoming increasingly annoyed that we were stuck in their drop off and collect zone, bingo, my bodge was working, that is for about a minute and then Svetty's remaining oil started to seep out under the zip tie.

Plan C or whatever we were now on. I looked up where the nearest car parts place was. Being in the city center the nearest was about a kilometer away so I took a photograph of the missing part, obviously I didn't as it's missing but a photograph of where it should be would help to explain what I needed as I don't speak Spanish and a picture as they say 'says a thousand words'.

I walked briskly to the parts store and attempted to commence a conversation with the jolly rotund man behind the oily counter. Firstly I asked if he spoke English or French, no was the answer. Mr Rotund got his phone out and using Google translate we commenced our conversation. I told him the make and model and he looked in an oil smothered parts book. After a few minutes he shook his head and I think he said it's a very old and rare engine we don't have anything, but I might be able to get something that will do the job. Mr Rotund asked if we could bring Svetty to the shop so he could see what size the oil filler cap needed to be. Sorry no we can't, Svetty is stuck in the city center and without said part she's not going anywhere other than on a tow truck.

I rang the wife and asked if she could take a photograph of a tape measure on top of the hole where the filler cap should be and send it to me. Fortunately our general tool box has useful things like rulers, tape measures, bottle openers and wine cork screws in it so the dutiful wife did as she was asked and sent me a photograph. I showed the photograph to Mr Rotund, he nodded. A few phone calls later between Mr Rotund and someone else he said that if I wait 15 minutes, someone would arrive with something that might solve my accidentally self inflicted problem. I called the wife to say hopefully we would be on our way again soon, I stood waiting outside and had a smoke.

A man turned up and gave two small bags to Mr Rotund. I asked how much I owed him, they are 12 euros but don't worry about it. What the fuck, you have just gone out of your way to help me and you are giving them to me for free. He said if one of them works drive up and pay, if not don't worry about it. I think he could sense I was on the edge of a mental breakdown. I hot footed it back to the wife and Svetty to see if we had a solution.

Bollocks! Although they looked the business in the bag they were actually radiator caps and had a spring thing on them so they wouldn't fit in the hole without some modification and we didn't have an angle grinder or hack saw with us so it was time to come up with another plan.

We had got this far from the hotel, albeit hemorrhaging oil and there was still some oil in Svetty's engine so lets top up the oil and go back to the hotel. We affixed the silicone cup cake thing with a cable tie in place of the filler cap and returned to the hotel to book a room for another night as we weren't going to magic an oil filler cap out of nowhere today.

I abandoned Svetty outside the hotel and went in to book ourselves back in. Proper job, we got a room facing the park opposite the front of the hotel. I deposited the oil dripping Svetty back in the same place in the underground carpark. Fuck me there was oil dripping everywhere. As you now know is tradition we set up the bar in the bedroom and started our search for an oil filler cap.

My first search online with the comfort of an IPA by my side was a search to see if there was a Spanish NIVA parts supplier, it appeared that there was not. I had a look on the Toute Le Niva Web site in France and they had one in stock. I messaged Toute Le Niva explaining our current Clusterfuck and asked if we could order it but pay for a 24 hour delivery service to Spain. I think they couldn't be arsed as I received the reply saying, sorry the Web site hasn't been updated we don't have that part in stock any more, have you tried a plastic bag and elastic band? Yes we have thankyou fuckwit. Time to look down further avenues to procure the filler cap.

After some searching and stressing we realised that we were missing the fucking obvious trick here, probably due to being stranded in Salamanca city center all morning and anxiety induced stupidity.

We have the wife's Loony LADA parked outside the house in Le Bost and my accident damaged Mr Putin rusting away in a neighbors barn. They both have the same filler cap, we'll just get the babysitters to take one off pop it in a jiffy bag and have it couriered to us at the IBIS Hotel in Salamanca. The wife promptly rung the babysitters and plan D, E, or F whatever plan we are now up to was hatched.

Granddad Steve procured an oil filler cap off the Loony LADA but wasn't sure where to start, being in the middle of nowhere as to where he would find a 24 hour courier. We suggested he went to see our near neighbor Dutch Louis, he knows everything and if he doesn't know he will find out what you need to know and will help. During the conversation the wife was having with the babysitter or shall we now revert to the babysitter as mother in law for simplicity, mother in law advised us of an issue with the children. Steve was heard in the background saying, Audrey it's not important right now but the favorite mother in law was adamant to share the issue with us. Apparently Billy our middle child had become very aggressive and violent towards Desmond our youngest child to the extent that they couldn't be in the same room together. I suggested that if Granddad Steve does go to see Louis for help apropo having the oil filler cap couriered to us he can recuperate our big child cage from Louis that we lent to him a few years ago for him to put something or other in and they could incarcerate Billy in a caged enclosure for his bad behavior.

Bless Steve and Louis, after some internet searching Louis drove Steve to Gueret to a courier depot, I can't remember which one but apparently when they arrived they said, no sorry we can't do that you will be better off at the post office. Steve after visiting the post office with Louis and successfully sending the jiffy bag some time later sent us a photograph of the label on the package so we could track where it was. I'm thinking that as its now late afternoon the 24 hour delivery promise won't apply. Normally you need to send something before 11 am for it to arrive the next day so I didn't expect the jiffy bag to arrive in Spain until Friday. We would be enjoying the sights of Salamanca for at least one more day.

It's Thursday and we have little else to do other than wait for a jiffy bag that probably won't arrive until tomorrow so we went sight seeing. The good thing about staying in a hotel is that you don't need to wait in to receive a delivery. The reception will take care of it, that is unless you are staying at the Bates Cold Hotel. We did the tourist thing and visited many places, the view from the top of the towers in the cathedral were epic. As I've said previously I'm not writing a Salamanca travel guide so we will regroup when we have news of where the jiffy bag is or when it arrives, I don't think there will be anything happening today.

Friday morning and a quick check online to see where the jiffy bag is. It is in Spain, about 80 kilometers north of Salamanca at a depot awaiting distribution. We should now be in France on our last leg back to Le Bost.

If the jiffy bag arrives before lunchtime we will set off today, if not we will set off tomorrow morning at dawns crack and go as far as we can in one day. We are running out of time, the babysitters need to leave on Sunday and we have two days of driving to get back home unless we travel through the night. We tossed it off all day checking the Internet every now and then to check on the delivery status and it appeared the jiffy bag wasn't moving anywhere.

The jiffy bag didn't arrive on Friday, do the Spanish couriers work on a Saturday? Probably not, but if they do it will only be on a Saturday morning. We sat around all Saturday morning and the jiffy bag had not moved so we instigated plan Y, I selected plan Y as I have no fucking idea where we are in the count of plans as I've lost track of how many plans we have instigated and failed at in the last few days.

Plan Y was instigated, we would find a way using public transport for the wife to travel back to Le Bost within the next 24 hours to relieve the babysitters and send them on their way home before Sunday evening, I would wait at the hotel for the jiffy bag to arrive which I'm sure now won't be until Monday. When the jiffy bag arrives I would apply the oil filler cap to Svetty and drive her back to Le Bost on my own.

Firstly we looked at train travel, there was nothing feasible, next we looked at busses, why not, we have spent most of this trip on one. Boom, there was a Bla Bla Car bus picking passengers up at the bus station in Salamanca at the incredibly unsociable time of quarter to midnight and would arrive in Bordeaux at 8 o'clock in the morning, the wife could then get a train to Limoges and then another train to La Souterainne where Steve would pick her up and take her the last few kilometers home. I booked the bus ticket and that's it, plan Y is sorted.

The bus station was half an hours walk away so we set off walking at quarter to eleven to give us plenty of time. It was Saturday night and Salamanca was in full party swing, it was busier than during the day, that was until we arrived at the bus station which was worryingly quiet considering the size of the place. The departure boards showed a few local buses on them which came and went but nothing saying Bla Bla Car to Bordeaux or wherever it's final destination was. I was getting worried that this might be like the CTM busses in Morocco and the bus picks you up from somewhere random. I checked the pick up location on the phone and we were apparently in the right place.

Quarter to twelve passed and there was no bus. We waited a few minutes more and then went to find someone to ask if we were in the right place. There was no one about to ask so we wandered across the concourse to where there were buses parked and a bus driver was milling about doing whatever he was doing. We asked if we were in the right place and he gestured over there 10 minutes away. We were later to discover that much was lost in translation. We walked in the direction the bus driver had pointed and there didn't seem to be anything resembling a bus pick up office or anything. We walked back to the bus station and I triple checked the address, I was certain we were where we should be. We gave it a few more minutes, it wasn't as if there were even any other passengers waiting to ask, there was just us. We agreed we had fucked up somewhere and walked back to the hotel.

The wife is such a fucking dick! As soon as we arrived back at the hotel she got her phone out of her pocket to ring the babysitters and advise them that we had somehow fucked up and she wouldn't be arriving back in La Souterainne tomorrow morning. Before she did this she said, I've got a text message from Bla Bla Car, the bus is late it will be arriving at quay 12 Salamanca bus station at 12.50! Fucking brilliant, that gives us four minutes to get from the hotel back to the bus station for you to get on the bus in the exact same spot we had been waiting for it. What time did you get the message? An hour ago. Fucking dick.

We looked on line to see when the next bus was, the next bus is the same time Sunday night! I was feeling very sorry for the babysitters, not only were they now going to have to drive non stop on Monday in the region of 1500 kilometers back to Wales but have also had to resort to imposing the incarceration of our middle child Billy in the child cage they had reclaimed from Louis due to Billy's increasingly violent behavior. We booked another bus ticket for Sunday night and plan Z was in place, if Sunday night goes wrong we're fucked as I've run out of letters in the alphabet for anymore plans. We will regroup at the bus station tomorrow.

24 hours after the first attempt we're back at the bus station for a second try, same time same place. Considering it's nearly midnight on Sunday the bus station is unusually busy.

A big red bus arrived with Bla Bla Car emblazoned on the sides. The wife showed the e-ticket on her phone to the driver, it was the right bus. Off she went and I walked back to the hotel and went to bed.

Good morning what to do today? If the jiffy bag doesn't turn up early doors then I'll leave it until tomorrow to head home. I loitered around until 11 o'clock and I checked online, the jiffy bag was out for delivery but without any delivery time. I had a look online for somewhere to have lunch and boom, there was a Chinese buffet just outside of the magnificent city square, only a few minutes brisk walk away. I would pop in there for lunch.

I don't know how we had managed to miss an all you can eat Chinese in the last few days we have been loitering around in Salamanca, but somehow we did. The place was a dump but the food was good, I ate far too much and consumed a bottle of Marquis De Caceras white, I took the liberty of sending the wife photographs of the many plates of food that I had consumed and I received the romantic short reply 'CUNT'. I returned to the hotel for a well earned afternoon nap.

It's mid afternoon, I'm napping away and there's a ringing in my ears. It was the room phone ringing, this must be the jiffy bag, I answered, the receptionist said your delivery has arrived.

I opened the jiffy bag and there it was, never in my life have I been so happy to see an oil filler cap. I went down to the underground garage to present it to Svetty, she was very happy with it. I topped the oil up, making sure to firmly apply the filler cap. There appeared to be a miniature beach that had appeared underneath Svetty, the hotel staff had obviously seen the oil slick and put a few sacks of sand on the floor to soak up the oil. I packed everything but essentials into Svetty ready for an early start tomorrow. I checked that she would start and all appeared to be OK. The wife messaged to say that she was home safe and sound. It was great news all round.

The wife later messaged to say the children were actually ok and behaving. Possibly Billy was just missing his Mama and Papa. They had been taken out for their evening exercise without any issues.

Good morning Mr Anxiety, lets get on the road. I have no idea where we are going today, I don't mean that from a direction point of view, Google maps will take care of that, it's more about how far my anxiety will stay under control without my trusty co pilot. Hopefully I will make it into France which should be about seven hours of tootling. During the journey I will occupy myself en route by rolling smokes and playing make a sentence or phrase out of number plates, yes I have the skill of rolling smokes while driving which is probably as illegal as texting while driving but it's something I've done for at least the last thirty years.

I stopped three times to top up the oil and fuel, always checking the oil filler cap is securely put back in place. It's now mid afternoon, I'm back in southern France and without a copilot to keep me occupied I'm bored. I've done 600 kilometers so it's time to get Google to find me a stop over for the night. Fifty kilometers ahead just off the AutoRoute there is a B&B hotel, Google maps tells me they have rooms available so I headed there for the night.

B&B hotels don't have a reception, you use a machine in the lobby to book and pay for a room. I had to wait for ages while an English couple in front of me tried to fathom it out. I could have translated what the check in machine was saying or told them to touch the English flag icon at the top of the screen but I was in no rush so I just stood there waiting enjoying watching their increasing frustration and despair. Welcome to my world. When the English idiots had finally booked themselves in I booked myself a room.

Proper job, in the room, there were two USB chargers on the bedside lamp. This might appear mundane in our modern world but every hotel we have stayed in during the last three weeks had none. I took a photograph and sent it to the wife with a few words asking if everything was good at home. There was no immediate reply from her. I needed food so had a look where the nearest eatery was. Just over the road about five minutes walk away there was an upmarket looking burger place. I would have preferred something more substantial but that was all that was in walking distance and I do like a good burger, not the shite with an M on the box that I would feel obliged to throw on the floor on the way back.

I wandered over and ordered something that looked good on the menu and waited for my carry out. Meanwhile the idiot English couple I had encountered checking into the hotel came in to order their food. They opted for the speak very loudly in English and the French lass that was taking their order would understand them. Fucking dicks, it's moments like this that I am ashamed to be a British passport holder. Anyway my burger was ready, where's the chips? For just under 10 euros I was expecting chips but no they were an optional extra. I took my not very big burger back to the hotel, it was despite the price disappointingly tasteless and unfulfilling. There's still no reply from the wife.

I rang the wife rather than just messaging, just to check that everything was OK, still no reply, I then tried a messenger call and still no reply then as a last resort I rang the house phone and there was still no reply. I reclined on the bed and found some rubbish to watch on the television and nodded off.

The phones ringing, it's the wife, hello darling bitch wife how are you? Well I've just got back from a day at the urgence department at the hospital in Gueret. Why?

I'm now going to summarize the events that had happened today, at this point even though I didn't now all the facts and events until I eventually return back to Le Bost tomorrow but I think it's best to explain as a third party to what transpired all in one go.

The wife had taken the children out after breakfast for their morning exercise, not far from the house Billy decided to attack Desmond. Let me elaborate, Billy is a small ageing 18 kilo spaniel cross with spinal arthritis that has been treated for the last three years with injections of steroids every six weeks rather than us having him put to sleep on account of the pain he would otherwise be in. Desmond is a two year old St Hubert hound crossed with what we assume was probably a Doberman. Desmond although still a baby is 30 kilos of pure muscle and has the most adorable massive floppy St Hubert ears. Desmond doesn't have an aggressive bone in his body, that is unless he is provoked and then he will protect himself and how his breeding instincts tell him more importantly he will protect us or in this case more importantly the wife.

Apparently Billy had gone psycho and attacked Desmond, the wife was tethering Billy on a lead, she slipped and hit her head on a stone and was then stuck on the ground between Billy going psycho and Desmond protecting himself and the wife. Fortunately for the wife black van man farmer from one of the local farms was passing and came to the rescue using a pitch fork to get Billy psycho off Desmond and the wife. The wife had returned to the house saying she was ok with blood pouring out of her forehead and only vision in one eye.

We will now welcome back to this story our idiot neighbor. Bless the idiot, he had taken the wife to urgence at the hospital in Gueret, and had spent the day there while the wife had her forehead stapled back together and her eye lid stitched followed by many eye tests. I am fearful of what sort of devastation I will return home to tomorrow.

Bless idiot boy, after returning the wife home from the hospital he then took Desmond to the dog hospital to have a gash in his cheek apparently big enough to see his teeth through sewn up that Billy had administered.

This news has put me off wandering off and going to get another overpriced shit burger, hungry as I am. I topped Svetty's oil up ready for tomorrow and had an early night, tomorrow is another day and I still have the anxiety stress of getting

Svetty the last 500 kilometers back to Le Bost. I probably won't sleep well tonight.

Up and at em, we'll not really. Google maps tells me I

should arrive home in le Bost at 2 o'clock in the afternoon, what Google doesn't take into account is the required oil top up stop checks and Svetty's speed. The drive home was uneventful and I arrived triumphant mid afternoon. I thanked Svetty for getting me home, got out and went towards the front door to greet the wife.

# 20 Aftermath

What the fucking fuck, the wife looked like she had been in some sort of unlicensed cage fight or had taken a night out at fight club. When she said they had stapled her head she wasn't fucking kidding, I've used smaller staples to fix cattle fencing to wooden fence posts. As for her eye, well, you couldn't even see her eye, there was just a swollen mess where her eye should be. The wife looked a fucking mess, not that she was ever an oil painting but she was now in a different league.

I gave Desmond and Pippa a fuss and ignored Billy who was enclosed in the sin bin cage. The babysitters had left plenty of refreshments so we sat down to reflect on the current situation.

The first and to be honest the only subject to discuss was that Billy had to go, he couldn't and we couldn't continue to live with his behavior and it's no life for him to live in a cage. If this incident had happened in a residential area and people had seen it, Billy as the instigator would have been immediately taken away and euthanized, sadly also would Desmond as he was involved. We decided to give it a day to decide, maybe as Mama and Papa were back Billy would calm down but I wasn't convinced. Like humans who for whatever reason pump them themselves full of steroids they will in rare cases go totally off the rails in an aggressive psychotic way, this appears to be what has happened to Billy.

We decided to have a family evening walk to see how Billy behaved. Billy and Desmond were administered with muzzles and both of them were on short leads. The wife applied some rather large sunglasses for vanity reasons should we happen to meet anyone. Pippa bless her, the old lumpy bird just ambled along looking like she was waiting to die. We didn't get far before Billy kicked off, I dragged Billy back to the house by his collar while the wife continued on a pleasant walk with Desmond and Pippa. I decided that Billy wasn't coming back in the house so I put him in the gayrage to let him calm down for a few minutes.

When I went back to the gayrage to see if Billy had calmed down, I opened the gayrage door and he went for me, I don't mean just went for me he took a chunk out of my arm, this was even through his muzzle. I'm not cruel towards animals in anyway. Child cruelty I have no issues with but animal cruelty is a great big no. I did however put Billy in the work pit for his and my own protection with a bucket of water should he be thirsty, he would stay down there for at least a few hours or possibly until tomorrow morning.

We looked into the possibility of having Billy rehomed but I wasn't keen on this idea as his behavior was increasingly sporadic mainly on the aggressive side and who knows what he might do next, possibly to a new owner, I wouldn't be able to live with myself if he attacked someone other than me or the wife.

There was an option that he could go to the SPA in Limoges in exchange for us taking on a hound that had been there for six months that nobody seemed to want to adopt. I didn't want him to go to the SPA as he would just spend the rest of his days in a cage albeit a larger one than the one he has been living in at home.

We wrote a letter to take to the vets, it was easier than trying to explain in French Billy's issues and what he had done. We went to the vets in La Souterainne to book him in for euthanasia. The appointment was arranged for tomorrow.

We arrived at the vets and Billy was as good as gold, it seemed weird that we were having him put down. We really wanted him to have one of his episodes but there was nothing. This is fucking heart breaking but it needs to be done. I won't continue with the details but ten minutes later Billy was gone and would be taken to Poitiers for an individual cremation and returned back to us.

I could carry on and tell you about the Clusterfuck that was the inside of Svetty's engine when I took it out and found out what a bodge job the cunts at the market stall garage had done, the untimely death of Pippa puppy from a stroke and the wife's ongoing weekly eye retraining sessions in Gueret so I'm going to leave it here.

Just so I don't leave you in tears we did take the unwanted hound from the SPA and named her Stella, she is now Desmond's best friend.

I'm all dobbered out and you are probably bored as fuck that is if you are still reading.

There is one final issue to resolve and that is how to get back to normal life and stop the Clusterfuck, I can see there is only one way of getting out of the world of ClusterFuck and that is to reverse how it started and remove myself from the forces that created it. Those forces have been in play since Audrey became my mother in law. There's only one thing for it, suicide or divorce!

# 666 THE END

The end of my life or marriage?
Who can say?
That's just how it is. (Thanks Elaine)
Reet then, I'll see you.

Printed in Dunstable, United Kingdom

75285066R00131